Devil IN THE DETAIL

MAX HENRY

DEVIL IN THE DETAIL

Published by Max Henry

Published July 2015, by Max Henry **maxhenryauthor@outlook.com**

Edited by: Lauren McKellar

Cover Design: Louisa of LM Creations

Image from: DollarPhoto Club

Formatting by: Max Effect

Something In The Way – Nirvana
Waiting Game – Banks
I Will Buy You A New Life – Everclear
Every Day Is Exactly The Same – Nine Inch Nails
Snuff – Slipknot
Shadow Flash – Indiana
I Need A Doctor – Dr Dre, Eminem, Skylar Grey
Fix You – Coldplay
Big Girls Cry – Sia
So Cold – Breaking Benjamin
Pistols At Dawn – Seinabo Sey
I Alone – Live
Heart-Shaped Box – Nirvana
Fell On Black Days – Soundgarden
Blue Monday – Orgy
Lean On – Major Lazer, MO, DJ Snake
Never Gonna Change – Broods
Change Your Life – Far East Movement, Sidney Samson, Flo Rida

Guilt is bad,
and sadness is bad,
but regret is the sickly
combination of both

- unknown

prologue

TY It's the little things that make us. And sometimes, they also break us.

Little things, like a droplet of blood on my foot.

My world ended and started in that droplet. It changed, broke, fell apart, and never really came back together the right way. I regret everything that happened, the *reason* for that little drop of hell marking me, scarring me, and staining my soul. And yet, in a sadistic, morbid way, I love everything that perfect shade of crimson represented.

It made me who I am. That droplet bled from a life, a life that ended at my hands, but that droplet created the need in me to help, to heal, and to protect. The values that make me the man I am today. The values I'll need to face the damage that droplet also caused.

Every journey is unique—every man or woman's self-discovery personal to them. There's no 'one' way to find your place in life, no 'one' answer that covers us all. What changes me for the better may scar you, but the thing that guides you might also send me off the rails.

What's important is that you recognize that moment in your life, that sign that things are about to change, for what it is. The experience might hurt, in fact, it probably will. But, in enduring that pain of loss, rejection, or regret, we need to remember that nothing worth having ever comes easy. What scares us challenges us, and what frightens us strengthens us. Embrace your moment, revel in it, and don't let it go to waste.

Shock yourself, dare yourself, and step out of that fucking comfort zone. Make friends with people you'd never think you had anything in common with. Mix it up. Break the mold. *Let people see the real you.*

I fought against showing my true colors for so long, hiding behind a façade of success and style. But I was wrong. I relented and let the people around me in, and once I did, I realized the most important thing of all.

Nobody deserves to fight alone.

betrayal

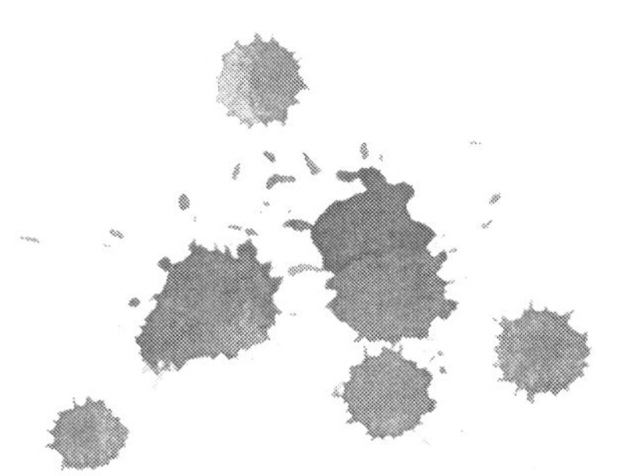

RAMONA The afternoon sun streaming across the porch does nothing to warm my flesh as I relax in an old timber chair; the light breeze peppers my arms and legs, carrying a chill warning of the weather to come. Sonya, and Jane sit in amicable silence, also enjoying the fading sunshine while my son, Mack, plays at my feet with an old toy car—a red Nascar replica that one of the boys at the club gave him years ago. It's his go-to toy when we travel, his comfort, and one he'll need in the hours to come.

His father's leaving us—going home to *his* father to face the music for the horrific crimes he's been committing these past years in the name of impressing the lunatic. Crimes I had gladly been turning a blind eye to.

I'm no fool; the things he did were impossible to hide completely, but I was careless. I thought if I paid no mind to the atrocities my man committed—murder, torture, blackmail, and extortion—that they'd never come home to us, that they'd never affect my son and I.

Shame on me.

They've not only impacted our future, but they're putting our lives at risk. I danced with the devil and now I'm scrambling to save myself from the fire. And for what benefit? Where do I stand now? With a man who doesn't love me, a son losing his father, and an uncertain future—one where I have no idea what I'm going to do to shield my child from any further heartache at the hands of this lifestyle.

How could Sawyer do this to us? How could the father of my child go this far? Our club president, King, packed Mack and I off to a safe house, fearing Sawyer had finally cracked one too many times. So one guess as to how I felt walking in the place to find the asshole restrained on the sofa. Callum, our VP, had his work cut out holding me back, bearing the brunt of my flying nails and kicking feet. I could have killed the smug asshole with my bare hands—I'm positive of it.

But one look at Mack's face as he walked in to the house and zeroed in on his father, bound like a wild animal, and I knew my energy was better directed elsewhere. Our boy's only five, and he's about to face the ugly truth of the life we live. For four years I've managed to keep him sheltered from his father's illegal activities, only revealing the better parts of club life to him. I went without, isolated us, and for what? All those years of hard work and calculated efforts have been a waste. With one murder, Sawyer's unraveled the web of lies I'd created to shield our child. With one foolish decision, he's tugged us into the line of fire.

And he doesn't care.

Shaking free of Callum, I had stormed out the back, taking Mack with me to do what we are now—hiding. I want so damn badly to keep Sawyer from seeing his son before he leaves, hoping that in some small way he might feel an ounce of the pain he's given us. But mostly, I think that I hoped the problem would disappear if I pretended it didn't exist—just like I always do.

Yet there it is—the raw truth of the person he is, hog-tied and catatonic as he waits out his final hours before he faces his fate at the hands of his father.

"You need a top-up?" Sonya gestures to my glass.

I shake my head, glancing inside at Sawyer and the men—Callum, Vince and his boy, Malice—as they sit around with stern faces, discussing something in depth. The men move, pinning Sawyer to the sofa while they retie his binds. I look away, ashamed at the blatant evidence of what a threat they think he is, this man I've had a child with.

How could I have slept next to a monster for so many years? Easy, I guess, when I think about how many times he *wasn't* home.

"Hey, Mom," Mack calls out, breaking my gaze away from the two new faces who've just come through the front door. "Check out this truck."

He shows me a small Hot Wheels rig that smashes

apart when you drive it hard enough into an obstacle. I smile at the humor he finds in the destruction of this little toy as he crashes it into his car, happy that *he's* happy.

"Oh, good. Bronx and Ty are here." Jane pushes out of her chair. "Come meet them, Ramona."

Pushing back the urge to protest returning indoors, I hold out a hand to Mack, and he replies by lifting his arms. Hefting him onto my hip, I relish the connection and giggle. "Baby, you're getting too big for this."

"You can still lift me, can't you?" He gives me that cheeky grin, identical to his father's.

Regret wars with pride as I look at my boy—this child so full of love and joy, qualities so unlike those of the man he resembles down to the scruffy mop of blond hair.

"Typical male," Sonya says as she reaches for the door. "Always getting the woman to do his work."

We step inside, laughing, and my gaze catches Sawyer's. He shrugs, lifting his eyebrows at the same time. My brow furrows as I scowl at the mongrel, wishing a plague of a thousand herpes-ridden whores on him. *Bastard.*

I run my gaze around the living room, placing Callum on the far side. Malice's father, Vince, leans on the dining table, watching his boy introduce these two new men standing behind the sofa, near the door.

"Guys," Malice announces. "This is Ramona, and her son, Mack. They're friends of Dad's."

"Hey," the first one answers with a nod. He's tall, but not as much as his friend. Definitely a gym addict, judging by the way his T-shirt holds to his wide chest and hangs loose at his narrow waistline. Tattoos cover his left arm, and he has that short hairstyle which is neither laid-back, formal, or even attempted at being styled either way. It's just short and choppy—that's the only way I can describe it.

The taller guy's gaze burns into me as he stares, and I realize that I'm now doing exactly the same. He's just . . . beautiful. Unlike his 'singlet, shorts and running shoes' friend, he's perfectly put together. He wears a lightly patterned button-down, held at the cuffs by skull-shaped links. The denim of his jeans is a perfect shade of pre-worn grey. A thick studded belt is looped around his trim waist, drawing my gaze back up his body to those striking brown eyes. He lifts a hand to nervously stroke the short beard he's sporting, ducking his head and letting the longer lengths of his undercut fall forward.

Sawyer chuckles over on the sofa, breaking my focus off this work of art before me and reminding me of the fact we're not alone. Before I can open my mouth, Vince takes a large step over and gives him a firm smack to the back of the head. Sawyer goes quiet with a scowl, much to my pleasure.

"They'll be staying for a while," Malice continues, gesturing to Mack and I, "so let's all act like family, huh?"

"Sure thing," Gym-Boy says, nodding.

I don't have a clue which name belongs to which man. Malice introduced them as Bronx and Ty, but he never gestured to either one as he did. The tall eye candy still stares at me, heating me from the toes up.

"Ty?" Jane asks.

The beautiful creature's gaze breaks from mine. "Yeah . . . sure." *So he's Ty.*

I catch Jane's eye, passing her a silent thanks for clearing that up.

Callum's phone rings, and under the scrutiny of the whole room, he smiles awkwardly and pulls it out, walking out of earshot as he answers.

"Mom?" Mack moves his arms to wrap around my shoulders, hands linked behind my head.

"Yeah, baby?"

"Can I go see Daddy?" he whispers, leaning in close to my ear.

Reluctantly, I set him down, touching his head as he moves away to go sit with Sawyer. I couldn't deny him the one-on-one time forever—it would have happened sooner or later, but my emotions are too raw for this. I can't handle seeing the connection, knowing it won't last, and that I'm going to have to be the horrible person who explains why to Mack afterward.

"Mommy said you'd been naughty," Mack exclaims when he reaches his father.

Sawyer smiles, and leans down so his face is level with Mack's. "I have, Son. So you make sure you're good for Mom, okay? Because this is what happens to bad boys."

A lump forms in my throat as Mack clambers up to sit beside his father. He leans in, resting his head against Sawyer's arm like he has with me so many times before. I can feel the pressure of his head against my body, the memory so vivid.

Crossing my arm over my chest to coax the sensation away, I place my fingers to my mouth, willing the congestion in my throat to ease. Yet it doesn't. The damn thing grows and grows. I focus on not showing it, on hiding the pain welling within me.

"I'll help you make some lunch," Sonya says, directed at Jane. I barely notice them leave the room.

Bronx clears his throat, pulling Ty to the French doors that overlook the yard. Tension radiates from everybody in the room—nobody knows what the hell to do. Malice can't even look at my son and his father, it's that bad.

"Can we watch some TV?" Mack asks, breaking the awkward silence.

Sawyer glances over his shoulder at Malice and Vince, seeking approval.

"Don't see why not," Vince answers with a shrug.

The men move the sofa so it faces the TV, and Malice flicks through the channels, stopping at some old *Looney Tunes* cartoons. The two boys in my life sit in silence, giggling every so often at the stupid shit the characters are doing. They shouldn't be doing this on Sawyer's last night as a 'free' man, the last time he'll get to see his son for quite possibly forever. *This* is what they should have been doing all those times I nagged and begged Sawyer to spend time with Mack.

It's too little too late.

I can't contain the pain any longer. Slapping my hands

to my mouth, I fail to disguise the gasp that breaks free. Heat scores my shame across my cheeks, spreading down my neck in a wave of fire. Determined to hide my mini-breakdown from Mack, I tear up the hall to find a quiet space to regroup as the tears start to fall.

Ironically, the room I end up in is the same room Jane has put Mack's and my bags in. Just the sight of his *Incredible Hulk* backpack sets me off on a new wave of self-pitying misery.

How did I end up here, stuck with the predicament of how I'm going to break the news to my son that his father has been hurt, or even killed, at the hands of his grandfather? Nobody has voiced such an outcome, but we're all thinking it. Carlos isn't known for his compassion, and from the stories Sawyer has recounted on many a drunken night, he doesn't exactly hold a soft spot for his son.

I guess that's one point where Carlos and Sawyer differ—although they're both absent role models, I know deep down Sawyer loves Mack, which leaves me again questioning why he'd do this to us? Were we not incentive enough to stay out of trouble?

heartache

TY She gave a little whimper, one slight sound, but that gasp for solace revealed everything she'd been holding in for too long. Slender fingers across her lips, a painful note slashed across my heart. One tiny second of my life, but the most pivotal one yet.

From the minute I laid eyes on her I knew I had to know her, because in that small moment we shared, the honesty in her sharp blue irises eased the ache in my soul.

I could breathe clearly for the first time in years.

Standing on the wrong side of the door, I recognize the sharp intake of air as she starts to sob. My mind's eye pictures her sitting there, lips slightly parted, eyes glassy as she tries to suppress the pain. I don't want her to hold it in, though. Bottling the pain only poisons a person's soul. I've done it long enough to know what that kind of living-suicide feels like.

It's a suffering worse than death.

My knuckles tap against the wood, and I wait. Will she let me see? Let me listen? My heart thumps a steady rhythm in my chest, gradually building toward a more staccato beat the longer I wait. A sniff sounds, and then footsteps.

"I just need a minute," she calls through the door.

Not happening. "Can I share that minute?"

Silence. Hesitation. *Pain.*

The handle rattles, and my gaze is drawn to the source of the sound. The changing hues of the brass handle intrigue me as I watch it turn. The house is mine, I've been here a hundred times before, but never have the flecks of gold and amber in the handles captured my attention like this.

The door eases open, and she stands in the gap, the side of her face resting against the lip of the wood. "I wasn't expecting it to be you."

Nobody ever does. It's what makes me good at what I do. "Can I come in?"

"I'd rather be alone."

Ramona moves to shut the door, but my foot slips in the gap, forcing her to still.

"What are you doing?" Her eyes are wide, concern mixed with fear.

"Don't shut me out."

A slight frown mars her features, and she pushes against my foot. "Move . . . please."

The same whimper, the same shock escapes her mouth as I shunt the door against her, forcing her to step back and let me in. "I'm not walking away and leaving you to handle this alone—deal with it."

Checking the hallway first, she shuts the door gently behind us, and then turns to confront me. I expect anger, indignation from her, and I get it. Her arm lashes out and she belts me—palm open, square on the shoulder.

"Why don't you men ever listen? Why?"

I lift an eyebrow.

Ramona belts me again, this time harder, her frown deep enough to turn the flesh between her eyebrows white with force. *Keep it up, baby. Let it go.* I smirk, knowing it'll help speed her along.

She lets fly with both hands, beating me about the shoulders and chest. A couple of times I'm forced to lift my chin a little, but I'm not concerned with receiving any accidental injuries to my face; she's barely five-foot-seven, and I'm six-two. Tears streak over her sharp cheekbones, running down her neck and into her shirt as she sobs.

"Fuck you," she moans, still pummeling her tiny fists into my chest. "Fuck all of you."

She throws hit after hit, gaining momentum, finding strength in each strike that connects with my body. After a while they actually hurt, leaving a sting in their wake. Still, the frustration hasn't left the glazed stare she has, fixed on my chest. I'm not putting a quit to this until she's got it out, bled the well.

Plus, I'm kind of enjoying it.

When her fists finally slow, and the sad sobs outweigh the blows, I reach out and wrap my hands around her, pulling her shaking frame to me. Predictably, she resists, moaning complaints even as her fingers knit in my shirt, and she presses her face against my body. Everything about the moment feels so right, and yet so wrong. I'm enjoying the excuse to get close to this mad little woman way too much. I'm a sick fuck for taking advantage of her weakness.

"Got any more?" I ask.

She shakes her head against my chest, burying her tear-streaked face far away from my eyes. I drop an arm and tuck my hand beneath her chin, pulling her head up toward mine.

"There's no shame in it, Ramona. You've got yourself a shit of a situation and you have every right to feel messed up over it."

She smiles weakly and shakes her head. "I'm not messed up, Ty. I'm disappointed."

"In what?"

"Myself. I knew it would end up like this—still, I went there." Her voice is hoarse, and barely above a whisper. "I set us up for this; it's my fault Mack will be hurt."

"Bullshit," I snap. "You can't be held accountable for what Sawyer is. As far as everyone out there is concerned, this whole thing lies squarely on his shoulders."

"I can be held accountable for bearing his child though, bringing an innocent soul into this mess."

Squeezing her shoulder, I ask, "You love Mack, right?"

"Of course." She pulls free, and looks into my eyes, confusion clear in her frown.

"Then what's the issue? He's loved, he loves you, and he'll get over the fact his father's a douche."

Her brow furrows further, and her fists clench at her sides. "That's a cold thing to say to somebody you don't really know, isn't it?"

"It's the truth, too."

"Is this meant to be making me feel better?" she asks, stepping backward. "Because it's not."

I shrug. What can I say? I'm not trying to gloss over the fact of the matter—Sawyer's a complete and utter idiot. She's better off without him around. "I didn't intend to make you feel better about it all, Ramona. I just wanted to open the discussion with you, stop you bottling this hurt away."

"What's it to you?" Her slim arms cross over her chest as she stops, and I'm drawn to the tattoo on her breastbone of a dove among roses.

"I have a problem with caring too much," I say with a sigh. "But so far, that problem hasn't given anyone grief but myself. So as long as me being a nosey bastard pays off for the people I can help, I'll keep on being just that—fuckin' nosey."

Her shoulders drop and she makes her way to where I stand at the foot of the bed, falling to her ass on the mattress. "You're the only one who came to check on me. I should be thankful for that I suppose."

"I'm not the only one," I correct, taking a position on the bed as well, "just the one who got here first."

"Why?" she asks, truly stumped.

Good question, too. Why, in a room full of her closest friends, would a guy she's only just been introduced to be the one who feels the greatest need to comfort her? There's no glossing over the awkward intentions behind it, and no point denying it for fear of making things look even worse.

So I give it to her straight. "Because the minute you walked in to the room everything about you struck me hard, and right now, I want to know why."

Her hand moves to her chest, hovering over the image inked there.

"Why the dove?" I ask, gesturing to her piece with my chin.

She traces the outline of the bird with a finger, down to the tail feathers, which are sheathed in a black fog that extends behind the roses. "It symbolizes my struggle for peace. The roses are the beauty of life hiding the darkness that consumes the dove."

A large lump forms in my throat, and I bring my gaze up to meet hers.

She shrugs. "It just fits me perfectly."

It shouldn't. A fire ignites inside of me. One day I'm going to change the way she feels about that—I know it. It pains me to see such a breathtaking woman so upset. Miracles of beauty shouldn't express such an ugly side of life. It's just wrong.

"Come here," I instruct, holding out an arm.

She shakes her head, huddling her hands to her chest.

"It wasn't a request," I tell her. "Come here."

Her shoulders heave, and she closes the space, sitting close, but far enough apart that even the dip of the bed doesn't give us reason to touch. *Not cool with that.* Ramona gives in as I wrap my arm around her and pull her to my side. The point of her collarbone digs into my chest and I heave a sigh. Her rigidity tells me she noticed.

"If I'm putting you out, then you're welcome to go." Her words are polite, but the tone far from it.

"And leave you here?" I scoff. "Doubt it."

"I'm not your problem, Ty."

"Anything else?" I ask.

"What do you mean?" Her slender features tilt toward me and I meet those gorgeous blue eyes.

"Any more excuses why you don't need my company?"

Her face lights a little at my cheeky smile, but she hides her joy quickly. "Not yet."

"Then shut the hell up and just sit."

Minutes stretch into what could have been hours for all I know. Her breath is steady, and a few times I lean my head forward to check she's still awake. Those cobalt irises stare out at nothing each time, unwavering. She's gone somewhere else, but wherever it is, I'm pretty certain I'm giving her confidence to do so, a safe place to come back to.

My arm grows weary; still, I sit. The tones of blossom flowers drifts up from her hair, and after waging an internal war with myself, I give in and rest my nose in her fire-red locks. She hums, lets out a little vibration from deep in her chest. I place a gentle kiss to her head, and pull back before the intimacy overwhelms me.

"You ready to face the others?" I ask.

She shrugs. "Not sure."

"What scares you most about going back out there?"

"You've done plenty giving me company—I don't want to burden you with all my problems at once. It's not exactly a stellar first impression, is it?" She smiles weakly.

"Tonight's going to be one long night. You're going to have way too much time to think while the guys are out dropping Sawyer off at the meeting point. I think it'd be a good idea to lessen that load a little, don't you?"

Her shoulders jump. "Probably, but I don't want you thinking I'm this crazy little messed up woman." She does a little wiggly thing with her fingers, emphasizing the 'crazy'. "I don't know you from Adam."

"Trust your gut when it comes to people's character. Do I make you anxious?"

"No," she says with a laugh. "Far from it. That's what I can't understand."

"Why not?" This time I smile. "Do I look that threatening? I thought I pulled 'respectable' off pretty well until now. You've got me double-guessing myself."

She looks up at me and smiles, melting any apprehendsions I had at being here with her. "You look anything but threatening. You look very appealing." Her eyes dart down before she drops her chin, hiding her flushed cheeks.

I chuckle, giving her shoulders a squeeze. "Relax—I'm not passing judgment on you. Promise."

"I can't believe I said that," she murmurs.

"If it makes you feel better, I think you look very appealing, too." I match her smile. "Now we're even."

Ramona sighs, her mood shifting as she fidgets with the edge of her shirt. "I have a lot of things I'm afraid of, but I guess the biggest one is losing Sawyer for good, losing what family structure we have, and what that'll do to Mack."

My gut flips. The fact she's decided to open up is a start in the right direction. "What do you think will be the most important thing for Mack, to help him through?"

She draws a laden breath, and rubs a hand over her throat. "Me."

"Exactly. You are his everything, and you will be the only person that can bring him happiness no matter what the world throws at him. Yes his dad will be gone, but every kid needs their mom, and he's going to need you to be his rock. Whatever you're dealing with, whatever guilt you have, he doesn't give two shits about that—he just needs you. He'll need your love and the healing it will bring him."

She tugs away from my side, and stares silently into my eyes. It hurts in my chest to have her look so deeply inside of me. My skin heats at the fear she can see it all, see my façade, and I throw a few extra covers over the darkest pits of my soul, hiding the scared, sad man inside from the truth of the world.

She needn't speak a word—it's all there in her silent assessment of me. I speak from experience, knowing the pain an absence of love so deep from my own mother caused. And yet, she grants me dignity by briefly touching my jaw, and then turning her gaze away.

"I get the impression you know what you're talking about."

"For the most part."

"Will we recover from this, Mack and I?"

I pull in a heavy breath, and let it out slowly. "That's up to you."

"I hope I'll be able to do this," she whispers to the room. "I mean, I think I can."

I shake my head, and tuck her hair over her shoulders. "You don't *think* you can. Saying you *think* is only admitting the chance of defeat is higher than that of success. Positive, Ramona. Think positive and say 'I *know* I can'."

She nods, and stands. "I know I can do this." Her hands knot before her as she restlessly paces between the bed and the door. "When I think back on it, I've had worse, and I've survived. As long as I can still cuddle my baby at the end of the day, there's no reason why I can't deal with whatever comes my way. I need to remember what I have, not cry for what I've lost."

"Exactly."

Turning to face me, her fingers find my beard and she strokes the lengths away from my chin. "Thank you." My composure is dissolving.

"Any time," I murmur.

A smile graces her lips, and she nods toward the door. "Come on. I'll feel like a right dick if I go out there on my own and draw all the attention. What say you help take the heat off?"

I stand and walk to the door, taking the handle in my grasp. "Gladly."

a time and place

RAMONA "Can I help with anything?"

Sonya gives me a warm smile, and tugs me into a tight hug. "No, sweetheart. You just kick your feet up and leave it to us." She pulls her head away, hands still on my shoulders. "Take the opportunity to let us look after you." Sonya winks, and turns me around to face the living room. "Now, scoot."

Laughing, I take my cue and leave the kitchen. Since emerging from the bedroom, I've spent the better part of two hours on the sofa beside Sawyer and Mack, watching them, committing the moment to memory. There are so many things I want to say to him—good and bad. Yet, for my boy's sake, I keep my trap shut and my opinions to myself.

In the four years since Mack was born, I've never seen this level of calm intimacy between father and son. There was never a doubt in my mind that Sawyer loves his boy—it was there in every proud smile he showed when Mack reached another milestone. Still, they'd never spent one-on-one time like this, ever. I can't be sure if it's from a fear on Sawyer's behalf, or simply the fact that he hasn't a clue what he's doing since his dad is the coldest, least parent-like father a man could have.

Either way, the moment is rare, and I cherish it for what it is.

Mack fidgets beside Sawyer, and twists his little body to look over the back of the sofa at where I stand. "Mom. Is it dinnertime yet?"

"Not far away, baby. How about you go wash your hands?"

He nods, and drops off the seat, sparing Sawyer a quick glance before he runs away to the bathroom. I round the sofa and take his place, the warmth still in the cushion from where he'd been curled up beside his father.

"How you feeling?" I ask.

Sawyer stares at the TV, but his mind is a long way away from where we are. I've seen the vacancy in his eyes many a time before, always after he'd done something bad. I place my hand gently on his arm and he jerks, twisting his neck to look down at me with a fire in his eyes that scares the living daylights out of me. As the color drains from my face, the storm subsides from his gaze.

I can breathe again.

Sawyer frowns, and sighs. "Shit, I'm sorry, babe. I was thinkin' about somethin' else."

"I can see that," I deadpan. "I asked how you were

feeling."

His nose twitches on one side, and he smirks. "Like I'm gettin' everything that's due."

My smile is weak, my sadness laid out bare. "You have it in you to be better," I remind him. "You can change."

He chuckles, and lifts his bound hands to capture my fingers between his. "Babe, you need to stop bullshittin' yourself. I can't change, I never will, so stop hurtin' yourself waiting for the day that'll never come."

A loud clearing of the throat pulls my head around. "You good, Mona?" King's arrived.

"Fine thanks. How was the ride?"

"Good. Where's my little trooper?" he glances around for Mack.

"He's washing up before dinner." The last word is barely off my lips before Mack comes thundering into the room.

"Uncle King!"

"Hey, buddy." He gives Mack a hug, and then sets him down to ruffle his hair. "Been good for your mom?"

Mack nods enthusiastically, and I give a small smile and nod when King looks up to check if Mack's answer is correct. "Yeah, he's been good."

"You eaten?" Sonya asks from the doorway to the kitchen.

King shakes his head at her. "No, darlin'. Love a feed if you've got enough."

"We'll make do if we don't," Sonya responds with a smile and turns her attention to me. "Mona, can you help us with the table?"

I nod and get up, making it halfway to the kitchen when King pulls me aside. "How's Sawyer been?" he whispers.

"Bad," I answer in earnest. "He's shutting down, going to his 'happy' place."

King's shoulders rise and fall as he steals a look over Sawyer's way. "It's probably the best thing for the bastard, really."

"Yeah," I agree. "Probably."

With the kind of shit Sawyer's been getting up to in the name of pissing off his old man, I can't expect the reunion to be pretty. Whatever solace he finds in his madness, he'll need that comfort to make it through the coming days.

King gives me a gentle rub between the shoulders, and smiles at Mack as he wanders past with his toy cars. King's head swings back toward the sofa. "I guess I better go have a word with the idiot." He draws a deep breath, and makes his way over to where Callum is now interrogating Sawyer.

"You coming?" Sonya calls gently from the kitchen.

I turn and head in to where she stands beside Jane, mashing a pot of potato. "Yeah, I'm here. Sorry, babe."

"Don't let that boy get to you," Jane says with a small smile. "Nothing you do will change what's already passed."

"I know." I busy myself pulling out knives and forks for everybody. "Thanks girls, just for, you know, being there."

They both dazzle me with their pure, genuine smiles

before Sonya replies. "That's what we're here for. Us girls have to stick together, especially with what our men put us through."

That we do.

I set the table and help the girls plate up meals for everyone, chatting about everyday topics like which store has denim on sale, and the TV programs we're all engrossed in right now. The moment is a slip of the normal—exactly what I need to calm my apprehension at what tonight brings.

Ty's place doesn't have enough chairs to accommodate our cramped guests at the table, so I turn a laundry hamper upside down to seat Mack and take my dinner in the kitchen. Conversation floats across from the gathering, and I let my mind relax, listening to their banter. After scoffing down all I can stomach of the meal, which isn't much, I plate up a serving for Sawyer and head to the sofa as the boys continue to make small talk over their dinner.

Sawyer watches me approach, his eyes now clear and with me as he smiles. Taking a seat beside him, I look down at his bound hands and sigh. How exactly did the guys expect him to be able to eat like this? Did they even plan on feeding him? Tucking the fork into the potatoes, I lift a portion to his lips and hold it steady as he accepts the bite. His sharp eyes lock onto mine, and as I have a million times before, I feel a mixture of exposure and sadness. His gaze punches a hole straight through my false bravado to my heart, and spreads its inky black through the warmth I'd been carefully cultivating since speaking with Ty.

How am I supposed to be brave when the totality of my fears sits mere inches from me?

I feed Sawyer, bite by bite, all the while acutely aware I'm not only being watched by him, but by pretty much everybody at the table as they all take turns checking out the show. My neck burns. They must find me so weak, so pitiful, catering to a man who's done nothing but cause me hurt and misery. Yet, I remind myself, they don't know the Sawyer I do. They haven't heard his cries in his sleep. They've never had to rock a full-grown man in their arms while he worked a bad trip out of his system. They haven't witnessed the broken child that hides inside of this twisted man.

I push their judgments aside and focus squarely on the task at hand—giving Sawyer one last act of kindness before his world shifts on its axis. To most he doesn't deserve this, any of it, but a part of me harbors a ridiculous notion that perhaps this will be it? Perhaps this will be the final step toward him changing? That my act of selflessness will touch something inside of him, and start a chain reaction?

Sawyer finishes the last of the food I brought over for him, as the discussion behind us grows heated. I glance behind me, and notice Ty has left the table; the remaining men all sit in various positions of defense. I've been so engrossed in caring for Sawyer that I never noticed anybody move. The raised voices behind me send a wave of anger surging through my chest. The guys are arguing, swearing at one another while my child sits at the table with them.

"Was that enough?" I ask Sawyer, lifting the plate a little with a painted smile.

He nods. "Yeah, babe. That was perfect."

My ass is out of the chair, and the plate in the kitchen before I can count to five. I swing past the table and scoop Mack from his seat. "Time for a bedtime story, huh? What do you think?"

He smiles and rushes ahead of me down the hallway, checking the rooms until he finds the one we're sharing. I round the doorway to discover him already halfway into his pajamas. He points a short finger at one of the books we bought from a gas station while we were stopped for fuel on our way down here. "Can we have that one?"

"Sure," I answer with a smile. "Don't forget to do your teeth, though."

He tugs the top of his pajamas on and then sets about rifling through the bag of toiletries for his toothbrush. Holding it high, he charges out of the room and toward the bathroom to clean his pearly-whites. While he's gone, I flick through the storybook, checking how long it is, and simultaneously loathing the fact I'm terrible enough to be hoping it's short so I can have a shower and slip into bed, too.

Mack returns, replaces his brush, and we go through the book in record time. His eyes are shut when I leave the room to shower, and by the time I return he's dead to the world. I sit for a moment, watching him, as a slinking sadness creeps through me at how much he resembles his father. The familiar ache starts in my toes and fills me like lead, weighing my limbs and leaving me physically and mentally drained. The tax on me to stay strong, to stay calm and composed while Mack is awake is already hard. How the hell am I going to cope in a week, a month?

I've barely pulled my sleepwear from the small bag I brought when Sonya's head pops around the door. "You up for a game of poker?" she whispers. "Our boys left with Sawyer a few minutes ago, and Malice's lot have disappeared to the garage."

"I didn't hear them leave," I mumble, a little upset that I never had a final moment to say goodbye to Sawyer.

"They left when you were in the shower," she explains. A soft smile graces her lips. "Didn't want to upset you, I think."

Nodding, I wring the over-sized T-shirt in my hands. "A game of poker could be fun," I whisper. "Give me five."

Sonya nods and disappears silently up the hallway. I tug the T-shirt and shorts on under the towel, dropping it at the last second. Mack stirs slightly when I place the damp bath sheet over the footboard of the bed to dry for tomorrow. Leaning over, I lift the blanket up over his shoulders before heading out to join the others.

Jane has the dining table set out for a game with Hershey's Kisses in the center as our chips. The lights are off, all bar one hanging lamp over the table setting the mood. Sonya pours us each a glass of wine, gesturing to a seat as she finishes, while Jane shuffles the pack. I slip on to the chair, drawing a deep breath as Sonya doles out our 'chips'.

"So?" she asks.

"What?"

"How are you doing?" She pushes the final chocolate my way, and then leans her forearms on the edge of the table.

I shrug, looking down at my cards. "Hasn't sunk in yet. There's still this part of me that's stopping the reality of it all taking hold."

"Let me know when it does," she says, squeezing my hand.

I nod tightly and turn my attention to the table. "Who's going first?"

Jane smiles and picks up her cards. "Anybody but me. I'm terrible at this."

Before long, I've lost myself to the game. The girls never ask anything else about Sawyer the rest of the night, and none of us speak about a single thing to do with the club or what Malice, Bronx and Ty do. The three of us spend a few happy hours ignoring the stark truths of our lives, and it's heaven.

We're still laughing when the boys return, looking every bit as sullen as I've been pretending I'm not.

"What's so funny?" Malice asks.

"Nothing," Jane sings in reply, sashaying her hips toward him and very effectively drawing his attention away from what we were talking about.

"Look what we stumbled across outside," Bronx calls out, wandering through the door with King, Callum and

Vince in tow.

The absence of Sawyer smacks me square in the face—they've done it, traded him out.

Ty steps to the side to let them all past, having come in after Malice himself. His gaze catches mine, and he smiles sympathetically. I drop my line of sight to the floor—looking at him only fed an urge inside of me to cross the room and seek out the comfort of his arms again. Everybody here is willing to support me through this, but the lack of a person to hold me and make me feel loved with the intensity that only a person your truly intiate with can, amplifies my loneliness. Knowing Ty's able to give me that comfort, but also knowing I can't have it for fear of how it would be perceived by my friends, is torture.

I walked a fine line when they found out about the affair I had going on with Bruiser—making the same mistake twice would surely lower whatever esteem they might hold me in. I can't risk that when I know without a shadow of a doubt I'm going to need these people around me for support while I rebuild Mack and my lives. I can't continue to chase love where it doesn't exist.

The boys all rib each other while I'm lost to my thoughts, warmed by the beers they've been sharing. Voices are raised, and for a fleeting moment I consider going to check they haven't woken Mack, but after I look up, I find I can't move. Ty's eyes are still locked to me and although I try, I can't bring myself to look away.

"Eww, Dad. Take it behind closed doors, huh?" Malice's

protests about his father kissing Sonya finally draw our attention away from each other.

I busy myself watching Jane usher Malice off to bed before he can do any more harassing, flashing us all an apologetic smile. Warmth envelops me before I even register Ty has stepped beside me.

"You okay?"

"I'd be a lot better if everybody stopped asking me that."

"They're only concerned," he says, brushing shoulders with me as we watch Jane wrestle Malice through the bedroom doorway.

I inch a little further from him, unnerved at the buzz tickling my flesh where we connected. "I know. In a way I'm just waiting for tonight to be over, to wake up tomorrow and feel a little more like this was all a dream."

"But it's not."

"That's what scares me. When did this become my life?"

"Things have a way of sneaking up on you," he says with a shrug. "The biggest changes are always the ones we have no control over because we never see them coming. They're always an accumulation of tiny steps in our life that we paid no mind to given they were so inconsequential on their own, but when you analyze them all together, you wonder how you never saw the end result for what it was, how you could let things go that way without doing much to stop it."

I stare up at him, his flawless profile, as he clearly

speaks from experience, from an understanding of what this is like—this feeling of helplessness over your future. "You're in my head."

He tilts his face down to me, and grins. "It's unnerving, isn't it, to have somebody understand so intricately."

"A little," I answer, heat spreading my across the crest of my cheeks.

The clatter of glassware from the kitchen snaps me back to my senses. We're in a room full of people, and here I am having an intimate moment with a man I hardly know. How would that look to everybody else?

Glancing around I feel a little better when I realize there isn't a single soul in the place who's paying us any mind. Callum's busy shaking out a blanket while King cracks the top off a bottle of Jack. Bronx emerges from the bathroom, completely oblivious to us as he staggers past—too consumed checking out his reflection in the glass doors that lead to the porch. Vince and Sonya are also so engrossed in each other I doubt they'd notice a bomb going off.

"If it's all good with you lot," Callum says, whipping my head about, "I'm going to crash. It's been a long day." He flops down on the sofa, settling himself in for the night.

"Night," I chorus with the others.

Ty's fingers brush against mine, drawing my attention toward the tall man who stands patiently by my side. Vince and Sonya make quick work of disappearing to their room, leaving us alone with Callum, Bronx, who is organizing his spot for the night, and King, drinking himself into a stupor alone on the sofa.

"Try and sleep," Ty says quietly. "I'll be here in the morning if you want to talk more."

I nod, biting my lip to stem the raw emotions building into tears of desperation: at the loss of Sawyer, at this strange connection to a man I barely know, and mostly at the thought of facing a new day where Mack is without a father.

"Let you in on a secret," Ty whispers, bending a little to place his mouth closer to my ear. "If you fill your head with happy memories before you go to sleep, you'll be sure to make your dreams good ones." His beard tickles the point of my jaw, just below my ear, as he closes the small space between us and places a gentle kiss to my temple.

My eyes flutter closed, my effort on pressing the lids tight, on bottling the rush before I fall apart on a few simple words. "Thank you." My fingers tangle in his, and he responds, tightening the grip.

Silence hangs thick as I stare into his brown eyes, lost for a moment in what it would be like if I hadn't bound myself to Sawyer, but instead, had met a man like Ty. I don't want him to go—I don't want the loneliness of the night to hit me yet.

Making the first move and disengaging my fingers from his, I take a step back and hesitate, before turning and making my way up the hall to the bedroom I share with Mack. The day has been nothing short of a ball of conflicting emotions.

Every fiber in my body reaches for the comfort of bed, for the recharge a few hours sleep will provide. But as I lie in the dark having climbed into the king bed beside Mack, I stare at the deep grey shadows on the ceiling wondering what Ty's thinking. Is it about me? Have I affected him at all? Or is this curiosity one-sided and he's out there focused on something other than me, another woman perhaps?

With a laden sigh, I slip my eyes closed and furrow my brow. Why is it on the day my partner returned home to a father I know loathes him, am I thinking of another man? What the hell is wrong with me? I'm selfish, unfaithful to the man who will forever be tied to me because of one beautiful blue-eyed mistake.

What sort of woman am I?

midnight snacks

TY Pale light illuminates the room as I tap my phone to check the time. *Two in the morning.* King snores on the sofa next to me in his intoxicated state. Callum lies curled up on the other armchair, legs and arms at all angles. Leather and denim is strewn about the room like confetti, the men having peeled off the layers of their image to find some sort of comfort with their temporary sleeping arrangements.

Stretching my legs out, I rub the heels of my hands in my eyes. I'm tired, I should have gone home, but hanging out here seemed like the only option the moment Ramona's fingers sought mine.

Sleep eludes me. Not only because King is currently sawing down a damn forest, but because my mind wont still. Facts, figures, scenarios all swirl through my head in a kaleidoscope of information. Over half of all single mothers in America live in extreme poverty, a third receiving food stamps to feed their family. What if that's her? What if she becomes that statistic now Sawyer isn't around to support her?

Why do I care?

None of this is any of my business, but I've never been one to walk away from a person in need. *Sucker for punishment.* Pushing out of the chair, I make my way quietly to the kitchen and draw myself a glass of water. Apart from King's snoring, the house is cloaked in silence. Even Jane's dog is fast asleep on his bed by the door. With a hand on my waist, I toss back the last of the water and move to place the glass down.

My arm freezes, suspended over the sink. *Am I hearing things?* My senses attune to the scuff of feet, and the soft inhale, exhale of somebody nearby. Resting the glass softly in the sink, I head around the corner toward the hallway, wondering who's sneaking around at this hour.

We collide.

Ramona yelps, slapping a hand over her mouth. Both of us turn toward the sleeping men on the furniture, waiting with bated breath.

Nothing.

"Sorry," she whispers beside me. "I can't sleep."

"Neither," I answer under my breath. I rake my gaze down her body in the low moonlight, noting her T-shirt and short fucking shorts. "Where were you headed?"

"I hadn't thought that far ahead." Her arms cross over her body.

I shake off the fact her head's tilted in such a way she

can only be checking out my state of mostly undress, and thumb toward the armchair I'd been on. "Let me grab my clothes and a blanket. We can sit outside and talk for a while if you like; save us waking this lot up."

Her fire-red hair bobs as she nods, the waves flowing free of her earlier ponytail. "Sounds good."

Snatching my shirt from where I left it on the back of the chair, I shrug it on over my head, leaving the top half of the buttons undone. She watches me untangle the legs of my jeans, and tug them on. With the blanket in my arms, I gesture to the doors leading to the porch. "After you."

Ramona stills before the glass, taking her time to depress the handle and edge the door open. I check over my shoulder at the others while she creeps out onto the porch. Nobody has moved, and King's still going for some record with that God awful sound. I follow Ramona out, patting Rocco on the head as I do, and close the door with the same care she took. Turning, I find her curled on one of the chairs, knees to her chest and the T-shirt stretched over top.

"Here," I say, handing her the blanket. "Wrap that around your shoulders for a minute."

She watches me drag a chair over and position it facing hers. I take a seat, and set my legs wide. "Come, sit here." I pat the seat between my thighs.

"Uh . . ."

"With your back to me," I explain. "Sit over here so I can wrap the blanket around both of us."

She hesitates for a fraction, and then twists in her seat before scooting backwards onto mine. Grabbing her by the waist, I shunt her closer so there's barely a gap between us. She passes the blanket over, helping me tuck it in around her legs after I've thrown it around my shoulders and placed the ends over her.

"This is weird," she says with a nervous giggle.

"You'll get used to it." I relax my legs so that she's trapped between my knees. "Feeling warmer, though?"

She nods, still leaning forward so her head isn't resting against me.

"What was keeping you awake then?" I ask, wriggling my feet up onto her empty chair.

"Guilt." Her shoulders relax.

"What about?"

A resigned huff escapes her nose. "I should be crying, Ty. I should be heart-broken about what they've done with Sawyer, but I'm not. How wrong is that?"

I don't know if it's wrong, but it's most certainly odd. "You must miss him?"

She shrugs. "I miss the idea of him."

"What do you mean by that?"

Her hands fidget under the blanket, letting gusts of cold air in. "Sawyer was never a great father," she explains. "He loves our son, but he was never there for him. They haven't done a single thing together, just the two of them, ever. I think I miss the idea that he could have changed. I regret not having the chance to know if he would have."

"Perhaps not having him around isn't such a bad thing given his mental state?" The man's a damn lunatic. Why would she want that influence in her child's life?

"He was never like that with us—not really. I saw glimpses of it, I knew he had issues, but I chose to ignore it because, for the most part, he was fine when he *was* home."

"Did he hit the road a lot?"

"I shouldn't be talking to you about any of this," she murmurs, shaking her head. "You don't know us."

"Fix the problem, then," I reply. "Tell me all about you."

Her head twists so she can look up at me. "Are you like this with everyone?"

"I'd like to think so." *First time for everything.*

"It's awkward enough sitting out here in the middle of the night with you like we're a couple of kids sneaking around or something. I don't know if I can be comfortable telling you more than I already have."

Pushing back the need to squeeze her, force the secrets from her, I slip my arms between the chair and my legs. "Do whatever helps you," I say, dropping my head back and closing my eyes.

The dynamic between her and Sawyer is interesting. She cares, but there doesn't seem to be *love*. Why does that intrigue me so much? Why do I feel like that's the detail I want to exploit about her?

She's beautiful; delicate features contrasted by her alternative appearance. Her hair is the first thing you notice—fire engine red and long, flowing to half way down her back. But the more I look at her, the more little details I find, the more things that captivate me. A nose ring fitted snug over her nostril, a piercing on the inside of her ear, tattoos over her chest and side of her neck. How many more are hidden below the clothing she wears?

Why does the need to know leave me restless?

"What had *you* still awake?"

Her question shakes me from my spiraling thoughts. I snap my eyes open, and drop my head forward to find hers resting against my chest. *Feels so good.* "I was worried about you."

"Why?"

"I don't know. I think it's because I feel like I could help you."

Her hands move under the blanket and slender fingers rest on my shin. "I didn't ask for help, though."

"People who need it never do."

The sound of her swallowing echoes off the confines of the porch. "I think I should try to get some sleep again." Ramona pushes forward, the blanket falling free of her legs.

I reach out, capturing her arm in my hand. "I'm sorry if I made you feel uncomfortable. Can you stay a bit longer?"

"There's no need. You don't have to try and help me, Ty—I can do this alone." She moves out of my hold and stands.

Frustration wedges tight in my chest. What can I say? That having her close seems to ease the perpetual ache I carry with me? "I feel better when you're around," I admit.

"It calms me."

"You don't strike me as a very high-strung guy."

"Then we really *don't* know each other that well."

Her brow twitches. "I can't do this. I'm sorry." She steps away, heading for the door.

Lunging from the chair, I catch her shoulder and spin her to face me. "Can't do what? Why are you running?"

"Because being around you makes me feel things, and I know it's wrong to."

"Ramona, you need to tell me," I plead, heart beating erratically. "What kind of 'things' are you feeling?" I need to know if they're the same.

"Like you could be something incredible for me. But . . ."

God, she's killing me. "But?"

"It's not the right time." She smiles softly.

A beat passes with us staring at one another. I don't want the moment to end. I don't want her to walk away. "Do you love him?" My tongue is thick in my mouth.

She shakes her head, smiling, yet her eyes are sad . . . so damn sad. "Not like you think—that's the problem."

Breathing is a concentrated effort, the air running thin about me as she ducks her head and turns away. With each step she takes toward the door, my anxiety builds once more, climbing to a new height as the catch clicks behind her. I stand like a fool—a love-struck fool—watching her shadow disappear toward the hallway.

I met the woman who will change my life.

I think, in a way, she already has.

distance

RAMONA "Do you ever wonder what's happened with Sawyer?" I ask Sonya the next afternoon.

We're curled up on chairs in the living room, enjoying some sun while Malice and Vince see Bronx and Ty off outside. The mood in the house has been awkward to say the least since I told Ty I needed to keep away from him. He did his part; each time I walked in to the same room he discreetly got up and left.

It burned.

It shouldn't.

I asked him to give me the distance, I needed it, and yet, it hurts. The sooner I can move on with a fresh start for Mack and I the better. The distraction is very, *very* needed.

"Sometimes." Sonya answers my question, her mouth screwed to the side in contemplation. "But we need to make peace with what he's done, Mona. The man had it coming; it just sucks we had to be the ones to deliver."

I nod, closing my eyes. Why did the people who were supposed to love him sell him out? "I'm getting tired of this, Sonya."

"Of what?" she asks, shifting in her seat.

"Being so emotionally invested in a lifestyle that only leads to heartache." I open my eyes, finding some peace in watching the sunlight dance across the ceiling. "It seems like every time I think the club is finally settling down, something else comes up. I don't know how much longer I can stay strong for Mack like this."

If nothing else, talking with Ty gave me reason to think outside the square. What *if* I had a life apart from the club? What if I *did* find a man who genuinely cared for us and could support us the right way—the *legal* way?

"What are you thinking of doing?" Sonya asks, setting aside the book she'd been reading before I interrupted her.

"Leaving the life. Starting again." I watch her closely, gauging her reaction to my decision.

"Where?" she asks.

"Here. I've been looking around at schools and housing. It seems pretty good here, plus I'd have these guys as support. Jane's lovely." She jumped right on board when I tested my plan on her this morning, pointing out where I could look to find information on what options there are for Mack and I.

"She is," Sonya agrees. Her gaze moves to the porch,

looking over where the men stood moments before. "How do you think Mack would take it?"

I shrug, wondering how much worse it could be than dealing with tantrums over what he's allowed to eat . . . like I just have. "He's young enough still to adapt. And quite frankly, I'd rather he was upset about moving houses than having another 'uncle' at the club die." A drastic statement, but nonetheless true.

Sonya goes quiet, seemingly thinking things over. "Have you told King how you're feeling?"

She knows as well as I do that he'll take it the hardest. "Not yet." I can't bring myself to face his disappointment just yet.

Sonya moves forward in her seat, brow furrowed. "Sweetheart, you have to do what is right for you. Don't you worry about the opinions of others. You trust your gut, and if it says you need to leave us behind and start afresh, then do it."

Her words touch my heart—it's that kind of love I'm going to miss. "I wouldn't leave you all behind. We'd still visit, but I need that distance . . . for Mack."

She reaches out, taking my hand in hers. "I get it. Just make sure you have a spare room for us to visit you as well."

I nod, smiling. "I will."

"Now," Sonya exclaims, standing, "I better go find my man so we can organize what we're having for dinner."

She heads for the door, pausing when I call after her. "Sonya?"

"Yeah?"

"Thank you for everything you did over the years. For me and Mack. I don't think anyone ever tells you that enough, but we all need you. We'd be lost around that place if you left." Lord knows, I'm going to struggle enough as it is not having her close by to lend a hand when I need it.

"Good thing I don't have any plan to," she says turning away.

I watch her go, drawing a deep breath. The fresh start will do us good, at least, I try to convince myself it will. Mack doesn't need the heartache I've seen the people I love go through when our shady lifestyle catches up to us. He needs stability, *normality*. He needs to never touch a bloody motorcycle as long as he lives and be somebody other than what he sees all around him.

He needs to become anybody but his father.

Regret twists my gut when I think of where Sawyer is right now. How is he faring? How badly has Carlos hurt him? Because I have no doubt he has. Why didn't I take the opportunity to set aside my anger at what Sawyer had done to our family, and ask him what *he* wanted for Mack's future?

All I can hope is that I'm doing the right thing. If not, then I'm at a loss of what *is* right. Taking us away from the influence of the club seems the last option for saving Mack from a future behind bars, injured in a turf war, or worse.

My duty as a mother supersedes any anxiety I have at leaving the only family *I've* known behind. What I need doesn't matter. The future is Mack, and I need to give him the best start possible.

Even if that includes turning down the chance at what I've wanted most since the day I discovered what a double-edged sword a man's attention could be—to be loved.

game not over

TY Malice is yapping on at Bronx about something while I sit in the driver's seat of my Audi, waiting for them to finish their afternoon gossip. I check the side mirror, glancing back at the front door of the house.

She's not coming out again—I know that, but it doesn't stop me from hoping.

Ramona approached me while I was packing my stuff into the car, clearing the air before we went our separate ways. It's nice, being able to leave without things remaining unresolved between us. But at the same time our discussion has made it harder for me to even imagine I could simply walk away from her. She's dealing with *so* much stuff right now, and if anything, I know after our talk that the stress is taking one hell of a toll on her.

She tells me she needs to go it alone, but her sad eyes tell me otherwise.

I want to do something nice, something to ease her

burden, but I can't think what wouldn't come off as inappropriate from a guy she barely knows. All my ideas are toeing the line of the 'friend zone', which is where she's so readily put me.

It's not the right time—her exact words. Painful, but true.

My fingers skim the edges of my phone, the idea turning over in my mind of sending her a message, something to brighten her day. But again, friend zone, I need to stay in it—at least, for now.

A smile curls my lips as I think back on how easy it was to get hold of Sonya's phone and pilfer Ramona's details. Women—they never keep track of where their shit is. She never had a clue anything had moved in her purse. Never said a damn thing.

Never thought the skill learnt from being a pick-pocket would ever come in handy like that.

I place my phone in the center console as Bronx opens the passenger door. "Finally," I tease. "You two could gossip for hours."

"Fuck up," he says with a laugh, pulling the sun-visor down.

"Headache?" I ask, turning the key.

"Yeah." He drops his head back on the rest as I pull away, giving Malice and Vince a wave. "You know I'm not a huge drinker. It hits me hard when I do."

"Then don't do it."

He shrugs. "Needed to clear my head."

I glance over at him, wondering if the decision we

made last night is the right one. "How you with our plan? You up for it?"

"If it means cuttin' the assholes who used Tigger off at the knees, then hell yeah, I'm up for it."

I'm not convinced by his over-zealous enthusiasm. "You realize what you'll need to do . . . to fit in."

He rolls his head to face me. "I'm not stupid, Ty."

"Didn't say you were," I reply, flexing my knuckles on the steering wheel. "Just checking in."

"Yeah, I know."

We travel in silence for a while, heading toward town. I'd been so wrapped up in working out what it is that has me infatuated with Ramona, I hadn't stopped to think about the obvious issue with the boys—our lives are about to change course dramatically.

"I hope we're doing the right thing," I say, drawing Bronx's attention. "I always thought that this gig we had would be temporary, you know? Like, when we started this thing I was so convinced that it was a means to an end, a way to get us off the street. But now I'm not so sure."

"I understand," he says quietly. "I think about it a lot too, and I know Malice does as well."

"We fucked up, hey?"

"Massively."

"I should have turned down that first job, told the guy to get fucked and walked the other way."

"He would have shanked you, dude." Bronx straightens in his seat. "You didn't have an option, and fuck man, we were desperate."

"Just wish I know now what I did then."

"Don't we all."

The car falls into silence once more, enough having been said.

I drive on, pulling up eventually at Bronx's house, setting his dogs off. He hesitates as he gets out, looking down at the floor of the car while he speaks.

"None of this is your fault, Ty."

He steps out of the way, and the slam of his door echoes in the confines of the car. I watch him walk up the path, disappointed that I can't feel the same way about how our lives have turned out.

After all, if it wasn't for my bright fucking idea, none of us would have ever lifted a knife to another mans throat in the battle to survive. A hard decision each of us willingly made given we all would have chosen to starve to death before we returning to our respective families for help.

How fucked up is that?

duty

one week later

RAMONA I told King I'd do it, and I fully intend to keep my word. Still, I've never been the kind of person who can just barrel up to a total stranger's door and make conversation happen. I don't even know what the fuck I'm going to say first. 'Hey, how about we sit down with a coffee and organize your relocation?' or 'You don't know me, but in the next however-long-it-takes I'm going to convince you to move out of your house.' Yeah, easy as. Seriously, what am I worried about?

Here goes nothing.

Sonya reaches for my hand and gives it a little squeeze. Vince's old lady stands beside me outside Elena's house—the ex-girlfriend of one crazy-ass motherfucker drug-lord, and apparently, the mother to our president's child. How's that for sins of the heart?

Kind of makes my indiscretions pale in comparison.

"You ready to do this?" she asks.

I look up to the blue sky and listen to the soft laughter of kids playing several houses down. The day is perfect, and right now I'm not sure if I want to ruin it. I've had a lot of shit to deal with myself this past week, what with Sawyer being returned to said drug-lord—his father—organizing my own relocation to a whole new town, and the fact I can't stop thinking about a man I have shouldn't be so interested in. One lazy Saturday filled with sunshine isn't too much to ask for, is it?

"I guess so." I give Sonya's hand a squeeze back and step towards the house.

Delicate blue flowers fill the garden beds either side of the wide entrance steps. They're pretty and scream of summer, but something else about them gives me a shiver—there are clumps of them crushed under the front window, as though someone had stood on them. My eyes trace the yard and I notice tiny details that had been oblivious mere seconds before: a spot of blood on the path, a broken shutter on the window, fresh paint on the side of the garage where writing has been covered up, and the overwhelming silence that envelops the property, so at contrast from the hum of the neighborhood.

Sonya sucks in a deep breath beside me as we come to a stop before the plain white door. She lifts her hand and raps her knuckles three short times on the wood. We exchange glances while we wait for an answer. My gaze drifts from her face, over her shoulder, and to the black SUV parked down the road. The vehicle itself is creepy in that every-window-is-tinted-so-I-can-murder-you-inside way, but the thing that has my heart quickening is the white emblem on the front guard—Carlos's.

The door cracks open and a single brown eye peers at us from the gap. "Can I help you?"

Sonya points to her flouro vest and the charity logo stuck on the chest. "King sent us to speak with you. This is a guise for our friends down the way."

A beat passes during which no words are spoken. I watch the face behind the door, wondering if she'll let us in, or if we're going to be left out in the cold. Eventually, the woman, who has to be Elena, sighs and shuts the door to remove the chain. She swings it wide and nods for us to come in. She's strikingly beautiful: large eyes framed with dark lashes, glossy black hair, and a beautiful caramel complexion. In her presence, I immediately feel ten times worse in my stupid fucking disguise: blonde wig that itches like a bastard, and makeup covering the tattoos on my arm.

She leads the way, pausing for us to catch up at the doorway to the living room after Sonya shuts the front door behind us. Elena holds a hand out toward the sofa.

"Please, take a seat." Her Cuban accent is slight, but still fairly obvious.

We settle on the edge of the seat cushions, more rigid than a couple of girls in a school photo. Elena takes a quick look out the front window before joining us in the opposite armchair. Her long slender legs appear to go on for miles before meeting the frayed edges of her denim shorts.

"Thank you for allowing us to talk with you," I say. "We weren't sure if you'd even let us in." I smile nervously.

"I would have preferred not," she says bluntly, bobbing the foot of her crossed leg in the air, "but Dante was up late last night and he's having a quick sleep before dinner. I'd rather avoid the drama if it means he gets to stay resting."

I look to Sonya, praying like hell she has something to say. Right now, I'm done. This woman looks like a tough nut to crack.

"How long have Carlos's men been watching you?" Sonya asks.

Elena cuts her gaze to the window. "I don't think that's the reason why you're here, is it?"

Sonya flexes her fingers in her lap, and draws a deep breath. "King hasn't told us much of what is going on at present, but enough for us to understand the urgency of the matter. I don't want you to think your privacy has been compromised; we're the only ones in the club besides King who know of you and Dante."

Elena rolls her eyes to the ceiling and shakes her head. "Typical. He wouldn't want to be shamed in front of his men. How would that look, huh? Fathering a child to the enemy's ex?"

"I don't think that's the case at all," Sonya snaps, frowning. "King simply respects your privacy, and given the situation with Carlos, he probably assumes the less people that know what's going on, the better. Would I be right, you think?"

Elena nods, running a hand through her locks to push them out of her face. I shrink into my seat, sneaking a hand to my head to scratch beneath this God-forsaken wig.

Tension hangs thick in the air as Sonya's no-nonsense side comes out full-force. "How about we cut to the chase, bypass the niceties that you obviously don't have time for, and just talk about why you're ignoring King's offer of help."

Elena switches her tanned legs over, and leans back in the armchair. "I spent many years afraid of Carlos, doing as he pleased for fear of his punishments. It took me a lot of work, and a lot of unhappy days to get to where I am now. I'm not running from him again. I will fight before I lose what I've struggled to gain."

"And risk Dante's safety?" I ask. I could never put my pride before Mack's well-being.

She sets her steely gaze on me and I begin to question what the fuck I was thinking agreeing to do this. "He is with me, therefore, he will be safe."

Sonya rubs a hand over her forehead and sighs. "Tell me, Elena, if you were faced with Carlos at your door just now, do you think you would have been able to overpower him?"

"I have the security chain," she says defiantly.

I can't help it—I snort. "I've seen those things fly apart after a good boot on the door from a teenage girl. They don't do squat if the person is hell-bent on getting in."

"I beg to differ," she answers, turning toward at me.

Her holier-than-thou arrogance is starting to really grate. "Want a demonstration?" I snap. "More than happy to help, you know."

She glares at me, nostrils flaring.

"Anyway," Sonya exclaims loudly, clapping her hands together and snapping us from our showdown, "I want to propose a compromise."

"I'm sure I won't agree," Elena bites, "but go ahead and waste your breath if you must."

Looking at the stone-faced woman as she sits there, defiant and stubborn as hell, I struggle to imagine her afraid and cowering under Carlos. If the guy came up against her now, I kind of have to wonder what he'd think. Did he know this was how defiant she could be, and that was what drove him to try and break her?

"Two weeks," Sonya says. "Tell Dante it's a holiday to see his father, and move out of the house for two weeks. Come back with us. Let the boys do what they're best at and give them that time at least to make it as safe as possible for you when you move back."

Elena twirls a strand of her long black hair around a finger. There's consideration of the idea at least—that has to be a start. "I'm not sure. I'd want to know—"

She never gets to finish her sentence. All three of us snap our heads toward the front door after two deafening thumps. "Elena Burgadas!"

Her eyes go wide, and then quickly narrow on us. "This is all your fault." She stands abruptly and heads for the door, calling over her shoulder. "They've never approached me until now."

Sonya and I stay rooted to the spot. The rattle of the chain is followed by the click of the door. I move from the sofa and creep closer to the doorway, out of sight of the entrance, to hear what's going on.

"Why are you here?" Elena asks. "Carlos's time is wasted on me. He has no right to have you thugs following us around."

"Who are the women?" the faceless man asks.

"Nobody," she snaps in return. Elena's certainly not sparing any of her rage on the guy.

"Can I speak with them?" he taunts.

I cut my gaze to Sonya, and she shrugs, validating my thoughts. What do we do?

Elena scoffs at the guy. "You most certainly can not speak to them. Now go, and tell your *jefe* that if he does not call you off and leave my family alone, I will go to the police with all that I know."

I cringe, grinding my teeth together. The fucking woman has just signed her bloody death warrant.

"You're a stupid fucking cunt." Our unwanted visitor hisses. "You have any idea what he'll have us do to you for making such threats?" The thud of something against the door precedes Elena's grunts.

"Stop it!" she protests.

"Who are the women?" the man repeats, followed by more thumping.

"Nobody important; charity volunteers. You are

scaring them!"

"Liar!"

Sonya steps up beside me and leans in close. "Should we do something?"

"No," I say, pulling my phone out. "Not yet." I hammer a quick text to Callum. *'SOS.'* "Give the boys a chance to get here first."

"You can't come in," Elena shouts. "I am warning you—step away."

Laughter follows, deep and menacing. "I know who they are, Elena. Open up and this will be over a lot faster." The moving door makes repeated thumps as it strains at the full extension of the chain. A clatter of metal and ping of flying shrapnel indicates the guy has won the fight with her frail security system. *Wonder if she believes me now?* Sonya touches my arm, moving forward to intervene, but stills just through the doorway as a loud bang resonates through the house.

"Mama?" Dante calls from down the hall, his small voice shaking.

I rush around the doorway to see what's happened and am confronted with the sight of Elena, shotgun in hand, standing over the body of one of Carlos's men. Brain matter and fragments of flesh are splattered all over the front door. She lifts the barrel and points it toward the street, letting off a second deafening shot.

"Go!" she hollers, breaking the gun and reaching for more shells. "There are two more men coming."

"Go get Dante out," I tell Sonya, my voice strange with

the ringing in my ears. "Take him the route we talked about."

She nods, and darts off down the hallway to where Dante is crying in his doorway.

"Elena," I call, "we have to go now."

"Not until these two are dead as well," she growls, lifting the re-loaded gun.

Boom.

"Now!" I scream at her. "If you want your boy to have a mother, you run!"

She glances my way, pain in her eyes, and nods. I shove her down the hallway, gun still firmly in her grasp. She bolts past the bedrooms for the back door that Sonya and Dante went through mere seconds before as the heavy thud of boots on the front step gets my blood racing. Everything is a blur, my body on autopilot. I don't think where to put my feet, just that I need to run. I don't think about shutting the door behind me—I just do. And thank fuck because I swear it's the two-second delay we need to have a chance at this.

We skid into the alley that runs behind the houses on Elena's street. The mad woman pushes me aside and discharges her last shot at the back of the house. Sonya is powering ahead of us, Dante clinging tightly to her back like a baby bear. A sob breaks from Elena as she drops the gun and sprints towards them, the sight of her child all the motivation she needs. I rip the pointless wig from my head, my red ponytail falling free. It irritated, and the heat was already unbearable.

Behind us, the clatter of the gate hinge and the deep baritone voices shouting at us to stop indicate the men have made it into the alley with us. That damn black SUV screams to a stop at the intersection ahead of Sonya, and she dives through the nearest gate to her right, cutting through a property to the street. I shove Elena through the next one we come across, and the two of us leap the vegetable beds we find like champion hurdlers as shouting echoes behind us. Elena's neighbors scream and yell, ushering children to safety as our circus tears through their properties.

Gunfire rings out, and I cringe, yet never falter in my pace. Elena swears in front of me, and finds another gear, charging ahead of me into the street. I crest the path, and turn left mid-stride toward Sonya, praying that the boys have arrived. The suburban neighborhood has quickly become a ghost town. Nobody is to be seen, and the only sound is that of our feet pounding the cement, and our breath rasping into our lungs. Dante still clings to Sonya as she reaches the intersection and pauses, checking both ways. She hesitates, and then bolts right.

"Follow her," I yell to Elena, and pause at the intersection to check behind us.

Carlos's men careen out of a nearby property, and I see the handgun raised at me the exact moment I hear the sweetest sound in the world—the rumble of Harley pipes. A shot rings out, I dive to the left, and the sting is incredible. Pain radiates from my hip, accentuated by the jolting of my movements as I push up and run toward the bikes.

Sonya is already climbing on behind Vince, Dante now in Elena's arms. Callum reaches out and takes Elena by the arm, wrestling her onto the back of his bike, placing Dante between them, while I power forward with my gaze fixed on Mighty, one of our lifers, as he yells at me to hurry.

I reach him, my head swimming from the incredible pain in my side, and collapse onto the back of his bike as he flicks his wrist and sends us screaming down the road after the others.

Well, that went well.

substitution

TY "Wow, this is a really nice house."

My eyes fix to the brunette wandering through my living room, her slender fingers trailing over the furniture as she goes. Two days ago I bumped into her, quite literally, at the supermarket. She apologized profusely, bending at the waist to pick up the items that had dropped from her basket.

"How long have you lived here?"

Groceries retrieved, she'd taken off toward the checkouts with a sneaky glance over her shoulder. As chance would have it, we'd parked next to each other in the car park. After a brief awkward conversation about fate—mostly for her benefit, since I don't believe in that shit—she'd given me her number, which I saved under 'busty shopper'. That should have been my first sign. Still, when the need for a distraction arose, I gave her a call. She was more than eager, agreeing with everything I suggested. It should have been my second sign.

"Ty?"

I frown at the way she pulls my name through her nose, and turn away from her inquisition, dodging an answer. She's only here as a means to an end—to get my thoughts off of a redheaded woman who belongs to a rather psychotic biker. Who cares how her voice sounds, right?

My head's been in turmoil this past week, from the moment I wake up until long after I've gone to bed, wondering if the inexplicable pull I felt toward Ramona was real, wondering if there's such a thing as two people who are just 'meant' to be together. She makes me think there is, but again, she's already taken—isn't that enough of an indication that maybe I'm mistaken? I can't be that guy. I can't be the jerk who takes another man's woman, not when he isn't around to put up a fight.

I need to move on.

I need to figure out what exactly it is about a woman I've known all of a day that makes me so crazed with determination to learn every intricate detail about her. Mostly, I need to know if I can find that attraction in somebody else.

So I look for answers in places that raise more questions. "Would you like a drink?"

"I had enough at the club," she answers with a fake smile. "I'd hate for you to think I'm an alcoholic."

"An alcoholic wouldn't care about what anyone else thinks," I blankly inform her, tracing a pattern in the stone counter with my finger.

"In that case"—she grins—"the buzz is wearing off, so I guess so."

Honestly, why the hell did I think bringing her home would be a good idea? I'm already plotting how quickly I can get her out of the house when we're done. Whatever I'm searching for, it's not in her.

Trying to 'date' has never worked for me—why would it now?

"Whiskey okay?" I ask.

"Have you got any Merlot?"

Slamming my eyes closed, I hold on to the edge of the kitchen counter for stability. *What the fuck am I doing?* Trying to replace a Mercedes with a damn Honda, that's what. "No. Whiskey or nothing." Bitch isn't getting my best scotch.

"I'll pass then." Her grating nasally voice has grown nearer.

I open my eyes, reminding myself that she has a rather impressive rack, and spin to face her. "How about I show you around?" *Like right to the bedroom so I can shove your face into a pillow and pretend you're someone else?* No, scrap that, we'll go to the spare room. I don't want her tainting my sheets.

"Sounds great," she purrs, a hand reaching for my shoulder as she leans in close. "Although, I thought we might . . . you know." The dense bitch wiggles her eyebrows.

Seriously? "Yeah, that's kind of what I was implying,

too."

Her dark eyes light up, and she moves in for the kill. *The hell?* Is she trying to do me where we stand?

I turn my head to the side, avoiding her pouty lips, and clear my throat. "Follow me."

She stumbles to regain balance after I slip from her grasp, her heels clattering on the kitchen floor. They resume clicking behind me, beating an ominous tempo toward my awkward search for obliteration. Her bag makes a dull thud as she tosses it aside upon entering the room. Every muscle in my body tenses while the fucking woman skirts the spare room, taking in the details yet again. "Is this really your house? Like, do you own it?"

"Yeah," I say, fighting the urge to roll my eyes. People always assume I'm leasing, that a guy my age couldn't afford this without rich parents bank-rolling it.

"Mmm. Must admit, I didn't see you having such . . . bland taste. Although you obviously have a lot of money; the place is huge! I'd love to live in a house like this one day."

And there it is, like a flashing neon 'gold-digger' sign over her head. "I work hard for it." My ears are fucking alight. "Although, I'm not exactly out to impress anyone."

"Really?" she teases, eyebrow raised and gaze directed at my motherfucking crotch. "You've been impressing me all night." Her gaze lifts, dark, and hooded. "You're a real catch."

Why the fuck are still doing this, Ty? After staggering in a deep, cleansing breath, I turn away from the woman.

What was her name? Ugh, what did it matter?

"Wait here."

She plops her ass down on the edge of the bed, knees bent to accommodate her tight fucking dress, while I head for the door. "Where are you going?" she whines.

"To call you a taxi."

Her protests fade into a murmur as I stride out to the living room. I'm looking for sex, not a wife. Strike up a conversation with a woman like her, and next thing you know she wants you to take her on a date. Take the fucking woman out for a date, and she wants to fuck your brains out—which isn't all that bad. But go ahead and nail her, next thing you know she's begging you for the keys to your house. It's a slippery slope, and one I'm carefully backing away from before I find this bitch's toothbrush in my bathroom.

"You're a class jerk, you know that?" she hisses.

Oh God, she's back. "Well aware, darlin'," I respond, a little louder than intended. "But you aren't exactly doin' it for me anymore."

"Fuck you."

"And that just cemented the fact I'm not even goin' to ask what your name was."

"Cherise, you asshole. It's fucking Cherise."

I chuckle.

She scowls.

"Nobody's going to be 'fucking Cherise' tonight." My chuckle escalates into a full-on belly laugh as I dial the taxi company. Yeah, I'm being an asshole by saying that, but really—perfect lead-in.

Her red nails flash into view, and I swear the fuckers take a chunk of skin when she rips the phone from my hand. It skids pretty well across the floor given its lack of aerodynamics, and then promptly cracks as it collects the cupboards.

"Fuck your taxi. I'll find my own way home."

"Just get out of my house," I growl.

She huffs, hesitates, and obviously thinks better of whatever crosses her mind. Which is a good thing, considering I've never been violent toward women, and I don't fancy starting now. The *click-clack* of her stilettos stampedes to the front door, and I relish the familiar thud of the heavy wood as it slams closed behind her.

Flashing my gaze toward the ruins of my phone screen, I quell the building rage inside. How dare that desperado break my shit? Way past being over women who create as much drama as they solve, I snatch up my keys and storm toward the front door. It's the last time I try taking out a woman who doesn't have an hourly rate attached to her. At least a whore does what you need and leaves without question.

Time to go and *pay* for somebody to take my mind off the only woman I'd share my house with.

false façade

two weeks later

RAMONA "How's the hip?" Jane asks.

She's been calling me frequently since my stay down south. We've become pretty good friends, finding a lot of similarities in our personalities even though at first glance we're polar opposites.

I settle on to a stool at the kitchen counter, and pin my phone between my shoulder and ear. "Heaps better. It seems to be healing fast, really. I'm lucky it was a flesh wound for the most part."

"Well, I guess it helps that you look after yourself, too."

"I try."

"When are you going to be joining us down south?" she asks. "I can't wait to hang out and have a few girly nights while the boys are out doing their thing."

"Are you getting bored on your own?"

She chuckles. "Yeah, a little. Malice tells me I need a

hobby."

"How's the new job working out, though?" A couple of weeks back she started at a Lawyer's office part-time. I think getting out of the house is doing her good, helping her find her feet in public again and shake the fear her abusive asshole ex-husband is going to find her.

"Good. They've offered me extra hours, but I said I'd think about it. I'm just not sure; I kind of enjoy my free afternoons with my man."

"Make the most of it. As soon as you have kids they're pretty much gone forever."

"Agh!" she cries. "Settle down. I'm not thinking that far ahead!"

I chuckle, moving the phone to my other shoulder as I watch Mack wander around the living room trying to decide what to play with. "You're not writing it off, though?"

She sighs. "I haven't spoken to him about it yet. I don't really know if that's the kind of thing he wants right now. The guys seem kind of . . . distracted."

"Yeah," I agree. "They do." King's been buried in his office for weeks, losing his sun-kissed skin tone and weight hand-in-hand.

"You never told me when you're coming down," Jane prompts.

"It was going to be in a week or so, but after the trouble at Elena's, I'm not sure. I might just slow it all down and take our time—do it with less stress."

"Fair enough. I'm so sorry it all ended up like that,"

Jane says. "I'm just glad that poor boy wasn't hurt in all the chaos."

"Yeah, so am I," I reply, looking over at Mack flicking through the channels on the TV. "He seems to be okay though. We caught up with them at the clubhouse the other day."

"I bet you lot are giving them all the support they need, too. Hey, I need two hands to finish off this biscuit dough, so I'll catch you later, yeah?"

"Yeah, no problem."

We say our goodbyes, and I place the phone down, stretching out the stiffness in my neck. Mack is glued to a cartoon, his full focus on the colorful anime characters that dash about on a mission save the world. I stand for a moment, watching him while I figure out if I'll clean the bathroom, or fold the washing first. I hope that we did enough to shield him from what happened the day I went to Elena's. The kid doesn't even know I got hurt. If he ever asks, I'll lie to protect him from the truth that comes with the story of how I got shot.

I'll lie, because it's all I am most days—a liar who's perfected the art of presenting a mask to the world, and keeping my true face for when I'm on my own. I put up a brave front, but I'm anything but. I'm no braver than the blond-haired boy watching fictional characters fight for freedom. Then again, he's pretty darn courageous. My heart aches anew looking at our little creation, the kid who has a part of me, but so damn much of his father that he's almost a mirror image. Twice, only two times, has

Mack asked about Sawyer. And both times, thankfully, I've managed to dodge the bullet.

Three weeks have passed since Sawyer went home. I won't bullshit and say I expected daily updates, or even a phone call. But damn, I live in a world of underground activity and shady bastards—surely one of them has *some* news about him?

My fingers roam over the fabric of my tee, bunching it gently toward my waist so I can see the scab beneath. There's a rash of red around the wound, but nothing to cause any concern. Mighty rushed us straight back to the clubhouse after we lifted Elena and Dante that day, and carried me directly into the kitchen where he left me so he could search out Gloria, one of the old ladies who happens to be a deft hand with a curved needle.

Chomping down on a wooden stirring spoon, I'd let her clean, stitch and dress the wound. I have to say—she did a damn excellent job of it. Apart from some pinched skin, it looks pretty darn good. The scar should be relatively minimal; nothing my clothes, or a new tattoo, won't cover anyway.

One less-than-legitimate prescription later, and I was so high on painkillers I honestly can't remember how I got home. I'd slept the remainder of the night, never stirring. Mack had his work cut out for him waking me for his breakfast, and even then I slapped together some toast and went back to bed for another three hours.

Deciding not to disturb him from the program, I head outside to check the mail. The sunshine flows into the house when I open the front door and step out to the driveway. Walking to the end, I turn my head both ways and check the road. I'm not even sure what I'm looking for, but I know the absence of black SUVs gives me a ridiculous amount of comfort. It's been two weeks and there's been no sign of retaliation against me, so why would they turn up now? Wouldn't they have been here in the days following if what I did upset Carlos that much? After all, I'm only a little fish in a big ocean—what good would threatening me do?

I squash the thought, and turn for the letterbox. A flash of orange catches my eye. This morning's brief rain shower is still fresh on the ground as I wander over and retrieve the slip of card. I stare down at it, reading the words 'Sorry we missed you' over and over, wondering who would have sent me a parcel.

I head inside, turning the card over in my hand, to find Mack standing at the pantry, feet on the bottom shelf to reach the biscuits. He looks up and smiles at me . . . just like his father. I catch myself gaping at him, and quickly flash a smile in return.

"You hungry, sweetheart?"

He nods enthusiastically. "Can you make me a sandwich please, Mommy?"

"Sure, baby." I drop the card on the kitchen counter, and head for the fridge to get the makings of a cheese and ham sandwich.

Mack picks up the cars we've left free of the boxes I've packed in preparation for our shift, and starts racing them around the sofa, pushing them hard so they fly under the furniture and out the opposite side. I prepare the sandwiches, and slip them under the grill, picking up the card again while I wait for the cheese to melt. There's no clue on it as to whom the item's from, or even where. I rack my brain, trying to think who would have cause to mail us something. The fact only a handful of people know our address makes the list pretty darn short, and unlikely.

Mack continues to play while I carry the card to the bedroom and retrieve my phone; quickly dialing the number it gives to arrange redelivery as I perch on the edge of the bed. The operator answers, and I give her my parcel number. She goes through the options and I organize a new time for it to be delivered. Before she goes, I ask her a last burning question.

"Are you able to tell me who sent the package?"

"One moment," she says, followed by more furious tapping on the keyboard. Voices hum in the background. "I'm sorry, there's no name registered, only an address."

"Where is it from?"

"Ahh, let me see. Fort Worth, Texas."

My chest is tight, and my palms itchy. "Thank you so much."

"You're welcome." The lady disconnects.

I sit, staring at the phone in my hand as though it'll light up with the answers any second. Fort Worth? Does that mean Sawyer's left Carlos's compound and returned to the southern Fallen Saints' clubhouse? Is he coming home?

"Mom! The sandwiches!"

Cursing, I drop the phone and sprint up the hallway; smoke trickles from the grill. Wrapping my hand with a dishcloth, I yank the tray out and dump our burnt offerings in the sink. I turn and catch Mack smiling at me, arms crossed over his chest.

"Should we go get McDonald's?"

He laughs and nods. "Yes!"

Usually I'd be counting out the cost of the wasted food in my head, cringing as I deduct the dollars from our tight grocery budget. Not today, though. This time my lack of attention has given me the perfect excuse to swing by the clubhouse and ask King what the hell is going on down south.

scarred

TY Waking in an unfamiliar room, the events of last night come in as a flood. Sex, blow, and suffering. Unhitching my arm from the hooker sleeping beside me, I throw my legs over the side of her trailer-home bed and rub my eyes, settling my tired gaze on the mirror and blade perched on top of my discarded clothing.

Hell of a night.

With her blonde hair fanned out around her, and panties haphazardly skewed on her non-existent ass, the hooker doesn't stir as I stand and move the mirror to get to my clothes. Dressing, I look the woman over, remembering the hope in her eyes when I asked her how much for a full night. I don't think anyone's ever asked her for that before. Looking at her rail-thin frame, the telltale dark circles under her eyes, and the acne of a regular drug user, I can imagine why.

But fuck pretenses. So she's not the prettiest choice on

the street? That wasn't what I'd been after, and it wasn't what I got. I needed a woman who could do as I asked without question, and that was exactly what she did—delivered.

It's all the hired help has been doing for the past couple of weeks—delivering.

Last night was a first; I've never stayed over. But the pain inside of me is at an all-time high, and one or two hours of her time wasn't going to cut it. I needed more to ease my stress, and she gave me more, right up until dawn light cracked the horizon in a hue as orange as the shame that burns inside of me.

I'm not normal. Guys don't seek out this kind of abuse to get their rocks off. At least, I think they don't.

The hooker's eyelashes flitter in her sleep while I cinch my belt. What is she dreaming of? Is she remembering what we did? Lifting a hand to my throat, I rub the tender spot where her thumbs dug in to my windpipe last night. She had reservations at my requests, it was clear, but the girl handled it like a boss.

Stopping at a dirty, smudged mirror in the narrow hall, I take in my reflection. My dark hair is a fucking mess on my head, matted and sticking out every which way. I run my fingers through it, trying to coax the most of it into some sort of style. Settling on what could be passed off as artfully messy, I run my gaze lower to the dark area under my eyes. *Too many late nights, Ty.* Lower still my lips are flushed, a small split on the bottom one from where the whore's tiny fists cracked me mid-fuck. I keep perusing myself, the remainder of the marks invisible to the naked eye, but clear as day to me. For such small hands, she managed to deal the right amount of pain.

And I fucking got off on it more than her crack-addled ass did when I pulled out her down payment.

The woman still sleeps as I toss a roll of cash on the counter in her small kitchenette. I'm pretty sure there's twice what she quoted me in the pile of notes, but damn, I asked her to do some pretty fucked up things and she never once turned me down. She earned every dollar. Besides, looking around her shoddy trailer I have to wonder what the extra might do for her—if it doesn't hit her nose first, that is.

A framed picture catches my eye as I step toward the narrow door. It's a small girl wearing a *Frozen* T-shirt, riding a pony. An older gentlemen, grandfather age, holds the animal's reins, leading the kid around. The girl's cute and a pang lances my gut when it dawns on me—if the crack-whore wasn't so starved and sunken in the face, she'd look pretty much the same.

Running my eyes around the trailer again, I confirm what I thought—no kids stuff. The child in the picture is obviously her daughter, but it's also glaringly obvious she doesn't live with her mother. My heart aches as I step down the steel steps to the dead grass and gently close the door behind me. What do the hooker's parents think of her life decisions? Of the fact she's ended up a trashy whore who willingly leaves her morals at the door for a few grams of snow and a night of debauchery? A woman who's so consumed in her job that she's lost the only thing that clearly matters to her? Are her folks even alive? Was the man in the picture her father?

It's a thought I often play over—how do parents feel when they look at their children who haven't quite made the grade? Is it saddening to see their child never lived up to the dreams and expectations they had for them as a toddler, or even a teenager? Or are there parents who couldn't care less as long as their child is alive and well?

I sure as fuck know the latter kind isn't my mom and dad. They've never hidden from me how they feel about my choices in life, and it's the best part of why I avoid them at all costs. Twelve years it took them to find me—they were the best twelve years of my life.

My parents don't love me—they love the *idea* of what I could have become. And knowing it's too late for me to be that guy, they've all but given up on their only son. It's been close to six months since they last tried to make contact—the longest it's ever been between letters sent to my postal box, written on their lawyer's letterhead. I kind of wonder if they even write the things themselves? Or do they just pay the guy to send the same thing on rotation?

Knowing how they operate, I'm placing bets on the second option.

Starting the car, I take a last glance over at the whore's trailer, illuminated by crisp early morning light. I hope for her sake that her parents are dead, because damn, it's a whole lot easier to fantasize that they would have loved you anyway than see the disappointment in their eyes.

As far as I'm concerned, I never had parents—I had caregivers. And if proceedings go as planned, they won't even be legally that by the time I've finished with them. Emancipation when the child is no longer a minor is rare, but for me, it's the final key to unshackling myself from everything they represent. It's the only true way to move on.

In my world, I'm an orphan. It's just better for everyone that way.

home

RAMONA Mack tears off towards two of the other club kids with his Happy Meal clutched tightly in one hand. I watch him settle in with them and then turn to search for King when a commotion halts me in my tracks.

The door to his office flies open and an extremely pissed off Elena comes marching out, heading for the stairs. King's hot on her heels, grabbing for her arm to stop her, but she's cursing wildly at him, wrenching her arms over her head to evade his grip.

"Don't you dare talk down to me!" she screams.

"Fuck, woman!" He finally catches a skinny arm in his grasp. "I'm doing this to protect you."

"Why?" she hollers, beating his chest with her free hand. "You don't love me; you never did. Why protect something you don't want?"

His hand falls from her arm, and he stands shocked

into silence as she runs for the stairs, taking them two at a time to disappear from view.

"Whoa," Callum breathes from beside me.

"You can say that again."

We stare in companionable silence as King slowly makes his way back to his office and shuts the door. I glance over at the children and feel a wash of respite when I discover them all playing happily.

"How you doing, Mona?"

I turn and smile up at Callum, always entranced by his sandy blond curls. Giving them the obligatory ruffle I do every time I see him, I answer, "Pretty good, thank you."

"What brings you in today? You need a hand with anythin'? Moving something large?"

I shake my head. "Nah. I came in to talk to King, but I might just leave it a little while."

He huffs and jams his hands in the pockets of his jeans. "He might actually like it if you went in and had a word. You know he tells us guys jack shit."

"Yeah, I know." My gaze drifts to his door, and I sigh. "It's on you if he goes bananas on me."

"Taken." He slaps me on the back of the shoulder. "Go—sort the man out so we don't have to watch him lose his mind all over again."

A little under two weeks ago, right after we nabbed Elena, King broke down . . . massively. He'd been treading the fine line of insanity for a while according to the guys, but it seemed the stresses of the job got on top of him and he lost the plot. Callum found him rocking in his shower, water running cold over his back. He then sought out Sonya, who helped him get King into bed and nobody saw him, spoke to him, or heard from him for the following four days while he sorted things out. It was like a caterpillar going into a cocoon. He disappeared from view for a while, and when he re-emerged it was as though nothing had happened. He just walked down the stairs a new guy—a happy King.

Ever since, nobody has brought it up with him in case he cracks again. Nobody knows if this new grasp he has on things is solid, or if it's all a front, and really, nobody wants to find out which way it is. In all truth, it's a damn testament to the guy that nobody tried to oust him while he was gone. Callum tells me that the subject wasn't even brought up at church the day after he broke. Everybody just agreed in silence that it would work itself out . . . and it did.

Now I'm back to wondering how well.

"Can I come in?" I ask, popping my head around the door after he didn't answer my knock.

"Hey, Mona. Sure. Sorry, I ignored it thinking you were one of the guys." He steps around the desk and clears the seat of litter for me.

"Thanks." I drop into the worn leather and look around at the state of disarray everything is in. There's paper everywhere, guns lying in various stages of assembly on the desk, and a dozen or so empty booze bottles on top of the filing cabinet. "Been busy?"

"Yeah." He chuckles a low, hollow sound. "What can I

do you for?"

"Are you okay?" I press. Sure, I need answers, but he's more important than my conflicted heart.

"Not really." His face drops into his hands, and he groans softly. "Why can't people just let me get on and fix things for them?"

"Elena?"

"Yeah," he mutters.

"Some people don't like feeling out of control." It's the impression I got from Elena the day we met at her house. She likes to be in charge, probably because it helps her feel secure. "For some people, control is all they have."

His sharp irises lock on to me, and he quirks the corner of his mouth. "That's pretty much it, isn't it?"

"Maybe," I say, "you could try giving Elena the ideas so she thinks that they're her decisions? I don't know what you two were arguing about—it's an observation, is all. Feel free to ignore me."

King shakes his head. "I wouldn't ignore you. You're probably right anyway. Bitch was arguing with me because I want to organize another fuckin' house and she feels like I'm placin' her where I want her, with no input from her."

"Are you?"

He nods. "Yeah, but I want to be sure they'll be safe. Dante's my fuckin' son, too. I couldn't live with myself if he was hurt because I let her get her stubborn bloody way."

"Maybe you need to let her have some say in where they live," I offer. "She is the one, after all, who has to go back to the place you choose every day and feel happy about where she sleeps at night."

"Mona, if she had her fuckin' way the woman would be still in that damn house you visited."

"Try," I urge. "Let her pick from two or three places that you're comfortable with. She can't stay at the clubhouse forever."

He nods, shuffling a stack of documents to the side and bringing one of the disassembled guns in front of him. "What is it that you're here for?" he asks, pulling a cleaning kit from the drawer of the desk. "Everything okay with you? You healing fine?"

"Yeah, I'm healing fine," I answer. "Have you heard anything from the southern boys, though?"

"Just business. Should I have heard something else?" King proceeds to thread the rod with a square of cloth and then ram it down the barrel, all the while avoiding my inquisitive eyes.

"I got a FedEx missed delivery card at home today." His gaze finally lifts to mine. "The package is from Fort Worth."

"Saints?"

"Don't know." I shrug. "It's being delivered again in a couple of days."

"Don't open it," King instructs, placing the handgun down. "You leave it where the postman drops it, and then call me."

"Why? Do you think it might be dangerous?"

"Fuck, Mona. Carlos has been all over both of our asses.

It could be anything."

My stomach roils as my head fills with images of body parts—fingers, a head even. "Fuck. I never thought of that."

"Yeah, well, lets hope I'm reachin' a little far into the unreal, but we better play it cautious anyway."

These sorts of threats are the very reason why I decided to pull Mack from this life and move down south. Why the hell did I get suckered in with Sawyer? Why the hell did I turn a blind-eye to the connection he was to such a sociopath?

"Thanks, King. I'll be in touch tomorrow," I say quietly, standing and starting for the door.

"Take care, Mona," he calls after me.

I stop in the doorway and give him a smile. "You know I will. You just focus on looking after your boy."

He smiles and nods. A silent understanding passes between us. I muse how alike we really are as I make my way to where Mack plays with the other kids. Both of us are struggling to stay afloat in this world we've created for ourselves, both of us trying to do what's best for our kids when the odds are against us. Nobody really thinks of the long-term implications when they enter this life. It's all glamor, and badass appeal at the start. Living on the wrong side of the law is a thrill, but the thing neither of us realized as teenagers was that one day, we'd want to be rid of it. But now it's too late. A person can't just see the shit we do, hear the shit we do, and walk away.

Leaving is never really an option—ever.

intro

TY Raucous laughter fills the air as we cross through the main get-together area of the southern Fallen Saints clubhouse. People are crammed into the room, which was once two, now converted into a single space to form the heart of the old mansion the club reclaimed. Stories have it the place was on the list for demolition when their past president struck a deal with a council member, getting them an opportunity to put an offer on the table that secured the dilapidated property. The investor in me can't help but admire the bones of the pre-Civil War house and wonder what it was like in its hey-day.

"Hooch's office is just through here," the member we're following says, stopping in the hallway and gesturing down a junction. "He's expecting you two."

I look quizzically at the member, wondering why he isn't escorting us the whole way through. I'm pissed enough we have to meet with the VP, that we're not respected enough to be greeted by the president, Judas. This shit just adds insult to injury.

As though reading my mind, he tips his head in a one-shouldered shrug and explains, "Hooch doesn't let any club members apart from the officers in that part of the house." He spins to thumb over his shoulder at the 'prospect' rocker. "Respect comes with trust—you have to earn it."

I get the impression the latter part of his explanation is a veiled warning. *Fuck's sake.* If Hooch can't trust his own members, then what state is the club in? "Thanks," I offer, leading Bronx down the narrow hall.

We come up to a dark gray door, kitted out with at least three barrel-locks, and stop. I rap my knuckles against the chipped paint and wait. The locks click and the door opens on a smiling Hooch—well, I assume this is Hooch. We're pretty fucked otherwise. Every time I've dealt with the guy it's been non-verbal, and there isn't a singular picture of the guy anywhere on the web—which says a lot in today's age of Facebook and Instagram.

The guy takes a step back, running thick fingers over his beard as he moves aside to give us room to pass. The man's chest has to be as round as a keg. Glancing up as we move forward, I note the tiny camera lens hidden in the corner of the architrave. No wonder he opened the door so willingly—we've been watched the whole way in.

"Hooch?" I offer my hand.

"Sure am," he answers, taking my hand and shaking my arm within an inch of the shoulder socket's capacity. "You must be Ty, and this is Bronx, I take it?" Hooch says, tilting his head towards him.

"Certainly is," Bronx answers, offering his hand, and unlike me meeting the shake stroke for stroke. "Good to meet you. Thanks for having us."

"I heard you're going to be doing us a favor," Hooch states, wandering to the business side of a huge oak desk. "King tells me you guys have jacked up a plan to take the rungs out of Carlos's ladder?"

"That we have," I answer.

"Right," Hooch says, elongating the vowel sound.

"You think we can't do it."

"Did I say that?" Hooch leans back in the large leather chair, crossing his arms over his chest.

"Not in so many words," I reply, "but your body language kind of gave it away."

"Well, you'll have to excuse me for being fuckin' skeptical, but there are only two of you—"

"Three," Bronx quickly corrects.

Hooch eyes him warily. "There are only *three* of you and a whole fuckin' army on Carlos's payroll."

"That's why we need the club's help," I say, resisting the need to roll my eyes at having to state the obvious.

"What's in it for us?"

"You'll have to ask King that." Because quite honestly, I've been asking myself the same question. It's a lot of work on their behalf, solely for us to get ourselves out of the shit after Tigger's death. If it were our boys, I wouldn't have agreed to do a thing—the benefit doesn't outweigh the cost for King's club.

"I plan on doin' just that," Hooch drawls. "How did he get involved in the first place?"

Do these guys never talk? "Malice, our guy who isn't here today—his father is a member."

"Which one?"

"Vince, one of King's officers."

His lip twitches briefly. "Yeah, I know who Vince fuckin' is. Didn't know he had a kid."

"The connection wasn't exactly out in the open at our end either."

Hooch nods slowly, resting his hands on the desk and drumming his fingertips together. "What assurances do I have you guys aren't about to fuck us over?"

"The same assurances we have that you'll back us up one hundred per cent."

"Your word," Hooch fills in.

"Which, for us at least, carries our honor," Bronx finishes.

"Hmm," he grumbles, leaning back once more. "I'm really not into it yet, eh. You guys haven't convinced me why I should get our club tangled up in your mess."

Bronx shifts beside me, and I volley between my feet. There are two chairs in front of us, but Hooch has never offered us a seat . . . so we haven't taken them. The power play isn't lost on me. The whole meet-and-greet is weighing heavily on the 'disrespectful' side.

"Look, man," I start, "you might not find Carlos overly concerning or high on your list of things to be worried about, but it's a big deal to us. We need him off our backs if we're goin' to have a chance at carrying on our business without complications, and if this is what we have to do to make it happen for good, then so be it. Hey, I'm comfortable with us goin' in and doin' what we gotta without any support—it's how we've always operated—but the thing is, this business impacts on your club, and to be honest, I'd appreciate you givin' us some fuckin' understanding with that. Nobody forced us to come here, we came purely out of respect for you, for your club, and for what this will mean for *everybody's* future where motherfuckin' Carlos Redmond is concerned. So how about reciprocating the favor?"

Dipping his chin, Hooch peers up from under heavy brows, holding me hostage with an intense glare. We stay in the standoff for an eternity before the slightest twitch of his eye even indicates that the fucker's still breathing. He slowly leans forward, both elbows on the desk, and regards me for a little while longer before speaking. "You look like a fuckin' keyboard warrior," he bites, "one of those jackasses that plays pretend with his computer games, but you've got some fuckin' bite. Shirt's too fuckin' clean to have seen any blood, and those hands are too fuckin' soft to have ever got in on the rough shit. You mind tellin' me exactly what it is you do?"

"You want to know what I do? I make sure you walk out of this with same amount of assholes that you have walking in. I'm the guy that makes sure while you're all busy blowin' shit away, nobody gets themselves killed through a rash decision. I keep you *alive*." Although I seem to have a pretty shit record of that lately.

"We'd be fucked without Ty," Bronx interjects after being respectfully quiet my entire rant. "He's our eyes, our ears, and the guy who makes shit happen. You need something"—he thumbs at me—"he's it. You tellin' me you got a problem with how he looks, Hooch?"

The guy's gaze slides to Bronx, and he lifts his top lip in a sneer. "Nah, buddy. Just got a problem with you."

"Makes two of us then," Bronx leers back.

Great. "This isn't heading anywhere useful," I snap. "I think it's high time Bronx and I left you to whatever the fuck it is you're more preoccupied with."

Snapping out of the showdown with Bronx, Hooch pushes up from his seat with both palms flat to the desk. His chair scrapes across the wooden floor, the noise deafening in the enclosed room. "Before you go," he says, tipping his chin to the door, "I got somebody you fuckers will probably wanna speak with."

Bronx looks across to me. I look right back at him. *What the fuck?* My gut churns, and the warning signs I spotted on the way in of a club falling apart at the seams flash fresh in the forefront of my mind. I've never run the scenario that Carlos might already be in on these guys, that there's a chance the fuckers are all dirty.

How fucking distracted *have* I been?

"Follow me," Hooch instructs, opening the office door.

I tip my head for Bronx to go first, but he gives me a don't-be-so-ridiculous scowl and shoves me after Hooch, flanking me like some fucking bodyguard. I'll pick a bone with him about it later—right now I need to hustle to catch up to Hooch's long strides.

We weave through the darkened halls, past doors that have been boarded off, and across to the far side of the mansion. Hooch shoves a set of double doors open revealing the back balcony, wide and covered in people. Music pumps out of enormous speakers mounted on stands at either end, and the two tables are littered with an assortment of bottles at various stages of consumption. Two large glass-fronted fridges sit to the right, full to the brim with RTDs and beer.

I scope the range of people before us, noting an even mix of full members, prospects, and their women. A couple of them I recognize from photos King had shown me from Facebook of get-togethers held last year, but still, no names come to mind. For all the people here enjoying the afternoon sun, I'm still yet to see the president, Judas, anywhere. Turning toward where Hooch stands, I still when I notice the key detail that has somehow slipped by me until now—*he* wears the president patch.

His gaze meets mine as he turns, and he nods when I lift a hand to gesture to the back of his cut. "I didn't realize, man."

"We lost him a couple of weeks ago."

I duck my head quickly out of respect. "Sorry for your loss."

"Thanks, brother." His hand slaps down hard on my shoulder; his mood has shifted the full spectrum to that of camaraderie. "Shit's gotta happen some time though," he justifies.

"That it does." Still, the loss would have cut him hard. No wonder he was defensive, distracted. Probably explains why the place appears to be divided, too.

Bronx elbows me as Hooch wanders away through the crowd, and raises his eyebrows. "What was that about?"

"His old man, the president, recently vacated the position, so-to-speak."

Bronx nods, mouth drawn down at the corners. "Rough."

Hooch soon returns, nudging between a couple of guys with someone in tow. "Boys," he addresses us in a deep booming manner, "you'll want to hear what this sorry motherfucker has to tell you."

My eyes track the man who steps out of Hooch's shadow, and my gut sinks. *Fuck*. Bronx stiffens beside me, jamming his hands in the pockets of his jeans with a growl.

"Truce?" Sawyer asks, walking toward us with his hands raised.

My nostrils flare, and before I have time to get past bringing my own shit in line, Bronx flies forward and latches on to Sawyer, hands to his throat. "You want a truce, you low-life fucker?"

Somebody cuts the music as all eyes turn our way.

Oddly, Sawyer doesn't do a damn thing to fight back—just takes it, smiling. Hooch plants a hand on each man, trying to pry Bronx's hands from Sawyer and fails. If he can't pull them apart then there's no hope really for anyone else. I latch on to Bronx anyway, much to the entertainment of our growing crowd, and urge him to cool it. Attracting the attention of no less than a dozen men who are undoubtedly on their brother's—Sawyer's—side is not exactly the smart way to sort this out.

"Leave him," Sawyer chokes out. "Lay off."

"Are you fuckin' crazy?" Hooch asks, finally managing to rip Bronx off and tossing him toward the onlookers.

"Well, yeah." Sawyer chuckles, rubbing his throat. "But the guy has every fuckin' right to be angry."

"How the fuck are you even here?" Bronx shouts, elbowing off the grabby hands of a few Saints who are trying to restrain him. "You should be fuckin' dead."

"Fuck," Sawyer says with a chuckle. "He tried. He seriously tried."

"What happened?" I ask, sliding a chair over for Bronx and gesturing for him to sit his fucking ass down. I can't say I'm that impressed Sawyer's back either—equally for the hate I harbor against him regarding Tigger, and also because he'll be straight back to Ramona, complicating things more then they already were.

Sawyer drags a chair for himself and straddles it in a bear hug, resting his arms on the back. "Fate, Ty." His face drops and the life visibly drains from his eyes. "I met my guardian angel."

Either something profound happened within the walls of Carlos's compound, or the guy's totally lost his grip on reality.

It dawns on me that most of the people on the balcony have slowly cleared out while we were getting ourselves seated, leaving a handful at the far end, and a sullen-faced Hooch standing against the railing, lighting a cigarette. The pieces of the puzzle are there, laid out before me, but the picture isn't clear.

I run a mental inventory on what I know of the southern chapter, effectively starting with the edges of the puzzle. Judas had been the president, according to what I've been told, but clearly his death has made his only son, Hooch, take on that role. A part of me wonders why King hadn't said anything, but then with all the shit going down with Elena, King hasn't really had his mind on the task at hand for some time now.

Aside from Judas and Hooch, there were two girls: Mel and Dana. The center of the picture starts to form. Sources I managed to dig up told me Mel had fallen off the radar a few years back when Sawyer was booted out of the chapter—no prizes for guessing the connection there—but the verdict is out on Dana.

Still, a good majority of Hooch's family are clearly now missing from the picture. "Guys, I'm doing my head in trying to figure out what the fuck is going on here. Who's going to do me the honors of breakin' it down, from the beginning?"

Hooch remains with his back to us all, puffing on his cigarette. "Sawyer, you best be explainin' since your old man is the reason why we're all fuckin' here."

I move my focus back to Sawyer, noting his weary

position, and wait. Bronx crosses his arms, unconvinced. I give his leg a kick, reminding him to keep his shit in line.

Sawyer lifts his head from where he had it resting on his arms, and looks at Bronx. "I've got a lot to say and a lot of explainin' to do if you want to know what my old man's up to now. So if you could do me the favor of holdin' off on questions or givin' me an ass-kicking until I'm done, that would be tops."

Bronx's nostrils flare, yet he nods his acceptance. I tip my chin in acknowledgement and reach for a chair as he begins to tell us exactly what Carlos is planning on doing.

What a revelation it turns out to be.

attachment

RAMONA "You sitting down for this?" King asks after I pick up the phone.

I drop my armful of linens into an open box, and find a seat on an arm of the sofa. "I am now." I'd picked a date. Less than a week and Mack and I will be on the move. The house is so close to being packed.

"Sawyer's out."

My fingers grasp on reflex to keep the phone to my ear. I slowly slide off the sofa, crumpling to the floor. "Is he okay?"

"Bronx and Ty dropped in to see the Fort Worth boys. Hooch thought they'd like to talk, and yeah, Ramona, it's not good."

"How not good?"

A loud huff of air pierces the line. "Carlos has had eyes on you. That's how they knew it was you and Sonya at Elena's. The car wasn't there to watch just Elena that day, but you too."

"Fuck," I whisper, thankful Mack is now in bed. We'd only just returned from the clubhouse. I thought while he was out of the way it would be the perfect time to pack the rest of our stuff. "Are we being watched now?"

"I've sent Callum over to have a look around."

The words sink in, and they make sense to me on some level, but the shock has me in a fog. What do I process first? The fact Sawyer is out and relatively okay? Or the fact Carlos has been watching me? The second notion sends shivers crawling over my skin.

"Mona?"

"I'm here." My focus snaps on the wall opposite, out of the daze I'd lost myself to, and back to the room around me.

"Stay indoors until Callum gets there. We've got you."

"Thanks, King," I whisper, head resting on my knees. "I think I . . . I just need a minute."

"Take however long you need, but call me when he arrives so I can stop worrying."

"Sure thing." I cut the connection with tears in my eyes, my strength waning.

Slipping into the seat of the armchair, I pull the breaths in even and slow. I have to stay quiet—I can't wake Mack. He doesn't need to see me like this. I'm his mother, not his problem. Gaining confidence in the belief that I won't bust open the waterworks, I push myself to stand and set the phone aside. With careful steps, I creep up the hallway to Mack's room. Just seeing him grounds me, reminds me that all King is advising of is a threat, nothing more. For all we know, nothing will eventuate. There's no reason to hit the panic button just yet.

Still, with a ruthless and soulless man like Carlos watching every move, anybody would be terrified.

Mack's shrouded form lies still in his bed, blankets tucked up around his ears. How did I luck out with him? How the hell in this crazy world I brought him into have I managed to keep such a happy, pure child? My heart literally aches as my thoughts drift to the day it will change. How will I know that his innocence has left? Will he bring the cops home on his tail one day? Stop talking to me and hide his secrets until it's too late?

My entire body jolts as a loud thump on the front door echoes through the house. Mack twitches in his sleep, but the soft snores tell me he hasn't been disturbed.

I try and calm my shaking hands by wringing them together while I head down the hall, hooking a right into the spare bedroom. Peering from behind the bunched curtain, I sigh at the sight of Callum standing on the front step. Willing the adrenalin to piss the hell off so my jitters stop, I plaster on a brave face and walk out to greet him.

Callum scowls when I open the door without the chain. "Girl, you got a death wish?"

"What?" I ask. "I saw it was you. I checked."

"Could you see all around me?" he asks, stepping inside.

"No."

"So you didn't know if I had a knife to my throat, a gun

to my head?"

My blood surges and my ears burn. How could I be so lax, especially with Mack to think of? "Shit, Callum. I'm sorry."

"No sweat, honey." He smiles gently. "Just don't do it again, yeah?"

I nod and thumb toward the kitchen. "Would you like me to make you a drink?"

He shakes his head. "Just downed a fuckin' liter of coffee at the ex's." His boots clunk on the floor as he kicks them off, and the cushion protests under his heavy frame as he drops into an armchair.

"You sure it's wise getting that comfortable?" I wander over and check the locks on the door. *Yep, safe as houses.*

"I checked, Mona. Nobody suspect in your neighborhood unless they've taken to wearin' dresses and hangin' out in minivans."

I chuckle, and draw a sigh while I take a seat opposite to text King.

"Don't let me stop you if you've got shit to do," he says gesturing to the boxes. "I'm just here for a while to make sure nothin' is off out there. I'll check a few times, and if there's no activity, then I'll leave you to it for the night." He lifts a thick finger and jabs it at me. "You call, though. Even if it sounds like a cat has knocked over a trash can, you call."

"You don't need to tell me," I say with a smile. "I'll probably sleep with my phone in my hand."

"Whatever makes you feel better, doll." He stretches

out, dropping his hands over the back of the chair. "It's been a long day."

We sit in silence for a while before I switch the TV on, but even then my mind races elsewhere. I can't concentrate on what's happening in the program, let alone if it's ads or not. What good would hurting me do Carlos? I just can't work it out. Knowing how Sawyer's manic head works, hurting his family would only send him into a deeper craze. It would be the final motivation for Sawyer to head after Carlos, guns blazing to exact his revenge.

Unless that's what Carlos is counting on. But why?

"I don't understand why Carlos would want to hurt us," I voice, breaking our silence. "Wouldn't that just send Sawyer after him with a vengeance?"

"Probably, but it gets Sawyer's attention, doesn't it?" Callum answers.

"Did you hear anything about what happened while he was gone?"

Callum shakes his head. "Ty told King that it's changed Sawyer, but he wouldn't give details. Felt it was better comin' from the man himself."

"How is Ty?" Callum's eyes cut to mine. "And Bronx?" I add quickly to diffuse the obvious.

"Good. You can ask him yourself when they get here next week."

My stomach turns. "They're coming up this way in a week?" I'm moving in a week. We'll probably end up missing each other.

"Yeah." Callum smirks. "*He* is."

Fuck—even he knows. Was I that obvious when we were down there? Am I that easy to read?

"He's a nice guy, Callum. I'm just being me—worrying too much about others."

He smiles, and shakes his head. I can't fool the guy. I've known Callum almost as long as King. He probably reads me second best out of everyone I know.

"Everyone could see it," he says, confirming my fear. "You two were talkin' non-stop and then, wham . . . nothing. Have you spoken to him since you've been home?"

"No," I mutter. "Haven't had the guts."

"Babe, if he's used you or hurt your feelings, you know you have all of us to call on if you wanted to rough him up for fun."

"What? No!"

"So there is feelings," he taunts. "Care to share what exactly went down between you two?"

"Fuck off," I snap. "It's personal, and besides, after Bruiser, you probably think I'm enough of a bed-hopper as it is. I'll be the newest club slut before I know it."

He leans forward, his elbows on his knees. "Mona, you know who the club sluts are, and you also know you ain't anything like 'em."

"Doesn't stop me feeling like one if I do decide to pursue Ty," I grumble.

"Maybe you're just confused, lookin' for a man to take care of you. Fuck knows that hasn't been Sawyer."

"He has so taken care of me," I protest. "He's still giving us money, you know."

"The government gives you money. Doesn't make you feel the need to sleep in their bed, does it?"

"What are you trying to get at?" I ask, narrowing my gaze. "Spit it out."

"The man takes care of you financially—so what? Does he come straight back to you when he's not on business? Does he show you how much he cares with little gestures, like holdin' your fuckin' hand?"

He has a point, but there's still a part of me that feels the fierce need to defend Sawyer. "You know as well as I do he's not one for public displays of affection."

"Unless some guy's hittin' on you," Callum corrects, "and then he's all but pissing all over you to claim his territory."

"People show love in different ways."

"That's not love," he bites out. "That's abuse."

I'd beg to differ on that one. Abuse is what happened to Jane, not Sawyer being a little cold towards me.

"How is 'the ex'?" I ask, hoping to divert our conversation.

"Bitchy as ever," he replies with a lift of his eyebrows, relaxing into the seat. "Only wants me when she needs something."

"You don't have any ties to her," I remind him gently. "You've got no obligation to jump when she asks you to."

"I know." He nods. "Just can't deny that at one time I felt something for her."

"I get that. Just don't go confusing guilt with love."

His dark green eyes meet mine, and I shrink into the

seat. *Yeah, don't do that, Ramona.* "I think I might actually finish packing after all."

He smirks, giving me reason to smack him one on the arm as I walk by his chair. Damn bastards in that club—they all have my number.

warning shots

two days later

TY Paper is spread out around me like leaves from a tree in fall. Yeah, it's the digital age, I know that, but nothing beats mapping out a plan with bits of paper that you can re-order and remove or insert as many times as you damn well like.

I push the pieces of my plan around on the charcoal carpet, going over each step in my head as I place my fingers to the slips of notepaper. It's all here: backstory, connections, skill. He's set with everything he needs to make him invaluable to them, an opportunity to good to pass up. So what is it I'm missing? I beat a closed fist against my head, teeth gritted as I groan.

My mind wanders back to the raven-haired hooker last night and the sweet relief she brought. I came home and slept like a damn baby, which is why today I can't understand why my head is still fuzzy. Blowing off steam with a lady of the night usually clears my thoughts right up, but there's something in the background giving me static, and I can lay bets on what or *who* it is.

Seeing Sawyer stirred up the confusion about Ramona I'd somehow managed to bury under layers of paid pleasure. He was a slap in the face, a reminder that the first woman I felt any sense of true connection to on more than just a sexual level, is taken. And by a fucking asshole who doesn't appreciate what he's got, no less.

It's not fair. Never is.

Starting at the beginning of the plan, I skim-read my notes once more, trying to get my head focused on something less soul crushing. King seemed pretty happy with my idea to get Bronx into Edward Hennington's crew, but there's a detail that isn't quite right. I can't find which one, but my gut is never wrong when it comes to this kind of planning, ever. Right now, my insides are doing sixty-five miles an hour on the rollercoaster from hell.

My recently acquired phone vibrates over the black lacquer side table, clattering to the carpet as it topples off the edge. I reach out and snatch it up, swiping to answer.

"Hey, King. What can I do you for?" I pick up a slip of paper while I talk to him; something in the timeline on it itches.

"Your boy is giving me grief."

Bronx. "I knew I shouldn't have let him head up there early. What's he fuckin' doing now?"

"Pickin' fights with the younger hang-arounds. Being a general pain in my fuckin' ass."

"I'll give him a call." And a fucking reminder what he's there for—who it is we need to keep on our side.

"Plus . . ." King pauses. "I need a favor."

"Another one?" Aside from sorting out Bronx, the guy's already had me find temporary housing for his surprise kid and baby mama nobody knew about.

"Yeah." He chuckles. "Another."

"Sure thing. What do you need?"

King sighs heavily down the line. "That trip you were making next week?"

"Yeah?"

"Can you make it tomorrow?"

"Uh, sure. Can I ask why we're speeding things up?" Bronx isn't meant to make his 'chance' introductions until the end of next week. I'm not ready for this. I need to find that kink in the chain.

"Things got a little complicated here. I need to get the other chapters together and hash this shit out."

I slide the sheets of paper over top of each other, assembling them into a tidy, ordered pile. "What's happening? Anything I should know about?"

"I'll break it down when you get here," he replies. "Can you also run a trace on Vince, see what you can come up with?"

"Any special reason?"

"Asshole went AWOL a week ago and now he won't return calls."

"Taking Sonya?" I can't imagine him leaving her behind—not with the way they were all over each other when I saw them last.

"With Sonya," King confirms. "The woman jumped on the back of Vince's bike and that was that. Nobody's been able to get hold of him, or her. They'll come back, but fuck, I don't need this right now."

Fuck's sake. Neither do I. Last thing I want is another loose thread. I have to know where everyone is while this shit kicks off. *Fucking Vince.*

"Right, I'll be there tomorrow."

"Good." King sighs. "Fuckin' place is fallin' apart around me." He murmurs his last sentiment as an admission without need for reply. I feel for the guy; it has to be hard work keeping an entire club in line—fuck knows I struggle enough with the two meatheads that remain out of our lot.

My thoughts again wander, going to the brothers we've lost: Case, Seamus, and most recently, Tigger. All good guys, a little on the fucked-up side, but full of heart all the same. The familiar acrid guilt swims into my gut, thinking how I failed each of them; it's my job to keep us all in operation, and when a brother falls, I take that shit personally.

"We'll see you early afternoon?" King asks after a decent pause in the conversation.

"Yeah. I have a few things to tie up here before I leave, but should get away first thing."

"Great. Thanks, Ty. Catch you tomorrow then."

"No sweat." I end the call and toss the phone on the carpet beside my pile of papers.

Legs either side of my work, I lie back on the floor and stare at the ceiling. The silence in the house is deafening. Why the fuck didn't I turn on some tunes before I sat down with this shit? I should go pack a bag, get my stuff together, but there's too much chatter swimming in my head.

I'm driving closer to her. I'm heading to where Ramona is. What will I say? Things are . . . awkward, for lack of a better word. She made it clear we're just friends the day I left after Sawyer's exchange. I wanted to say everything to her then: tell her that the way I feel about her isn't the kind of connection you make with just anybody, that she does things to me, calms me, and gives me a peace that nobody ever has. Now I get a second chance. But where do I start?

Reaching out and making the first move is fucking hard. I'm not used to wanting that closeness with someone. I've never craved it, always run from it, scared that the self-hatred I bear is too much for a person to handle. I couldn't stomach breaking a person down with the burden I carry. I can't even entertain the thought of doing that to a woman.

But Ramona—there's this defiance, offset by her compassion. She has fight, a will to survive. Fuck, I don't know if that's all it is? How can I label that gut feeling you just *get* that a person can be everything you've been looking for?

I like the security that comes with my privacy, and relenting won't be easy. Trying to entice somebody in instead of pushing them away is so foreign to me that I may as well be reading a how-to manual written in a different language.

I want to believe Ramona can fix my fucked up habits, and that my gut feeling about her was right. But how can she be expected to do that when I'm always going to bring the rain? The minute she learns about the real me, the sadness I harbor inside like a cancer, she'll walk away. Anybody with the basic will to survive would.

I know I did once.

My world became too much to stomach, and I fixed that by shutting out the people close to me, bringing things back to basic. I ran away from home and made it all about me. The only person I had to worry about was myself. The only interests I needed to look out for were my own. And then my world grew again. I found people on the street just like me, and we banded together. We formed bonds so tight that when we looked out for each other we never saw it as duty or favor—rather as a second nature, as though we were taking care of ourselves.

Two were taken. That night, a piece of all of us who remain was lost in the mangled metal of a car driving too fast on a road too wet. I see the harm in their eyes: Malice and Bronx. They suffer that loss every day like I do. And I saw it multiply the day Tigger was killed.

I buried half of myself with those brothers. I live with the niggling ache that I'm missing something, and that I need something more. Until now, I could never place what, I just knew that searching for the answers in what I could do for others was a Band-Aid over the real issue. I needed to find somebody who could do the same for me, force me to face my own issues without fear. After one night talking so intimately with another man's woman, I think I could have found the person who could fill that role, and show me how take the emptiness away by facing a mirror to my issues.

Somebody who could give me direction.

Above everything else though, I'm terrified she's not real. I'm petrified that after this long I've built her up to be more than she was, that I'm simply romanticizing her memory. I'm shit scared of seeing her again in case this final grasp of hope for a future without regret and shame is lost.

In case I realize there isn't a person in this world who holds the ability to help me undo the damage I've done to myself.

I'm placing my last stand for freedom from the demons that taunt me every day squarely in the palms of a woman I barely know. Because I'm failing at life, magnificently, and without the idea that she could be it—that she is the person who can finally undo the knots of penance I've bound my soul with, I fear I'm lost forever.

a heart too large

RAMONA Groaning as I stretch, I push my legs out to full extension, ignoring the stiffness in my hip. The nap in the afternoon sun has done wonders; now I don't want to move. Glancing to my right, I note that the warm rays of spring have nabbed more than one victim. Mack lies sprawled on the opposite end of the sofa, book still in his hands, albeit skewed across his little lap.

Reaching over, I slip it from between his fingers and place it gently on the free part of the cushions. He stirs, smacking his lips a little, exactly how Sawyer does, and leans into the arm to continue napping.

It's been two days since King rang with the news that Sawyer was out, that he was alive.

Nothing.

I haven't heard a thing from him: no phone calls, no texts, nothing on Facebook, not even a random message passed through the club grapevine. I tried ringing him and left a voicemail, but either his phone is disconnected or he's avoiding me. Nobody can say.

The low murmuring of conversation to my right catches my interest, and I glance up to see a couple of prospects sitting with King and Mighty at the bar. My teeth grit and I groan at the cramp pinging in my hip while I hobble over to the group. The guys look up from their conversation. I offer a small 'I'm fine' wave and carry-on, grimacing.

"How you doing? Need help?" King asks.

I shake my head and bend, hissing through my teeth, to grab a bottle of water from the fridge. "Nah," I reply as I straighten. "I just need to stretch it out. A little stiff after that siesta is all."

"Dog, can you go get us something for lunch?" King asks, looking at a baby-faced prospect. "Nothing too greasy—I'd like to avoid an early coronary."

I pull pain meds from the first-aid kit on top of the shelving behind the bar, and absently pop two pills as the young guy nods and leaves without hesitation. He shrugs on his jacket as he wanders out the door, which is emblazoned with the same 'prospect' rocker in bold navy lettering as his cut. Letting my gaze drift back to the other up-and-comer as I place the pills on my tongue, I chase the medication with my water and feel a little ill at how young the boys who come in here these days are. Sure, there are worse places they could be, but they're barely adults, just kids.

"I meant to ask earlier if you'd heard anything new

about Carlos?" I say to King. Despite the rumor of threats against me, I'm yet to see any evidence of it.

He shakes his head, and leans an elbow on the bar. "Nah. It's been quiet, and to tell the truth I don't like it a hell of a lot."

"You wouldn't be very good at what you do if you didn't find it strange." I throw back another gulp of water. "Any news on Vince and Sonya?" The two of them took off last week, possibly after hearing Sawyer was hanging out at the Fort Worth pad.

"Nothing." King's face brews a deathly storm, so I decide to change the subject.

"Dante's cool. We hung out yesterday and built stuff with that Meccano you got for the kids around here."

"Yeah, he is pretty cool." King's face lights up, and I mentally pat myself on the back for avoiding a Sawyer-induced inferno.

"Never knew you had family until the other day, Pres," the prospect I know nothing about says. "Figures though."

"Yeah?" King scoffs. "How's that?"

"You're so good with us guys, like a big bro some days. Knew you couldn't be one of those cold son-of-a-bitches who avoid kids like a plague."

"I'll take that compliment," King says with a laugh, "but fuck, man, you dish that shit out too often, I may become soft, and that never bodes well."

The prospect laughs and stands from his stool. "Yeah, I'll remember that." He wanders off towards the garages with a bit of swagger.

“They’re getting younger,” I muse.

“That they are,” King agrees. “But I figure they’re better off here learning how to keep on the right side of illegal life than doing it all fuckin’ backwards with the likes of Carlos.”

“True.” I’ve never thought of it like that, but he’s dead on. If we don’t scrape them up when they poke their nose around this kind of life, then who will? At least with us they’ll be taught morals.

Us.

I’m getting ready to uproot my boy and start a fresh life for us, one without the dangers associated with the club, and I’m still referring to ‘us’. Too many years in these walls—too long in the life.

“What’s on your mind?”

I snap my gaze up to find King watching me intently. “Not anything of value.”

He smirks, getting under my skin the way only he knows how. “I beg to differ.”

“Of course you do.” I return the sarcastic smile. “You always differ.”

“Can just see through your bullshit, woman. What’s cuttin’ you?”

Pulling air into my lungs, I take the pause to find some sort of composure. I’ve never voiced the fears out loud, and just thinking of doing so has my eyes pricking. “I’m worried that I’ll miss this too much.”

“So what? If you do, you just come home.”

Home. Jesus, was the man trying to kill me, already?

"I can't do that," I whisper.

"Why the fuck not?"

My gaze drifts to Mack, and King follows. "I can't muck him around like that. We make this move? That's it. He's staying settled until he's old enough to make his own decisions."

"He's a kid, Ramona. He'll adapt."

"Yeah, but what if all the back and forth messes him up?"

King extends his arm across the bar and takes my hand in his. "If you push livin' someplace that ain't right for you two just because you don't want to uproot him again, what do you think will do more damage? One week of upheaval to a happier surrounding, or months, years even in a place where you have no support?"

"We have support there," I remind him. "Malice and Jane. Ty, I guess, and maybe Bronx, when he's finished doing whatever it is you guys keep talking in code about."

"It's not the same," he murmurs. "You've been with us since before you got your first fuckin' period, woman. You were a kid when you tripped in this place and found your family. Don't think you can shake us that easy."

"I'll come back and visit."

"I know you will," he says, "but it's what happens in between that worries me. You know we all got your back, and if you want to move Mack to a place far enough away from this life that he can grow up without the influence, fine, but don't take yourself too far away from where *you* belong."

I scowl at the big bastard. He already has me battling tears, and I was so damn determined not to give in. "Enough. I don't want Mack waking up and wondering why Mommy looks like a big red-eyed monster."

"Fine, enough for now," he says, slapping his palms on the bar. "But I want you to really think if movin' all the way south is the best thing."

"I did, and it's decided, King. I can't back out now."

"You can always back out." He tips his head toward the stairs. "Now go and have a long hot shower while the little guy's asleep. I know you haven't really left his side since you got shot, but you'll start attracting fuckin' flies soon."

I reach across the bar and whack him one on the shoulder. "Thanks, *pal*."

He chuckles, and points to the stairs. "Go. Take some time to slow down and look after yourself. I'll watch Mack."

"I'm serious, though," I say, walking around the bar to stop beside him. "Thank you. For it all."

Spreading his legs wide, he pulls me into a bear hug. "You're like my little sis, Ramona. I'd do it all for you all over again."

Fucker. I swipe the tears away and pull from his grasp. "You just wanted to see me cry, didn't you?" I tease.

"Not exactly, but it's nice to see that you care about us so strongly."

"Yeah," I whisper, "I sure do."

drive time

TY Being a Sunday afternoon, the road is quiet. The highway stretches before me, mirroring my life perfectly. It's a bland, functional resource to get you from one place to another. There's no joy in driving it—nobody *longs* to spend hour upon hour steering their vehicle along the concrete. It's just something you've got to do.

And here I am again, just doing it, thinking about Ramona and whether if I'd said anything about how I really feel to Ramona the day I'd left it would have been any easier than doing it now.

When I'm among the boys, I can fill my time with *their* lives. The more attention I give them, the less I have to spend on myself. Because paying mind to *my* life and *my* issues is just plain old depressing—especially when I start thinking about how much misery exists in my world.

I have no goal, no purpose in life. I'm treading water, blinding myself with everything shiny and loud around me that I can lay my hands on, all to ignore the heartache that surrounds me. Take away the people I give a shit about, and what do I have left?

Absolutely fucking nothing.

The radio cuts out and is replaced with the chime of my ringtone. I tap the button on the steering wheel and answer the incoming call. "How was the weekend?"

"I spent most of it dodging questions." Malice's chuckle reverberates through my speakers. "We're almost home."

Apparently Jane's mom wanted to meet the man in Jane's life responsible for getting her to leave her abusive jerk of an ex. They spent the weekend there, playing happy families. I can imagine that explaining exactly *how* they met to the woman would have been downright awkward.

"Sorry I haven't caught up much lately—been distracted."

"That shit with Bronx getting to you?"

There was no point lying to the guy; we've known each other too long. "Yeah. I have a gut feeling that something isn't tight, but everything looks okay at face value."

"As long as it's not critical, we'll work it out as we go. Try not to lose sleep over it." *Too late.*

"Where are you heading?" Jane joins in. "Sounds like you're in the car. Maybe we can catch up when Malice and I get home?"

"No can do. I'm headed up to Lincoln early."

"Oh. Where are you staying while you're there?" Her tone has shifted to low and suggestive.

"I hadn't decided yet," I inform her flatly.

"If the clubhouse is too rowdy, don't forget Ramona has a spare room."

I know what she's doing. So I call her out on it. "She's a taken woman, Jane."

"Is she?"

Malice scolds Jane for interfering, and then dives back in with the other sticky subject. "Sawyer goin' to be there? Bronx told me he's back. Didn't last long."

"No, it didn't. Given what King wants to do, I think he'll be at the clubhouse, yeah."

A couple of knowing grunts echo from the speakers in my car. The beep sounds to tell me I have another call waiting.

"I better wrap this up guys, I have another call." *Peak hour in the Audi.*

"Yeah, no problem. Just checking in."

"Bye, Ty," Jane adds before the call disconnects.

I tap the button to pick up the waiting line. "Go ahead."

"How far out are you?" King.

"About half an hour."

"I need you to swing by and pick up Ramona."

Fuck me. Is the universe conspiring against me? "Sure. Everything okay?"

"Yeah, just rather she didn't drive at the moment."

"Okay." I drag out the last syllable. "Guess I'll find out when I get there?"

"You sure will," King says. "I'll text you the address. Oh, hey, you know anything about a package from your way being sent to Ramona?"

"She got it?"

"Got the card to say she missed it. You send it?"

"Yeah. Just some stuff to help her with the shift."

"Right," King drags out. "See you in an hour. You can explain then."

"Yeah, catch you then."

The news Ramona needs picking up worries me. My mind boggles at all the things that could have happened to her for driving to be out of the equation in King's eyes. In an effort to calm my racing heart, I match each dire scenario with an equally mundane one—perhaps she slipped on the front steps, or simply sprained an ankle? After what King's had her involved in, I have severe doubts it's anything so innocent.

Still, I'm a little relieved to know my parcel is on its way to being delivered. I shouldn't have sent it to her—I should leave her alone, but who says I can't still look out for her under the guise of a friend?

Who the fuck am I kidding? I'm hoping it'll sway her feelings my way. It's a low play, but shit, I ain't below playing dirty if I feel it's warranted. Sawyer's back after all, and if she thinks he's what she needs, I'm happy to prove her wrong.

Fuck—listen to me, jealous as all hell. This visit's going to be nothing short of all out war.

ding-dong

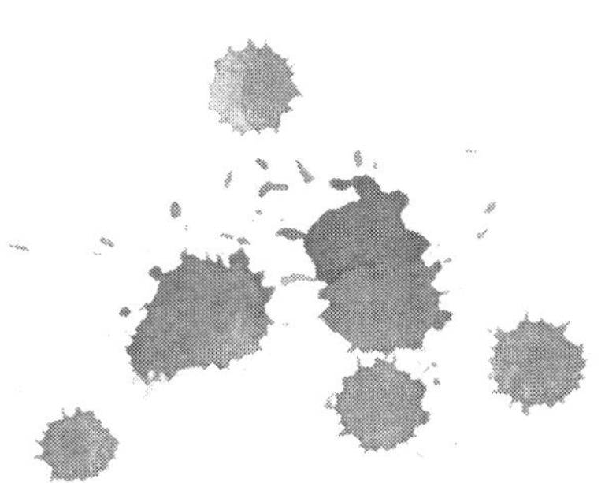

RAMONA I'm still wondering if I'm hearing things after the FedEx man's second knock when he tries for round three. I careen around the end of the hallway and skid to a stop in front of the door. The latches are undone in record time, and I swing the door open as Mack still hollers blue murder from his bedroom about having to wear sweats when he wants shorts on.

The poor guy huddles close to the door to get some shelter from the unseasonal rain we've been having. I offer him a smile, and accept the package as he hands it over.

"Can you sign here?" he asks, thrusting the handheld device at me.

I scribble with the special pen on the screen, and hand it back to him. He's barely accepted it from my grasp when his back is to me, and he's flying through the downpour to the safety of his vehicle. I close the door, shake the drops off the slim cardboard envelope, and flip it over to see no sender's name. *Damn.* A shiver zaps the length of my spine, and I drop the slim package on the back of the sofa on my way through to get my phone.

"Hey," King answers promptly. "You got your parcel, then?"

"Yeah. No name on it."

"You'll be good to open it. I asked around, and it's nothing to do with Carlos."

"Yeah?" I say, my gaze drifting back to the package. "Who sent it?"

"Ty."

A swimming, flapping sensation erupts in my gut. "Really?"

"Open it up, Mona. And don't forget to say thanks."

King ends the call as I stare at the cardboard envelope, wondering who gave Ty my address. I place my phone down beside it on the back of the sofa, and lift the package. *What could he need to send me?*

With tentative fingers I peel the perforated strip off the end, and balloon the sides of the envelope to see what's inside. A few slips of paper stare back at me, and I shake them out into my waiting palm.

The first is a generous petrol voucher that I set aside, heart thumping. Two hundred dollars. It'll cover my fuel expenses for the shift at least. Why would he send me this? My ears burn and my throat hurts as I unfold the second slip of paper. My gaze rakes the words, and unbelieving, I skim the document again, fighting for full breaths as I set it down with the vouchers.

My phone vibrates on the sofa, and I catch it before it drops to the floor. I swipe to answer without a second thought, and lift it to my ear.

"Hello?"

"Ramona, hey. It's Ty."

Silence. Long, awkward, silence.

"Hello?" he asks.

"I'm sorry—you took me by surprise."

"Did the gifts get delivered yet?" The husky timbre of his voice does weird things to my knees, turning hard cartilage and bone to some jelly-like substance unsuitable for standing. I drop to the arm of the sofa.

"I just got it. You didn't have to do any of that."

"Maybe not," he says, "but I wanted to."

"Why?" I breathe.

"You'll need something to give you a head start, and I'm more than capable of offering it."

"I don't like taking things from people that I can't repay. I told you that I don't need your help, and I meant it. We'll be fine. You'll have to cancel it, take it back, whatever."

"No, I won't. If anyone has somebody to repay, it's me."

My hand balls to a fist on my thigh. "What do you mean? I haven't done anything for you."

"You have," he murmurs, sending a strange euphoria skittering through my body. "Besides, it wouldn't be a loan anyway—it's a gift, Ramona." I wish like hell he wouldn't say my name. I can't bloody think straight when his tongue curls around the 'R' like that.

"It's a very generous gift, Ty."

"I'm generous."

My pulse has made an appearance on the inside of my elbows, my ears rushing with blood. "At least let me do something to say thank you when I get down there. I'll make you lunch when we're unpacked, or something like that."

"How about dinner tonight?"

"I'm not moving until day after tomorrow, Ty."

"I know." He sounds amused, and my curiosity is getting the better of me—how does he know?

"Then how can we have dinner tonight?"

"Hold on," he says. "I'm just parking. Let me get the phone off Bluetooth."

"Sure." I click my nails, listening to the sounds of him breathing, moving, and the scrape of his clothing as he gets out of the car—all of it doing strangely erotic things to me. Footsteps sound in the background, splashing over wet ground. Guess it's raining there too.

"Right, I'm good."

"So, dinner," I remind him. "How are we supposed to have dinner tonight if I don't move for a few days yet?"

A knock at the door has me rolling my eyes. What now? Callum checking up on the FedEx package? I walk with the phone to my ear and swing the door open, still unlocked after the FedEx guy. *Woops.*

"Pick you up at six?" Ty grins at me from the step.

I melt . . . and panic. The door slams shut with a

resonating thud. Heart hammering, I break out in a sweat, and gingerly open it again. "Shit, I'm sorry. You surprised the hell out of me."

"Again, so soon?" His full lips curve up on one side as he pockets his phone, and his dark brown eyes sparkle. "Can't say I expected you to do that though."

"What *are* you doing here?" As much as I try, I can't get the stupid smile off my face. He wasn't supposed to be here until after I'd left.

"Heard you needed a lift to the clubhouse."

"I, uh . . ." *King*. That bastard's dead. "No, I don't. I can get us there on my own. Thank you."

Ty stares. I gape. His left hand lifts to adjust the cufflink on his right wrist. I shift on my feet to ease the ache between my legs.

"Can I come in?" he asks, amused smirk still in place.

"Shit. Sure." I take a huge step back, and panic anew at the state I'm in: sweats, T-shirt, shrug cardigan with a hole in the sleeve, no shoes, hair unbrushed and thrown up into a messy ponytail.

And then there's Ty—a complete contrast to my mess with his impeccable style. His hair is freshly trimmed, longer on the top, and perfectly swept to the right-hand side. He's got dark designer jeans hugging toned and athletic legs, a tailored shirt tucked in, wide studded leather belt, and a dark grey waistcoat thrown on over top, unbuttoned. He's the perfect mix of badass and hipster.

My nipples are disturbingly tingly looking at him

standing before me, back turned as he checks out the house. Memories of him wearing a hell of a lot less when I crashed into that hard body assail me. I yank my cardigan tighter over my breasts to cover my clear arousal, and walk around in front of him.

"You thirsty? Hungry?"

"Thirsty," he answers, meeting my gaze. "You sure you don't need a ride? 'Cause King said he'd rather you're not driving."

"Did he now?"

"Nobody's told me much, Ramona, but I get the impression it didn't go very smoothly the other week. Did Elena agree to leave?"

I nod, walking past him for the kitchen. "Yeah, she did in a round-about kind of way. Coffee? Water?"

"Water's great, thank you."

I pluck a bottle from the fridge for him and one for Mack.

He accepts the bottle I hand over, and eyes me top to toe again. "Did you get hurt?"

"A little," I cede. "We weren't as inconspicuous as we thought. Carlos's men turned up at the door and things got . . . complicated."

His Adam's apple bobs before he speaks again. "How?" Ty twists the top off his bottle while he waits for me to explain.

I sigh and place Mack's water on the counter. Slowly, I move the fabric of my sweats from my hip, holding the hem of my T-shirt out of the way with the heel of my hand. "I got shot. Just a graze."

He splutters the drink of water he'd been mid-scull on, and places the bottle on the counter next to Mack's, wiping his mouth with his sleeve. "How bad was it? It looks like more than a graze." My skin heats in anticipation of his touch as he nears me, hand outstretched, staring intently at the damage.

The sensation of his fingertips skimming the flesh around the wound sets a shiver in my spine. "It was deep, but not serious. Gloria stitched me up and now it's just sore. It aches when I stretch out, or push down too hard with my foot. I can drive though."

His fingers drop away, and he meets my resigned gaze. "As much as I'm glad it not's more serious than that, it still fuckin' disturbs me that it happened. Where were the others?"

"Coming."

"Not fast enough," he mutters, turning away.

Mack chooses that moment to saunter casually into the living room, dressed in his T-shirt and sweats as though we never had a problem. "Hi."

"Hey, little man. You been behaving for Mom?"

He nods, and then brushes us off to take up residence in front of the TV, nabbing the bottle of water I had out for him on the way past.

"He hasn't, has he?" Ty smiles knowingly at the one eyebrow I have raised in Mack's direction.

"Not always," I say with a chuckle. "But he's good most of the time so I can't complain."

"You're the type of person who never would."

Meeting his gaze, I wonder how exactly it is a man I have yet to learn so much about seems to know me so well?

proximity

TY She smells like a fresh summer morning: flowers and dewy rain. It's exactly as I remember, exactly the same smell I've infused into my house after buying the same shampoo she uses—a little surveillance can uncover a lot about a person when you spend time under the same roof. Am I crossing an invisible line by doing that? Not sure. Don't care, either.

"I guess you've been busy organizing everything, ready to go," I say, looking at the boxes.

She pulls up the slip of paper from her purse again. "You sorted the only thing I had left to do besides packing, thanks."

Warmth spreads in my chest, and I'd lie if I said I didn't just experience a moment of male pride. "Glad I can help, is all."

"Ty," she admonishes, putting the paper away again, "paying my first three months' rent isn't just helping."

"It is to me."

Her eyes fix to mine and she fights a frown, her brow twitching. "Nobody's ever given me something like that without expecting some sort of favor, if you know what I mean, in return."

The air about me thickens. Yeah, I know what she's referring to—her time at the club as one of the whores. "I'm not one of those guys," I say. "I wouldn't expect that." Although the thought of her showing gratitude in that way is *very* appealing. "Like I said, you've already given me something anyway. I'm repaying the favor."

"What exactly did I give you?" she asks.

"Can't say." My eyes dart across to Mack.

"Of course, right."

"So, what brings you up here early?" She enquires, fussing with her purse. "Can't imagine you drove all that way to give me a lift."

"King needed to see me," I say absently.

"I forget—always with the club business, you lot." She smirks, letting her hands drop to the counter.

"You sure you don't need a ride?"

"Positive." She nods. "I was only popping over to visit. There's no hurry."

"King isn't the only reason I came over." My heart hammers so hard it's borderline painful. "I've got other business I want to sort out while I'm here."

"Yeah? Like what?"

"You." I freeze as her surprised gaze hits me. *Run with it, boy.*

"I'm sorry, what did you say?"

Don't back out now. "I said, you."

Her chin drops to her chest, causing her red hair to slip over her shoulders and shield her face from me. I can't tell what she's thinking, and my head goes crazy with worry. She stiffens when I approach and slip my fingers behind the lengths to tuck them behind her ear.

Ramona lifts her head and glances at Mack, still parked before the TV. "Can we talk somewhere private?"

"Sure."

She tips her chin, forcing my lingering hand away, and leads me down the hallway to her room. I walk in, uncertain where to park my ass, wondering if sitting on the bed looks too presumptuous while she gently shuts the door behind us.

"Are you giving me these things out of guilt?"

"Excuse me?" I give up finding the most polite place to sit and just drop where I am, onto her bed.

"Guilt," she repeats, hands on her hips before me. "Are you gifting me that stuff because of, you know, how awkward things got between us?"

"No," I protest. "I'm actually a little insulted you thought that."

Her head tips to one side, and she lets a smile slip through the angry façade. "I'm sorry." She moves to sit beside me the same as she did that first day—strategically far enough away so that the dip of the mattress doesn't cause our bodies to connect.

It irritates the hell out of me.

"You never called. You never said anything to me after we left," she complains.

"Uh, yeah."

"Why?"

"It has six letters, and stands about six foot tall."

"Sawyer," she says with a sigh.

"You're his old lady, Ramona." What the hell did she expect me to do? I kind of like my balls where they are.

"Why are you here now, then?" Her green eyes search my own.

"Call me stupid," I say, "but I had to come see if anything's changed since he's been gone. I need to know before you saw him again, and it influenced your answer, if you've been thinking about me at all."

"Every day," she whispers. "I think about you every day. But I also think about him every day."

In one sentence she wielded the power to give me confidence and then rip it away. "I can't compete with him."

I also can't be the guy who stands around and pretends everything's fine when it's not.

I need out of here.

Now.

"Why would you be competing?" she asks.

"Because you still love him." I turn away, burying my face in my hands. "In whatever way that is—it's still love."

Why *did* I come here today? She's fucking taken, spoken for, *and infatuated with the father of her child*. Have I deluded myself that much with all the fantasies I've divulged in this last month? Made myself believe there was any sort of a shot at this?

"Ty," she says, touching my shoulder. "Look at me."

I draw a heavy breath, and lift my head.

"I don't regret the fact there's this thing between us. Do you?"

No way. Never. I shake my head.

"I'm so damn confused," she confesses. "What do I do?"

"You're asking the wrong guy."

"Why? Can't you give me a reason why I should pick you?" She twists her body to face me.

I slip my hands either side of her jaw and run my thumbs over her bottom lip. "Babe, I could give you a hundred reasons why you should pick me, but that's the point—you shouldn't have to pick. The decision should be obvious. You need to make the choice based on what you know, the full picture. Only you can do that."

"I've missed you."

My chest aches at her admission. "I've missed you too. It makes no sense; we talked, it was one night."

"To me, it was the only night that mattered. You *listened*, Ty. You *cared*."

This fucking woman is going to tear me to pieces. "I still do." I search those beautiful eyes, looking for an answer I know is there. "Ramona . . ."

"Ty, don't tell me you're going to walk away. I don't want to lose this yet. I want that chance with you, I'm sure of it—I just need to get my head straight."

"I'm not walking away, babe." She sucks in a sharp

breath as I tug her face to mine, crashing my lips over hers. Allowing my tongue entrance, she kisses with the same passion that burns within me. It's everything I expected it to be and more: soft, angry, confused, and perfect. I break our union, pulling back and dropping my hands. My heart races, my breaths coming quicker. "This is just the beginning for us."

tug-o-war

RAMONA He walks out on me. Just kisses the living hell out of me, stands, and walks away. His deep voice murmurs through the walls as he says his goodbyes to Mack, and then the bang of the front door snaps me to my senses.

I rush across to my bedroom window and jam my face against the glass to catch a glimpse of the street from this side of the house. His white Audi backs out of the driveway, and then pauses. My heart stampedes, all sorts of scenarios running though my head where he pulls in again and gets out, coming back to me. But instead, the tires give a slight squeal as he takes off with speed.

Deflated, and more confused than I was to begin with, I trudge down to the living room and fall onto the cushion beside Mack's.

"Why was he here, Mom?"

"Dropping something off for us," I reply.

"Oh." He looses interest, the colorful cartoons snagging his attention once more.

I sit beside him, staring at the screen but a million miles away as I try to once again comprehend what he's given us. Three months of rent. Hundreds of dollars spent on people who have only recently come into his life.

If I don't allow myself to read into the gesture, I'll be a damned fool.

It takes me a moment to realize that the noise disturbing my thoughts is my phone, back in the kitchen. I dash through the house, and snatch it up before it goes to voicemail.

"Hey," I answer breathlessly.

"I didn't interrupt anything, did I?" King chuckles.

"You knew he was coming here," I accuse.

"Maybe," he teases.

Heat flames my face. "What were you ringing for? That makes it twice in a morning, King. A girl could feel special."

"Knock it off, woman." He laughs. "Nah, I forgot to ask if you could bring some of Mack's toys over. We've got a few more kids than usual here tonight."

"What's the occasion?"

"Members from the other chapters are on their way in. We've got what's going to be a day-long sit-down tomorrow about some shit that's coming up."

The reason why Ty drove up. "Do you need a hand with catering? Or is Sonya back?"

"Sweetie, if you could help, I'd love you forever. That

asshole Vince hasn't turned up yet with Sonya so we're completely out of our depth. Bones is in the kitchen, trying to work the damn dishwasher."

"No way." I chuckle at the imagery in my head of Bones, one of the oldest members in the club, trying to work out how to use the industrial washer.

"Yeah, so, ah, help?"

I laugh at his desperation, and agree to postpone my visit until just after lunch so I can help get things underway. King ends the call after berating me for not accepting Ty's ride, and I spend the next few hours just chilling with Mack, doing not much, but everything that I need to clear my head. We color for a while, build some interesting looking zombie apocalypse vehicles with his Lego, and then round out the morning with a walk around the block—at least, I walk and he rides his bike. My hip twinges in protest with every footfall I make, the pull of the scarring still causing problems, but I'm careful to check it every so often and the movement doesn't seem to have aggravated the wound.

After a long shower to ease my aches, I bundle Mack up and we head over to see the boys. Mack screams into the place, greeting 'Uncle' Callum and some of the other members who have earned the prestigious title of family even though the only member who shares blood with Mack is Sawyer. The kid has grown up with these men always being there to guide him, to show him how to do his 'boy' things, and generally provide male influence when Sawyer's been gone on a bender. The fact Mack feels so comfortable with them and insists on calling them all his uncles makes me feel even worse for removing him from the life.

Confusion reigns as I second-guess the motives behind my decision. What if having Mack spend time with the men from the club is the answer? I mean, I've always seen the guys as the problem, thinking their influence is going to cause trouble when Mack gets older. But I was only focusing on the bad side of club life. What if the *good* is what Mack needs? Having all of these people there for him; a bunch of men ready to do anything to protect my child—what's so bad about that?

Shaking the thoughts from my head, I make my way through to the kitchen area. Several of the lifers' old ladies are already prepping sandwiches, and boiling potatoes and pasta for salads. I greet them all and get brought up to speed on what they've got so far. Filling in the blanks, I let them get back to work with instructions on what we'll still need to get organized. Aside from Sonya, I'm the only other person who knows exactly what quantities it takes to cater to the whole club when they have these huge get-togethers.

I round up two of the prospects and send them out to the local butcher with a list of meat we'll need to keep the men sated over the course of the evening. While they're gone, I get Mighty to give me a hand bringing out the trestle tables and we set up the common room ready for the buffet-style meal later in the evening. Callum gets the fire pits ready with the grates that fit over the top to BBQ the meat. By the time the prospects return with the goods, the coals are red hot and we're on target to feed the masses.

Over the hours it's taken us to prepare, members from both Fort Worth and also our western chapter in Los Angeles have been steadily filtering in. I make a run out to the skip with a bunch of off-cuts from the sandwiches, and the sheer amount of bikes jammed into the yard is staggering. Faces are familiar as I head through to the kitchen again, but names elude me. I haven't seen most of these people in years, more than ten for some of them, and I can't help but wonder what is so important that all the chapters are getting together like this.

Being buried in the kitchen for the majority of the afternoon, I haven't been able to keep track on where Ty is amongst all these people. My gut flips every time somebody comes through the doors, but it's never him. I don't know what I'm more terrified of: bumping into Ty, or the realization that Sawyer is more than likely out there somewhere, too.

The kiss from Ty feels fresh on my lips, and I catch myself standing stock-still while I drift away with my thoughts. He seemed so put off by the fact I still feel emotionally attached to Sawyer—and I get that. Just thinking about the mess I've gotten myself in hurts my brain, so I head out of the kitchen to find where Mack has got to since I saw him last. When I finally locate him out in the backyard, playing with Tonka trucks and steel diggers, the sight damn near makes my ovaries explode.

Sleeves rolled up, and lying on his side in the dust, is Ty. He's engrossed in an excavation project with Mack and doesn't even seem to realize I'm approaching until I'm almost on top of them.

"How's the job?" I ask. "On target for the scheduled completion?"

Ty looks up and I blush at his fiery, panty-melting grin. "I think so. How you doing?"

"Busy, but the girls are pulling together. I think we'll manage to keep you boys happy." I place my hands to my face briefly, urging the heat to recede.

His eyes spark, and I falter under the familiar wave of physical awareness. "I'm sure you will."

"Ty, you need to unload!"

He glances down at Mack, who's pointing furiously at Ty's laden dump truck. "Sorry, man." He backs the truck up, complete with reversing beeper, and unloads onto their stockpile at the side of the work site.

With the truck in position for Mack to reload, he flashes me another smile. "You need help with anything?"

I'm sure I must look a dreamy fool as I stand and simply stare at the sight before me, but damn—can I be blamed? "You're helping heaps already," I reply, gesturing to the play area.

"Awesome. Well, just holler if you need me."

Holler, holler. God, do I need that man. But here? Now? Not suitable. Besides, I still need to work out if he'll accept me—complications and all. The impression he left me with after our encounter at home was that he won't be pursuing what we have until I've made a clean break from Sawyer.

Will that ever happen?

I leave the boys as they were and re-immerse myself in preparations. It's serving time before I next emerge from the kitchen, and my hands are wrapped around a hot tray of ribs when I spot trouble, staring at me as if he wants to devour me.

Shit.

The tray drops onto its placeholder with a clatter, and I feel no less than a dozen sets of eyes on me. The disturbance was loud enough to drown out the chatter and music pumping through the speakers in my immediate area. I sort out the serving tongs that had fallen off the tray with fumbling hands, and then go to make a quick exit when firm fingers encircle my wrist.

"Mona? Where you goin'?"

I want to scream. I want to cry. I want to let all my frustrations free in whatever shape or form they choose, and for as long as it takes to ease this welling pressure inside of me.

"There's still more to be brought out," I say weakly.

Sawyer looks into my eyes with a tender concern I have *never* seen from him, and I almost melt on the spot. I've missed him so much, but the air around him is light, and his entire demeanor toward me is caring, appreciative, and soft. It's not him. The true Sawyer doesn't give a shit about me. The Sawyer I know would have turned up here and ignored me all night while he got drunk with his brothers. The Sawyer who left me wouldn't now be holding my hand captive and staring into my eyes with a deep frown marring his beautiful face and asking what was wrong.

"I'll come help you," he finally says, releasing my wrist.

All I can do is nod, and die as I catch Ty's eyes across the room while I push the door to the kitchen open for Sawyer. Ty wraps his arm around Mack protectively, pulling him to his side as my boy takes a soda offered by Bones at the bar. My head is a whirlpool of indecision. I want Sawyer to be here; I'm relieved he's okay and have been waiting days for him to make contact, but at the same time I'm wondering if we've now ruined what could have been a pivotal night for Ty and myself.

Don't get me wrong, I love Sawyer in a weird kind of way, and want to work things out between us for Mack's sake, but Ty makes me *feel.* He shows me a level of attention Sawyer never has—at least not until all of a minute ago.

"Coming?" Sawyer asks, eyeing me from inside the door.

I break the connection with Ty, hurting as I do, and follow Sawyer into the kitchen to point out the dishes that need carrying out to the tables. He assists with setting up the last of the buffet, tracking me like a hawk. The minute the words 'that's the last one' drop from my mouth, Sawyer has me by the arm and is dragging me through the clubhouse to King's office.

The room is empty when he shoves me inside, and I

stumble, catching my footing while Sawyer shuts the door behind us. His intense blue eyes are on me, searching, asking silent questions of me. In a way, his sudden return to being abrasive and domineering comforts me. It's the Sawyer I know, the man I grew to love in our fucked-up way.

Yet, being as unpredictable as ever, he flips it all around on me yet again. Familiar hands find my face, softly holding me near him, and I allow it. I allow him to give the same intimacy as enjoyed with Ty mere hours ago. *Once a whore, always a whore.*

"How have you been?" he asks, frowning yet again.

"I've been okay."

Sawyer's lips find mine, but the kiss is quick, friendly, and lacking any passion. So vastly different to how Ty left me this morning.

"I worried about you."

"Likewise," I say with a sigh. "What happened?"

He moves to the chair, and gestures for me to go sit with him. I pause for a moment, but move with urgency when a flash of the old Sawyer shows in the dark flecks of his eyes. Taking residence in his lap, he twists me so I sit across him like a child. His large hand rests on the side of my knee, his other arm wrapped around my back.

"I'm not going to tell you what happened, sugar. It was fuckin' hell, and you don't need to know. All I want you to know is I learnt a fuck-load about myself in there. I learnt a lot."

"Yeah?" I whisper. I can't believe it, but it's there in his eyes. There's compassion, warmth, understanding—all the things I've missed out on during the last five years.

"You have new injuries," I say, looking at his arm resting over my lap.

"Yeah." The word is hollow, yet laced with so much unspoken pain. "Things got a bit messy."

"If you want to talk about it, I'm here. I know you said not now, but if you do . . . you know . . . in the future."

"We'll see." His large head rests against my arm, and my fingers find their way into his hair, stroking through the lengths to comfort him the way I always have. He hums beneath my touch, and cinches his arms tighter about me. "Can we just sit, do this for a while?"

"Sure," I whisper, settling in.

Despite everything he's put me through, I'll always find the time to give this man comfort when he needs me.

Because he needs me.

green

TY Yeah, I'll admit it—I'd hoped that asshole was going to turn up dead after we gave him back to Carlos. But he's not. He pissed me off by turning up at Hooch's club, and now the fucker is here, in my way, and his Goddamn hands are all over her.

Callum wanders past with some of the club kids. "Mack, you ever played Xbox?"

Mack shakes his head against my side.

"I'm taking this rough bunch upstairs for some games. You want to come learn?" His gaze lifts to mine, and a silent understanding passes between us.

"Yeah, okay," Mack answers pulling out from under my arm.

I watch them all file up the stairs, and then head over to nab something to eat before the buffet's all gone. Members mingle and chat, as if we're at some fucking bowling club reunion. It's so damn civil, as though it's not the norm for everybody in this room to have a criminal record as long as their arm.

"What's crawled up your ass, dude?" Bronx stops beside where I sit on the arm of a sofa, chicken leg in hand, gnawing at the marinated flesh.

"Fuckin' life," I snap back. "Kind of sick of it shittin' in my face."

"Dude," he says, dragging out the word. "Drink, relax, take a pill, whatever it takes to loosen up." He jerks his head to where Hooch and his crew are hanging out. "They've got some good shit over there."

"How would you know if it's good or not?" I narrow my gaze on the guy. He's never been one to shove anything up his nose, let alone in his vein. The only drugs pumping through his system are the ones found at a sports supplement store.

"Been learning a thing or two. You know, for what's coming up."

My gaze flashes to King's office, my face flaming redder than the desert sun when I find it still shut. Returning my attention to Bronx, I rise to my feet and get up close in his face. "King told me you've been trouble. What the fuck's going on?"

"Trouble?" he scoffs. "Shit, dude. If he thinks I'm trouble I guess I'm playing the role right."

I look him over, head to toe, as I toss the spent chicken bone in a trash can. He's been slowly prepping himself to become a part of Edward Hennington's crew. My best friend, who used to wear only running shorts and training shoes, now sports a pair of faded denim jeans and what appear to be steel-capped boots. His normal stringer singlet has been replaced with a black heavy-metal tee, and the boys have been inking him by the looks of the fresh design on the side of his neck.

"I get you need to come off legit, man, I really do. But, fuck, take it easy, yeah?" I've lost three of my best friends already. I'm sure as fuck not looking to add to the list.

"Don't worry your pretty little head about me," he says with a laugh, clapping a firm hand on my shoulder. "You know better than any fucker here I can look after myself."

"Yeah," I mutter. "Exactly what I'm worried about."

"I've been getting to know some of the other guys," he says, nodding again to the Fort Worth crowd. "I'll introduce you to the new faces before you get stuck around a table with them tomorrow."

I nod blankly and follow as Bronx leads us over to Hooch and his men. The lot of them are fucking huge, just like their pres. There isn't a doubt in my head that at least two of the three could bench-press a damn truck if they tried. What the fuck do they feed them in their clubhouse? Steroid-laced beef? The closer I get, the smaller I feel. For the first time ever, I wish like hell I wasn't so lean and well dressed. I stick out like a calf in a field of gigantic bulls.

"Hooch, you know this dude. Jo-Jo, Crackers—this is Ty." Bronx thumbs over his shoulder at me, but never actually indicates who is who with the two I haven't met before now. *Thanks for nothing*. "He's the brains behind this gig, and the bastard who has saved my ass more times than I can count." He slings an arm around my shoulders like a proud parent.

Hooch gives me a lift of his chin as the other men take turns shaking my hand. After the last jolt I cradle my injured paw to my chest, wondering how on earth I ever thought I was fit. "How's it, guys?"

"Heard a fuckin' ton of good shit about you," the shortest states. "You're a good bastard, yeah?"

Sure as hell hope so. Don't really want to find out what happens if these monstrosities think otherwise. "So I'm told," I reply.

The big guy to his left with a beard twice as long as mine—you know, because I couldn't be the best at anything with this lot—gives me a shove on the shoulder with his loose fist. "King tells me you're good at finding shit out."

"You could put it like that, yeah."

He nods knowingly, and gives me a wink. "Can you find out where a stripper works now if I give you a description of her?"

The short guy groans, slapping a hand to his face.

"No, I can't," I mumble. "That's not really what I do." I'm not about to waste my time searching out a woman this beast's got a thing for, just so he can get his jollies off.

I twist to take a quick look over my shoulder at King's office once more. The door remains shut. No prize for guessing what could take that long, and requires the privacy of a closed room. *Fucker.*

"Ty."

I spin back around and look at the guy with the flowing beard. "Yeah?"

"Why's your fuckin' hand empty?"

I drop my gaze to my vacant hands—as though it's a surprise. "Preoccupied."

"What's your poison?"

Something red with a full, rich flavor. I close my eyes, pulling at the memories of that kiss with Ramona, praying to get even a whiff of her scent again.

"Dude." Bronx elbows me. "Crackers asked what you're drinking."

So that's Crackers. "Scotch." Might as well get hammered if there's no point staying sober anymore.

"Coming up," Crackers answers with a grin and turns for the bar.

Hooch and the guy who must be Jo-Jo close the tight circle we have, shielding anybody else from even considering taking Crackers's vacated post.

"Saw you with Mack before," Hooch says out of the blue. "You know Ramona well?"

Fuck me dead. Let's just jump right in on the awkward shit, why don't we? "Sort of. I met her last month."

"When you assholes sold out Sawyer?" His gaze is tight on my face, waiting for a reaction that gives away my position on what happened. "Yeah, that's right—we've been talking about what the fuck that grief was the other week between you lot."

I deal. "Nobody fuckin' sold anyone out, asshole." His eyes widen, but he stays quiet. "That psychopath got what was coming to him. He's fuckin' lucky that none of my boys, especially Bronx here, took him out on first sight. You saw what happened when you sprung him on us; we've got a personal connection to all the fucked up shit he's been doing in the name of makin' Daddy proud, so don't you fuckin' shift this shit on us like we did *him* wrong. He got everything that came his way, and then interest."

Hooch's thick arms cross over his mile-wide chest as he glares down at me. Crackers has returned and watches blankly from behind him, while Jo-Jo looks as if he's reaching into his waistband in preparation for this going south.

A swell of pride washes over me, strengthening my position on the subject when Bronx steps in closer beside me, standing shoulder to shoulder like we've always done. My friends have my back—always have, and always will. It's a bond that can't be broken, no matter what.

"You've got a lot to say about it for a guy who doesn't look like he'd last very long in a fight," Hooch spits.

"Fuckin' A, I do." My frown is so heavy that my forehead literally hurts under the strain. It's all I can do not to wrestle Jo-Jo's weapon from him and prove a point; I'm not weak.

"Anything else you want to add before I give you my fuckin' side?"

I shrug, taking the chance to glance at King's office . . . again. *Still. Fucking. Closed.*

"You keep lookin' over there every chance you can get,"

Hooch observes, casting his gaze in the same direction. "That tells me one of two things: either you're waitin' for a second chance to take on my brother in there when he steps out, or you're watchin' for his missus. Either way, *Ty*, it doesn't fly with me." His gaze slips back to my face, the weight of his anger pushing me back into Bronx. "What you know of Sawyer is only a drop in the ocean," he hisses. "That kid endured more fucked up abuse at the hands of his so-called father in the first fifteen years of his life than you'll see by the time you're fuckin' seventy. I haven't got the full story from him yet on what happened when he went home, but I'll tell you two things, *Ty*: one, it didn't go well, given the state we dragged him home in, and two, he went above and beyond inside those walls doin' what he could to save my *sister*. Now, she's dead and he's hurtin'. I don't question it, I don't pass judgment, I just know that there is one fuck of a loyal man fightin' to dig himself out of the shit he's brought on himself, and the least dirty fucks like us can do is cut the asshole some slack while he finds his feet."

Where the fuck is King when you need him?

"Point made," I say, chin raised. "But perhaps if he expects people to cut him some slack he needs to start explainin' just what the hell goes through his head half the time. People don't change overnight, *Hooch*. They can make themselves a better version of what they were, but the bare bones of a person's genetic makeup will never be altered enough to take away what they truly are. He's a fuckin' killer, he's selfish, and only does what pays off for him. Until he shows me otherwise, I'll keep on watching his every fuckin' move, and when he fucks up—because he will—I'll be right there, shovin' your face in it."

Bronx rips me to the side as Hooch's fist flies through the air toward me. I cop a blow to the jaw, just below my right ear. He's got fucking stone mallets for hands. Fuck, it burns.

Hooch's chest heaves, his fists flexing. The asshole's ready to keep it up if I give him the cue. I take a step forward, get right up in his face and mutter low and level, "I might not get my hands bloody, you're right there, but I can fuck you up a hell of a lot worse in ways you won't even see coming."

A commotion breaks out behind me as I walk away, several of the men around Hooch struggling to hold him back. With my skin ablaze and my head pounding with each beat of my heart, I strut casually toward the exit, noticing one last thing about this fucked up place.

The door is finally open.

implosion

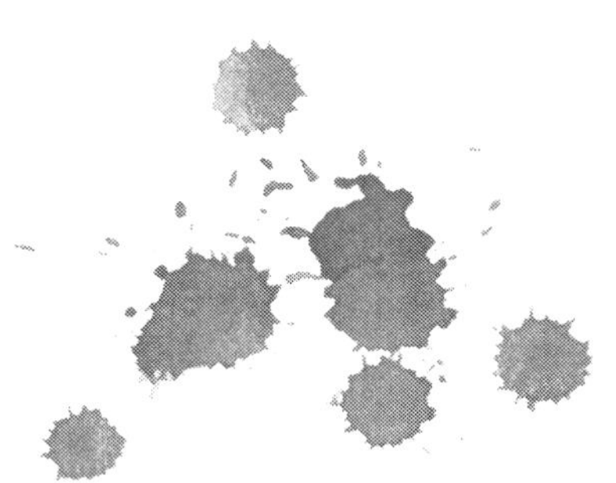

RAMONA Speechless. Sawyer heads across the room to where Hooch is going off like a cut cat while I gape at Ty's retreating frame. Whatever the hell those two just spoke about, it hasn't ended well.

Not that this will be the end.

Does Ty even know who the hell he's messing with? Surely he knows that our chapter is the tamest of the three. He's just walked in and picked an argument with the president of the most violent Fallen Saints chapter. What the fuck was he thinking?

My feet finally allow me to move from the spot, and I rush over to where Sawyer is standing with both hands on Hooch's shoulders, talking with him, forehead touching forehead, nose touching nose. The other boys have removed their hands, happy that Hooch isn't about to run after Ty, but he's sure as hell nowhere near calm yet. His chest heaves, his eyes dark and menacing. Knowing the guy, he's probably on his fourth line for the night already.

"What the hell did Ty say?" I ask Bronx, who stands a few feet back with his arms folded, watching the aftermath.

"A few things he shouldn't have, a few things we've all been thinking, and the rest you need to talk to him about."

Cryptic much? What is it with these Butcher Boys? Do they always just allude to what they're thinking, or am I the only lucky one exposed to that?

"Have you seen Mack?" My nerves are pinging at the thought he might have witnessed the exchange.

"He's upstairs in Sonya's room with some of the older kids. Callum pulled out his Xbox and they're all glued around it."

Bless, Callum. "Thanks, Bronx."

"You should go talk to Ty."

"Why?"

"I'm not the smartest kid out of school," he says, "but I sure as hell ain't stupid either."

My throat thickens as I stare into his brown eyes, reading every word between the lines. I break away from our silent conversation and touch Sawyer lightly on the arm. He says something final to Hooch, and then pushes him away gently, giving him a slap on the shoulder, telling him to go get laid.

"You okay?" he asks, turning his attention to me.

"Fine. Is Hooch?"

"He just needs to calm down and lay off the blow for a few hours."

Just as I thought. "Mack's upstairs in Sonya's room with the other kids if you want to see him."

"Yeah?" His eyes light up. "Can I go surprise him?"

"He'd love that," I say with a smile, giving him a gentle shove in the direction of the stairs. "I'll let you two have a moment without me hanging around." *While I go out and talk to Ty.*

Sawyer nods, and jogs off toward the stairs. I watch him go, waiting a few seconds after he's disappeared at the top to be sure. Hooch is at the bar, surrounded by the other Fort Worth boys and a few club whores who probably just creamed themselves watching that display of testosterone. I need to get outside without any of them catching on, but when there are this many members in the place, that's going to be near impossible. Making do with the fact the most important people aren't watching, I hustle down the front hall and out the door, giving the prospect on point a smile as I pass.

Ty drops in to his car as I step out into the night, his face shadowed through the windscreen by the lone light shining behind his parking space. His expression is hidden as I approach and butterflies flap mercilessly in my gut. What if he doesn't want to see me? What if I was the problem?

His driver's door opens again as I near, and one dark denim-clad leg emerges, quickly followed by the other. He rises from the seat, intense and strangely dominant in his refined attire. He swings his body around the door to meet my quickening steps as I close the last few feet to him.

Ty's hands wrap around my jaw as our bodies crash together, his lips on mine in a fever, and my answering whimpers doing nothing to slow him down. I've never just *wanted* a person as much as I do with him. Damned who can see us, damned who might know, I need this before I implode with reined desire.

He breaks free, still holding my face. "You came after me."

"I was worried about you. What did you say in there?"

His eyes close, and he turns his face away briefly. "I can't share that without upsetting you."

"Ty," I say with a lopsided smirk, "I don't think I could get any more messed up than I will if you won't talk to me. Stop making me guess; stop making me assume the worst. Just tell me."

"Come home with me."

"I can't." I twist my face in his hold to look back at the clubhouse. "Mack . . ."

"He can come too. Just come home with me, to my house, tonight."

"Ty . . ."

His hands drop away, and he paces to the far end of the car. "You want him more."

I long to fall to the ground and bawl my eyes out, but that won't explain any of this to him. It won't do much but ease the drowning feeling I have inside.

"I can't explain it, Ty. He's just always needed me."

"I need you," he murmurs. "Not that it matters,

obviously."

What the hell have I done? Still, if I could go back to that night and undo what we started, would I? No way—ever.

"Of course it matters," I snap. "Would I have chased you out here at the risk of wearing the consequences if it didn't matter? Would I have kissed you just now if *you* didn't matter?"

He spins on his heel, his eyes black in the low light. "I don't know, Ramona. Would you? Maybe I do matter, maybe you care. But fuck, woman! Do I matter more than that asshole in there?" His hand jabs angrily toward the clubhouse, his bicep pumping through the movement.

"I don't know," I murmur, dropping my gaze to my feet. It hurts me to admit I don't have the first clue which way I want to go—I can't imagine what it's doing to him.

The car door slams.

My breaths shudder, and my skin seems all slimy and alien. Ty's headlights snap on, casting a blinding sweep over the lot as he pulls from the park. I can't breathe properly. My chest hurts. I think I'm going to vomit.

I do.

How do I get myself in these situations? Tears break free as I stand with my hands braced on my knees, heaving through the last of the stench permeating from my spilled guts. I've heard that stress can make you physically ill, but until now, I'd never seen the truth in it.

Guess I just proved the point.

Swiping the back of my hand across my mouth, I stare

out the gate, watching where he went, aching in every inch of my bones with the hope he'll come back.

But he doesn't.

The prospect on the door gives me a tight nod as I enter the clubhouse. "I didn't see anything, Mona."

"Thanks, Tails."

I'm so lost in my self-pity that I don't even realize Sawyer has Mack downstairs until I near trip over them.

"Where'd you go?" Sawyer asks, Mack on his shoulders.

I look up and smile at our boy, longing selfishly to hold him to me so I can feel a little better. "Needed a breather."

"Fuck, babe, you smell like hurl. You okay?"

"Yeah. I think I drank too fast, or ate something off. It just came out of nowhere." With every word I say, I sink further into the comfort of this moment—of our family.

"I'll keep hanging out with my man here while you go get cleaned up. He wants to go home to bed, so we were looking for you."

"Sorry, baby," I say, reaching out and giving Mack's knee a squeeze. "I'll get myself sorted and we'll be out of here before you know it."

"It's okay, Mom. Take your time."

Tears sting anew, burning behind my eyes. Yeah, I wish I could take my time, but somehow, I don't think either man is going to wait.

self-destruct

TY "How long you after?" The hooker pops her gum, eyes running around the inside of my car.

"Hour."

She nods, and looks over her shoulder to an enormous black guy standing in the shadows. She fires off a hand signal, and he nods in return before she opens the door and slips into the passenger seat.

"Where we going?" Somehow she manages to get the question out although her jaw is still working the gum the same as a cow with cud.

"I'm not from around here—"

"I can tell." Her gaze rakes over me.

"—so, where's best?"

"Park up that way is usually quiet. Good secluded spots."

I nod and drive, needing to keep my hands busy and my mind at work before I toss her ass from the car in a hailstorm of expletives. *You need to do this—need to clear your head.* Need to unload. Working myself over with my hand only achieves so much, which is why I don't bother. Draining the reserves with the real, live thing will kill this insatiable need I have to turn the car around, ditch the whore, and go get Ramona.

She's not yours to have. She made that obvious.

I ease the Audi into a park under a large sycamore tree. The branches block some of the light from a nearby streetlight. It's perfect. Her face is mostly in shadows, obscured, and it's easier for me to pretend she's somebody else, somebody with vibrant red hair.

The girl gets to work like a pro. My jeans are open, my old fella hanging out before I can turn the car off. She's got him in a chokehold, working me with her hand and mouth, but he simply isn't budging.

It doesn't hurt enough.

Eyes closed, I grasp her hair in my fist, bringing up images of Ramona, imagining it's her in the car, her working me over. There's movement down below, but it's slight.

The hooker peels back, pushing against my hand. "You want me to fuck you instead?"

Hell no. She's a street-worker; there are more tracks on her arms than at Grand Central Station. Fuck knows what she's full of. I'm running a risk even using her mouth. "No, just keep it up. I've had a bit to drink," I lie. "You have to work harder for your cash, love."

She does. The woman pulls out the big guns, squeezing

and rolling my sack in her hand, tugging on the flesh, but still not hard enough to really hurt. I reach down, closing my hand over hers and force her to pull harder. Her nails bite into my skin, and I hiss at the blinding pain. *Heaven.* It's the distraction I need, the diversion from my reality. I let myself go to another place, another time, and before I know it, I'm convincing myself I'm back on the porch at Fort Worth, Ramona tucked to my chest.

The hooker gets into it, deep throating, and gagging as my cock hits her tonsils. I need more. Letting the fantasy go, I concentrate on the building tension deep in my gut. With a hand on the back of her head, I drive her further, harder, making her choke. Tears slip across her cheeks, and her eyebrows are drawn up in a pleading expression, but I don't give a fuck. She's being paid to give me what I need, and right now, I need to punish somebody for shit that's out of my control.

She moans in protest, her red lipstick smeared around her mouth as her saliva bubbles in the gaps at the corner of her hold on me. She's pushing against my hand on the upstroke, trying to get free, but I'm close—so close.

Gargled, pained noises slip from her, the vibrations exquisite on my length as I fall over the ledge into the pits of hell, shooting hard into her mouth. She swallows, gags, and swallows some more. Spent, finished with her, and only marginally sated after dealing out the abuse, I yank her hair hard, forcing her off me.

"There's clean wipes I the glove box," I tell her, looking at the mess on my crotch.

Where the hell did that come from? Until now I've always paid them to hurt *me.* Never have I done it this way, hurting them.

She's still gulping, trying to get her breath back as she pulls the wipes out and gets to work cleaning me up. Every stroke of her hand over the area, every breath the woman takes, my anger builds to a raging monster. It alarms me, being so out of control. It disgusts me more watching her clean away the reminder of what I just did.

Things shouldn't have come to this. I shouldn't have to go here, to take my pain out on someone else in this sick fucking way. Why am I so fucking broken? Why is this me?

She straightens her skirt as she gets out, taking the wad of wipes to the trashcan a few yards from the car. Her hands dispense the litter at the same time as I lunge across the car and slam the door behind her. The whore's head whips around, and I throw a bundle of cash out the open window at her, needing to get the fuck away from this place. It flutters to the ground, colors changing through the movement like autumn leaves.

The sad fucking woman doesn't even move as she shrinks in my rear-view, fading into the night.

I'm an asshole, an abuser, and I don't need a shrink to tell me I have some serious issues. The technical term for what I've just paid her for is 'transference'. Normally I use these women to inflict pain on me that I can't bring myself to do. This time, I've taken the hate I have for myself and forced it on another. As new as this role reversal is, I know exactly where the need for punishment comes from—it's an unhealthy by-product of growing up in a house where self-loathing, failure, and guilt weren't allowed.

My parents are both successful in their careers. My father is a pilot, my mother a surgeon. They barely see each other. I never recall a single time I ever saw the two of them hug, or kiss. My sister and I had it drilled into us every day on a regular basis that we were the only ones responsible for how our lives ended up, that the only people who could determine our fate were ourselves and that if we wanted to be the best, there was no room for feelings of inadequacy, regret, or self-hate.

I'd proved them wrong. My sister's maker wasn't herself—it was me.

My chest rises and falls rapidly, my palms growing slick on the steering wheel as I head God only knows where. I can't think about this now. I can't afford to take myself back there when we've got such an important meeting tomorrow that I need my full focus for. Shit, I wonder if I'm even welcome?

Shoulders heaving as I try to regulate my breathing and heartbeat, I do my best to keep my voice level and recognizable. "Siri, call Bronx." I need a familiar voice.

"One moment please."

"Where the fuck are you?" His deep baritone echoes through the car.

I flinch at the clear panic in his voice. "Trying to get my shit together, brother. What's going down there?"

"Ramona's taken Mack home, looking like fuckin' hell might I add, and Sawyer's over in the corner looking every much as fuckin' spaced out as he has all night. Seriously, don't know what's up with that dude—he's not the same guy we saw take down Tigger, but man, I can't figure if it's a good thing or a bad thing."

"Me neither."

"Hooch is playin' pool with King, and the rest of his boys are hangin' about the bar, drinking booze or drinkin' club pussy." He sighs. "You comin' back tonight?"

"Not sure if that's wise."

"Yeah, you're probably right, dude. Look, get a motel, find somewhere to lay up, do what you got to do, but get your shit squared away before the morning, yeah?"

"That's the general plan." Although it's failing miserably so far as I find myself turning down the street two blocks from Ramona's. "I'll see you first thing. Behave, for fuck's sake."

He chuckles. "Fuck, man. I'd have to do a hell of a lot to take the shine off your stunt tonight."

"Guess that gives you a pretty broad pass then, huh? You can thank me later."

We both chuckle before he ends the call, perfectly timed as I idle to a stop outside Ramona's house. There's a single light on in her bedroom, and the street is quiet. I've got no idea if she can see me from here—I just pray the dimly lit street hides who's outside her place if she does happen to look.

I want her. I need her. But I'm not chasing after a losing battle. I need to know she wants *me* over *him*. She has to prove that it's me she chooses before I give in to the urge to lay her down and show her how a *real* man would worship her.

Fuck, I hope she picks soon though because this burning pain inside can only stay contained for so long before the resulting actions become dangerous.

A man in pain is a man to be feared.

And I'm fucking hurting hard.

simplify

RAMONA The pink glittered pen twirls between my fingers as I stare down at the mostly blank sheet of paper. I'd managed to keep myself together long enough to get Mack into bed, and then I cried. I'd bawled my eyes out like a damn baby, and although none of the tears eased my pain, it did clear my head enough to see what is it I need to do to move forward.

So now, I sit here staring a sheet of paper, which has two headings on it: Pro and Con. On the left, under the pros, I've managed to scribble down two reasons to stay with Sawyer—Mack, and familiarity. On the right are four for why I shouldn't, all centering around the fact that the love I have for him isn't how it should be between two people who have produced a child.

I love Sawyer, unconditionally, but there's never been that rush when he's touched me. I've never felt that unexplainable heat course through me when I've watched him walk my way. With Ty, I've experienced both those things. Plus the insatiable desire to call him, just to hear his voice when he's not with me. And the unquenchable thirst for physical contact: fingers, tongues, lips, I don't care what as long as it's his meeting mine.

I tear the sheet from the notepad, and start again—pros and cons. This time, though, I list them for Ty.

The pros flow from my pen with ease, the letters scrawled in barely legible handwriting on the paper just to keep up with my rambling thought patterns. Compassion, consideration, loyalty, *attraction*—the reasons why I should pick the dark, mysteriously sensitive man in the sharp clothing spill over the page like a waterfall.

Cons.

I stare at the blank column, my hand twitching as I hesitate to write it: *hurting Sawyer.* I stare at the two words, frowning whilst I chew on the end of the pen. Is that my problem, though? After so many years of neglect from him as a partner and a father, do I really have any grounds to feel traitorous if I leave him for another man?

I can't shake the niggle that if I'd been able to see my relationship with Sawyer for what it is six months ago, I would have looked at everything it lacked and walked away, choosing Ty without a second thought. But now, I know why I struggle—because Sawyer's *different.* All those hopes and dreams about him changing suddenly have basis, and I wonder, was I right after all? Could I save our family unit if I just stick it out and gave him a bit more time? Whatever happened to Sawyer when he went home rocked his foundations enough to strip him of the cold, jaded façade he held on to for so long. Perhaps it was the final push he needed to realize what his priority should be?

Us.

Setting the pen and paper aside, I flick the bedside lamp off and slip under the covers. My phone lights the room as I wake it from its sleep and do the obligatory scroll of Facebook before settling in for the night. Photos litter my newsfeed from people still at the clubhouse. There's several of King and Hooch doing shots, a couple of Bronx with one of the newer club whores hanging off his hip, Mighty carrying a prospect around in some game, and then a few of the Los Angeles Saints leaving on their bikes in the night.

Nowhere is there any trace of Ty.

A heavy dread settles in my gut knowing he didn't return. He stayed away from what was meant to be a wind-down before meetings got underway because of me. I made him miss out on the fun he could have had with the guys.

Still, a small part of me revels in the fact that staying away kept grubby club whore hands off him. I'm selfish, and I have no right to be, but I can't stop the possessive nausea that overcomes me just thinking about any of those girls touching him.

Shit, I used to be one. I know how they operate.

A guy like him—flashy clothes and a flashy car—they'd

be all over him like ants at a picnic. He exudes security, safety, and a chance to be settled. What transient woman wouldn't want to score that as a package?

It could have been me.

But instead, I'm so messed up over what I feel for Sawyer, that I can't bring myself to feel right about deciding either way. What is right? Lust will drive me to Ty, but duty will bind me to Sawyer. I wish I knew which was the better emotion to follow. Which is the lesser evil?

I set my phone aside, plugging the charger in, and nestle under the covers on my side, hands clasped under my jaw. There's a barely distinguishable resonance in the room, similar to the engine of a car idling in the night. My legs itch to move, to go to the window and look, but I remind myself that Callum checked the neighborhood, and nowhere was there any sign of Carlos's men. My overactive mind is simply making the worst of the situation. I need to get some rest.

My eyes fall shut, heavy from my lack of sleep lately, and I drift away, listening to the low murmur of a car somewhere in the neighborhood, wishing it were Ty coming to solve this problem for me.

•• • ••

"You leaving?"

Ty lifts his head from where he'd been concentrating on putting his things back in the Audi, and frowns.

"I'm sorry if I complicated things for you," he says,

fiddling with a seatbelt. "It wasn't my intention."

"I'm sorry too," I murmur. "I didn't mean to cause a scene."

He gently closes the car door, stepping over to where I hesitate near the front steps. "You're doing an amazing job so far given the circumstances. Don't apologize."

I scoff. "Amazing job of what? Falling apart?"

As he comes to a stop before me, I'm struck for the second time by his natural grace. He holds himself well, dresses so sharply, and behaves with impeccable manners. The guy has to be from money and lots of it. He was never going to fully understand the situation I'm in.

"I'm guessing it was hard seeing him with your boy," he mumbles. "I never took that into consideration."

"It was, but I guess it was more the final straw than anything else. I'm stressing out about him being back there, like freaking the fuck out."

His dark brown eyes hold an unnerving level of understanding. "It's natural when you love someone."

"I told you, Ty, I don't love him like that." The thought's been rolling through my head for weeks now, but admitting it out loud to him for the second time now still sounds so filthy.

He lifts his face to me. "I just assumed . . ."

"It's okay. Our relationship is quite complicated."

Ty's throat bobs as he swallows, straining against the buttoned collar of his shirt. "If it's not that, then what else is upsetting you about him being gone?"

"I'm panicking about how we're going to survive, money-

wise," I say. "It's okay; I don't expect you to get it."

He jams his hands roughly in his pockets, kicking a stone into the bottom step. I inch back at the sheer anger that emanates off of him because of my flippant remark. The man's so damn beautiful, but his handsome features only add to the contrast of his anger.

"Why wouldn't I 'get it'?" he asks icily.

My gaze roams the length of him. The guy is GQ *material. Why would he?*

"You think I'm some rich kid who doesn't know what it is to struggle?" he asks.

Nailed it. *"Yeah."*

Ty leans in, our noses so close to touching. "Don't you know you shouldn't judge a book by its cover?"

"I've heard the saying," I reply weakly.

He grumbles and leans back again, allowing me room to breathe. It's so damn hot out here.

"I was homeless, you know."

"No way." I clearly sound as ignorant as I must look. "You don't look like you were homeless."

"There's a look for it?" he asks, an eyebrow raised.

I drop my head and smile. "I'm sorry. I must sound like such an asshole."

"It's a common misconception," he remarks.

"That I'm an asshole?" I ask.

"That I could never have been homeless at one point in my life."

"You've obviously recovered from whatever put you there, though."

"I did, and you can too, from all of this." He waves his hand around, gesturing to the house behind us. "You just have to want to work for it."

The slight humor I'd been building dies in a puff of smoke. "I don't know. There's so much to deal with: Mack's questions about where his dad has gone, losing Sawyer's financial support, and what we're going to do from here. I don't want Mack growing up in that club anymore—I know that much."

My head's a damned mess, and I'm struggling to come to terms with what Sawyer going home means. Even touching on the subject has my chest tightening and my gut churning. I push the thoughts deep again, struggling to control my tears.

"Hey," Ty coaxes, pulling me into his chest. "Just worry about getting through today; tomorrow will come either way."

"What if Carlos kills him?" I sob, fingers bunching his shirt in my grasp. "How can I explain that to Mack?"

"Just worry about today," Ty repeats.

I hiccup through the tears, inhaling his clean and spicy scent, finding comfort in the subconscious security being in a man's arms brings. His hold on me tightens, and after a while I realize his nose is buried in my hair. A hand fists the locks at the nape of my neck, and he tucks me into his shoulder.

I push away the feeling of being home, reminding myself that Sawyer is where I should find comfort. But then again, I never did and I think I never will. I close my eyes, my sobs having calmed, and nuzzle into Ty's shirt. His body is firm and warm, and like the harlot I obviously am, I allow my body to react to his.

Strong hands tip my head back, controlling the angle with the hold he still has of my hair. I stare into his chocolate eyes, my confusion and hurt mirrored back two-fold. His lips are so close . . .

"Are you ready to go face the world again?"

Only if he stays in it.

•• • ••

There's a child in my house—correction, a small girl—two, maybe, by the sounds of the conversation. My eyes crack open, and the giggling begins to make total sense. Mack's awake, and he has the TV on.

The images from my dream slip into focus in my mind, as does the fact I am very swollen, and very aroused . . . there. I dreamt a memory. I dreamt of the moment I fell hard and fast for a sharp dressed man. Does that even count as a dream? When it's something that's really happened, can you call it a dream? Or is it simply a memory while you're sleeping?

Whatever it was, I'm disturbed that it managed to get me so damn aroused. And a little frustrated at the lack of anything to relieve the tension. My thighs rub together as I roll from the bed, and a sigh escapes me at the sheer thought of how good it would feel to relieve the burden. Maybe I could slip into the bathroom for a bit? Before

Mack realizes I'm up?

All thoughts of sneaky masturbation are dashed at the echo of somebody thumping on my front door. I growl, tugging an oversized football sweater on, and trudge down the hall to answer.

"Hey, buddy."

Mack waves back absently from his pajama-clad spot in front of the TV.

The locks click, and I pull the door open to find a deliveryman standing there with a white cardboard catering box in his hands. The smell emanating from the parcel tells me what's in it before I even clap my gaze onto the bright red logo drawn on top.

Apple cinnamon waffles from the Engine House Café—my favorite local food, and a once-a-month treat for Mack and I.

"Ramona Seaten?" the guy asks.

I nod, accepting the box. Two simple words written on top leave me intrigued: *I'm sorry.*

"Bon appetite," the delivery guy says with a smile, giving me a wink.

"Uh, thanks."

I don't wait for him to leave. The door's shut in his face and I have the box on the counter, searching out two of the plastic plates I bought for us since the dinnerware is packed for the move.

"What's that, Mom?" Mack pulls himself up onto one of the stools on the opposite side of the counter.

I open the lid of the box, and inhale the heavenly scent

that wafts out on clouds of steam. "Breakfast, Mack. It's breakfast like no other."

"Do they deliver now?" he asks, peering in at the golden goodness inside.

"Not as far as I know." I'm still wondering just how much Sawyer *has* changed if he's sending me gifts like this. As out of character as the gesture is, it has to be him—who else would know I love them? Either way, it's not as though I'd turn down the one thing that makes me salivate like a dog.

I slip a waffle onto Mack's plate and get my own sorted. Fork poised, my phone rings from its position on the charger beside my bed. I glance down at the food, and frown. Whoever it is can wait. The first mouthful hits my tongue and I swear to God the same sensation I left bed with returns. Instant foodgasm. I'm about to take the second bite when the phone rings again.

Fuck it—it could be important.

Mack doesn't stir in his hoovering of the waffles as I dash past him to retrieve the phone. Out of breath, I snatch it up and answer without checking the display, hoping I've got it before it switches to voicemail. I really need to start leaving the thing within reach.

"Hey," I pant.

"Is it as good delivered as they are in-store?"

Jesus. How did he know? The area between my legs throbs anew hearing Ty's voice. "They're great, thanks. Hope you don't mind if I eat and talk," I say, walking back to the kitchen, doing a weird little shuffle to alleviate the pressure.

"Go right ahead."

I settle back at the counter, stabbing up another forkful. "Why?"

"Why not?" Ty asks.

I pause in my answer long enough to take a mouthful and swallow. "I caused the argument." If anything, it should be *me* groveling to *him.*

"But I was the one who said the things that hurt," he explains simply.

"I did some thinking about it all last night." I lift my gaze to Mack and find him slipping off the stool, heading for the fridge. "The answer is you. You mean more to me than he does."

Silence hangs thick on the line while I help Mack with a cup of juice.

"Are you still there?"

"Yeah," he answers breathy and quiet. "Are you sure?"

"Pretty sure." Especially if my lists have anything to say about it.

"So it's okay if I come in, then?"

pash & dash

TY "I thought you had a meeting today?" Ramona asks, pulling her front door wide.

"I do. Doesn't start for another hour." The scent of her breakfast hits me as I walk inside. It was a gamble, one I spent all night finding out the details for, but a gamble that paid off, evidently. I might not have won the battle against Sawyer at the clubhouse last night, but this war has just begun.

"How did you find out?"

"About the waffles?" I ask.

She nods, her red hair still mussed up by sleep. I rake my gaze down her slender body, encased in a college football sweater that's several sizes too large.

My gut twists at the thought it might be *his*. "When I want something, I have a way of getting it."

Her face flushes and she turns away, hurrying over to their dirty dishes. She drops the plastic plates into the trash, and turns back to me with her arms over her front.

"I'm going to quickly run through the shower and get dressed." Ramona thumbs over her shoulder toward the hallway.

"I kind of need a shower, too. Was hoping you'd let me use yours, if that's okay?"

Her eyes assess me, as though she's only just now stopped to take me in. "You're in the same clothes."

I wiggle my eyebrows at her, smiling.

"Have you not slept?"

"Caught an hour or two in the car, but I was kind of busy making phone calls most of the night." I let my gaze slip to the empty catering box.

"Oh."

She looks so fucking adorable, all shy and surprised that I'd do such a thing for her. My feet itch to carry me to her, but no shower and . . . hooker. No way I'm getting close to her until I've washed the filth from my skin.

"You have the first one," she exclaims, snapping into action. "I'll get you a towel. Everything you need should be in there. I think Sawyer left some manly stuff under the basin." Her gaze lifts when she realizes what she's offered.

Yeah—I don't plan on smelling like him for her either.

"There's some stuff in the shower too, if you don't mind smelling like lavender."

"Whatever gets me clean."

Five minutes later I'm standing in the bathroom, butt naked, looking at the 'manly stuff' that Sawyer left under the sink. Mental notes made on what brands never to buy,

I step into the shower cubicle and under the warm flow. Over the rush of water, I can just make out the murmuring of Ramona and Mack talking in the living area. I tip my head back, letting the warmth run over my face and down my neck to my chest, eventually reaching the part of me that needs the most cleaning.

I scrub, I lather, and I rinse and repeat, but the skin-crawling feeling of use and abuse remains on my flesh like a temporary tattoo. I crank the dial hotter and grit my teeth at the sting of the infernal water temperature. Red rashes break out over my shoulders and arms. My stomach and legs pink, the water searing my skin. I scrub again, harder, trying to erase every reminder—visual or not—from my body.

The towel, as soft as it is, hurts when I use it to dry myself afterward. I've burnt my shoulders in my efforts, but I'll take the pain over feeling as if I wear my shame for everyone to see any day. I tug the dark jeans from yesterday on, but leave the rest of my clothes off, carrying them in a bundle in my arms as I head out of the bathroom and toward the front door.

"Your turn," I say with a smile as I pass a wide-eyed Ramona in the living room.

My blood rushes, the vision of her blatant desire burnt in my mind as I deposit the dirty clothes in the car and tug a clean T-shirt from my duffle. Selecting a matching belt and leather cuff from the bag, I finish the look, hesitating while I decide if I should add the leather-bound watch or not. *Nah, probably overkill.* I wouldn't call myself fashionable by any sense, but I've always taken care in my appearance. It's the only part of me I can control to keep clean, presentable, and acceptable. Little details like accessories can be so easily overlooked by men, but I've always been of the opinion that they can take an outfit from mundane to stand-out with such little effort. Take some time, show you give a fucking shit, and women will notice the same.

The shower's still running when I step inside, and Mack is nowhere to be seen. I take a seat on one of the armchairs and check the time. Twenty-five minutes to go before the meeting gets under way The water shuts off, and Mack runs in the room with two Marvel figurines in his hands.

"Did you have these when you were a kid?" he asks, leaning a small hip into the seat part of the sofa.

"No, buddy. I didn't have many toys like that." They distracted me from the 'important' things in life, my father would tell me.

"You can play with mine any time you like."

"Cool." I give him a nod. "Sounds like a plan."

He takes off down the hallway as Ramona emerges, hair damp, and her body wrapped in a flowing, sexy-as-fuck sleeved dress.

"You didn't have to wait," she says. "I wouldn't have been offended if you left. I know you've got the meeting to get to."

I shrug. "Being polite comes naturally."

"You weren't polite last night," she says with an eyebrow raised.

"When I'm in a good mood," I add with a smile.

"Where did you go?" she asks, propping herself on the arm of the sofa, wringing the ends of her hair in her hands with her head tipped to one side.

"Drove around. Looked around. Tried to get distracted so I didn't think about you all night."

"Did it work?" Her hands still.

"Did you get waffles?"

Her lips curl at the corners and she drops her gaze. "Point made."

"I need to get going so I don't give them another reason to kick my ass," I say, standing and moving toward the door.

She follows. "I'll see you out."

Ramona trails behind me as I exit, shutting the front door and leaning her shoulders back into it as she waits on the top step. I stand on the bottom one, eyes level with her, and simply stare at the incredible creature before me.

"You better get going," she says quietly.

I swallow. I suck in a deep breath. The feeling stays. "I wish I could skip this, spend the day with you."

"Business is business." She knows—she's been around the club long enough to understand how the order of priorities works.

"Still . . ." I take another step up, standing on the one below hers.

"Still . . ." she echoes.

Her hands find my waist, and she runs her thumbs

under my T-shirt and over the grooves of my obliques, trailing down toward the restriction of my belt. I'm suddenly thankful for what else it restricts.

"See you tonight?" I ask. "I can come over after the meeting if you want."

She nods, biting her bottom lip. "I want."

I take that damn plump lip between mine, sucking on the spot she reddened with her teeth. She sighs into the contact, placing her hands behind my neck and lacing her fingers there, pulling me deeper.

As my world shrinks around me to focus solely on her, I realize exactly what it is about her that makes me crave such intimate moments.

She's the first girl I don't want to hurt me.

gavel

TY King cracks the top off a bottle of water, leaning back in his chair at the head of the meeting table and placing his booted feet on the edge of it.

"You assholes ready to get into this?"

A flurry of nods and a mumbled 'yeah' circles the room. King takes center stage, being that we're in his clubhouse, commanding the rest of us from the furthermost point in the room. To his immediate left is Callum, followed by Mighty and a newly returned Vince. On King's right sits the Fort Worth crew: Hooch, Crackers, Jo-Jo and their road captain, Murphy. At our end, opposite King, is the Los Angeles crowd and ourselves.

"Right," King exclaims loudly, pulling his feet from the table and leaning both elbows on the surface either side of his water. "Let's get you all acquainted. We, of course, all know who we are, but some of you ugly mugs don't know these guys down the end."

The stares of a dozen men who wouldn't be able to find their way back to the right side of the law if they were handed a map hit me hard.

"The one who looks like he could blend in with us is Bronx," King says.

Bronx lifts a hand and nods tightly.

"The other guy who looks like he's got lost on his way to the coffee shop is Ty."

I cock my head to the left and stare King down as the table erupts in laughter. *Really?*

"You two know our lot: Callum, Mighty, and Vince—who, might I add, has decided to grace us with his presence."

Vince flips King his middle finger.

"On the other side are your new best friends: Hooch, Crackers, Jo-Jo, and Murphy."

I fix my gaze to the table, not offering Hooch the pleasure of giving me the stink-eye.

"And at your end," King finishes, "are the Los Angeles mongrels: Tap, the president, his VP, Hando, sergeant at arms, Mick, and road captain, Brute."

The men all give us the obligatory tip of the chin and then swing their focus back to King.

"Right,"—he slams both fists down on the table, making those with their elbows on the surface twitch—"how we going to do this?"

Everybody looks at each other before the whole table takes turns to finally rest their gaze on me.

"Ty?" King asks. "Tell us what you've got."

I suck in a deep breath, ready for the performance of my life. I have five men who trust me, four who are undecided, and four who would love to see how long it takes before dragging me behind their bikes would kill me.

"Are you all familiar with who Edward Hennington is?" I ask.

They all nod.

"Somewhat," Tap says. "We've done a little research before we rode out."

"Okay. Good start, then."

"Stand up, for fuck's sake," King interjects. "Take the floor, man."

White, red, whatever the color—the rage is building. I know King's simply trying to make me feel like I fit in by giving me his friendly jests, but fuck, not all these guys are seeing the funny side. *Let's not belittle me before we start, huh?*

I move to stand beside the table, commanding the room's attention. I have to admit, the sensation is a little heady.

"Edward—or Eddie—Hennington is born and bred in Liverpool, England. He came out here just shy of two years ago. No solid answer why—some people say family reasons, others say he was pushed out of his hometown. He brought two friends with him: Easy and a guy called Taylor. The three of them found themselves a niche, beat out everybody who opposed them. They're rumored to have been the reason why Big Mike disappeared."

A few eyebrows lift at the mention of one of the West Coast's most prolific marijuana suppliers.

"They've been growing their numbers steadily, bringin' out ex-cons, unemployed, family, whoever they can from England, but that source started to bring them too much attention; the authorities tend to start lookin' into why twenty-odd people from the same part of England suddenly settle down in the one town. So, he's started recruiting locally. Problem is, the gang still thinks they're ten-foot tall and bulletproof because nothin' major has happened yet to shake the base they're building. Eddie is a pub-brawler at heart, and to him, anyone with strong fists is worthwhile. They don't do very detailed background checks, and they have limited knowledge of who is who in the area, let alone the country, mostly because they've been importing their own and haven't made many American allies yet."

I take stock of the fact several of the men have shifted position to get more comfortable, their attention trained on me and solely me. Hooch still stares at the wall opposite, but I have Crackers's undivided attention, as well as Murphy's.

"Given what we know of them, it's goin' to be dead easy to get Bronx in there by his skills with his fists alone." My best friend shifts beside me at the sound of his name. "He's a good fighter—it's how we met—so I have all faith in him. We get Bronx frequenting the same bars as Eddie's lot, get him in their face and noticeable. All it is then is a waiting game until they pay attention to one of his brawls and approach him. Bronx will drop hints around the place in the meantime, make them think he's solo, lookin' for a purpose, needing direction. They won't be able to resist."

"What's the benefit for us?" Tap asks, flicking his snakebite piercings with steepled fingers.

"I'll take over here," King says, rising.

I drop into my seat, curious as to what he has to say. His shifty eyes tell me it's something I'm in the dark on, and I don't like it one bit.

"The reason we got behind this to start with was a mixture of things. Carlos had a hit out on the Butcher Boys after one of Ty's boys was responsible for Eddie gettin' an in on the distribution Carlos had in their area. Word got out about the hits, and Sawyer thought he'd one-up his old man, show off a bit by getting them done first. He took out Ty and Bronx's guy, which kind of fucked things up, because then we lost our knowledge on what he'd given Eddie's lot and how we could undo the mistake." King reaches down and uncaps the water, taking a swig. "Carlos agreed to our proposition that if we got the distribution back in his hands, he'd back off the Butcher Boys." He catches Hando's eye and nods to give him the go-ahead.

"I've heard of you lot before. You're those muscle-for-hire guys, right?"

I nod at Hando. "Yeah, in a nutshell."

His eyes flick between Bronx and myself, and I know what he's thinking—how could I be a part of a bunch like that?

"Anyway . . ." King takes the floor back. "Carlos and I

have personal grievances that also got involved in the issue. Needless to say, things are a little more complicated, and I can't trust he won't out what Bronx is there for to set Eddie's lot on us as petty pay-back."

"What's the proposal?" Hooch asks.

"We turn the tables on what he's expectin'."

A few of the men look between themselves, unsure and confused. Fuck, *I'm* just as confused. When the hell did he plan on sharing?

King nods toward the door. "I'd like to bring in a non-officer, if I can, to explain things."

Yeah, he didn't plan on sharing at all.

Everybody gives him the go-ahead, and within seconds Sawyer joins us in the room. King offers his seat, taking up position in one corner of the room, leaning against the wall with a hand to his mouth in contemplation.

"Hey boys." Sawyer nods to the table. "As King just explained to you all, I was on a bit of a bender when I fucked these guys over." He gestures to Bronx and myself. "And for that, I truly apologize. As a sweetener to the deal to get my old man to lay off their unit, I was packed home minus the pretty bow." He smiles, and a few of the men chuckle. "I learnt some stuff while I was there—stuff I think you lot need to know."

A murmur sweeps the table and quickly dies down when King thumps his fist against the wall.

"My father plans on using the Fallen Saints as his new subcontractor, so to speak. You guys will get that distribution out of Eddie's hands, but he'll never let you give it up. You'll be blackmailed into runnin' it for him, taking the fall if anything goes south."

"Like fuck I'm doing any favors for that cunt," Tap bellows.

Most of the table agrees in a chorus of grunts.

"Plan B," King says, stepping back to the table's edge. "We do what Carlos expects, but we take it into *our* control. He won't see a cent from it. We'll take that channel from Eddie's lot, wipe them out, or send them packin' with their tails between their legs. But Carlos gets nothing: no control, no share, and no payout. It's ours—all of it. *We* keep it. *We* run it, and we fuckin' take *him* out next."

"You're fuckin' crazy," Hooch says. "You know what you're up against?"

"Well aware," King says, holding his steely glare.

"My old man is losing it," Sawyer explains. "He's unstable, clutchin' at straws to keep his crown. The whole reason why he kept me alive is because he wanted to get me into Hooch's role, take over the southern boys and turn the club against you all, convert it to one of his operations. He kidnapped Hooch's sister and held her as ransom to get Judas's cooperation."

"Why you still alive then?" Vince asks coolly. "Obviously you're not the pres for the Fort Worth boys, so what gave?"

"I escaped, with Hooch's help," Sawyer explains, addressing Vince. "Judas went in to secure his daughter's release, and paid with his life. When he didn't return, Hooch was on point to carry out his father's final wish."

"To get Dana out, or kill Carlos tryin'." Hooch fills in.

"And?" Vince asks. "That what happened?"

"Nah." Hooch shakes his head, solemnly. I almost, *almost* feel sorry for him looking at how broken he is about it. "Dana died, and we managed to injure Carlos pretty severely before we left. It was numbers, old boy. They had too many—we had what we could fuckin' spare at the time."

"And what can you spare now?" King asks, his eyes narrowed on the big guy.

"I'm not goin' to lie to you, boys," Hooch says, lifting his chin high. "Our club has gone to the dogs. Dad was too focused on my sisters to worry about the extended family, and unfortunately, some mongrels got brought in to the mix. We're cleanin' house now, but it'll take time."

"You think we need this pressure, King?" Tap asks. 'We've never dealt hard drugs before—never needed to."

"Apex ran our chapter into the red," King reveals. Looks of astonishment are aplenty. Seems this club isn't the best at communicating. "We're two mill in the shit to the Koreans."

"What the fuck?" Callum exclaims. "Does Jack know this?"

"Of course he fuckin' does," King snaps. "He's the motherfuckin' treasurer."

"Shit."

"Yeah, shit," King agrees. "We need to take this on before we wake up one day and find the clubhouse riddled with more fuckin' holes than a kitchen strainer."

"How long they givin' you to pay it back?" Tap asks. "The Koreans?"

"I've managed to work us six months." He rubs both hands over his face. "And it's all of us, not just our chapter. They see the club as a whole, lay the blame on all of us."

'Fuck' echoes around the room as the men all come to terms with the situation they're in.

"So how do we do it?" Jo-Jo asks. "How do you plan on taking it out from under not only Carlos's nose, but Eddie's?"

"Start with the small guys," I say, garnering the room's attention. "Those with the least to lose have the most to gain. We offer them a better cut at what they're sellin', take the little guys out of Eddie's operation and work our way up the chain from there."

"There's always a hundred more streetwalkers ready to jump the fuckin' game," Hooch says. "We steal one, two more will take his place."

"Not if we make it unattractive to work for the comp."

"How you propose we do that?" Hooch leans back, crossing his arms.

"Start a rumor, take a few of the low levels out who refuse to cooperate and blame it on Eddie."

"Stage the hits as theirs?"

"Exactly."

"It could work," King muses.

"We don't have many other options," I state. "You try and cut the serpent off at the head, the body will revolt. You need to work from the bottom, bleed the life from it before you deal the final blow."

"Where do we get the stock from?" Tap questions.

"The Koreans," King answers. "We owe them enough already—what's a bit more?"

"And then?" Tap asks. "Do we just knock on doors to find our turncoats?"

"No," I say, shaking my head. "You'd be makin' assumptions on who is aligned with who, allowing too much room for error. We start where we planned to, with Bronx going in to Eddie's crew. We need an insider who can get us the lists."

"It's time wasted," Hooch complains. "Just start with what we know and go from there."

"And then what? We fuck up because we didn't take the extra time to do it right? The whole thing is bust because somebody approaches one of Carlos's distributors and gives it all away?" I reply. "Just think about what's at stake, all for spending a month or two getting our shit straight."

"I'm with Ty on this," King rules. "We need to make sure we do our homework. I'll get in touch with the Koreans, work out a deal to secure some good quality dust, and you"—he points a thick finger in my direction—"can get Bronx in there as soon as possible. Start tomorrow. Take him to the bar and get introductions underway."

"You up for it?" I ask Bronx.

He nods solemnly; he's been strangely quiet throughout the whole discussion. "Yeah, I'm up for it."

"Right then." King leans across Sawyer to pick up the gavel. He smacks it down on the table twice. "Let's go have some fun."

fade to black

RAMONA The late-night movie struggles to hold my attention. Mack went to bed early, still exhausted from a long night at the clubhouse yesterday, and, sick of checking the street repeatedly, I sat my ass down on the sofa to wait out Ty. Pictures have been posted to Facebook showing King and Tap sharing a drink. The meeting is over and if he means to keep his word, Ty won't be far away.

My fingers brush across my lips, memories of his kiss fresh. Unspent energy buzzes through my limbs, only heightened by the fantasies I've been allowing myself, dreaming of what life with Ty is going to be like. The only thing dampening my spirits is the knowledge I still have to talk this over with Sawyer.

How's he going to take the news? Will he understand? It's not as though we ever had a traditionally loving and romantic partnership. It was always more of a team effort for Mack's sake.

Still, he's changed since the trip home, that's painfully clear. And change makes him unpredictable—more than ever.

A car door slams outside and I'm itching to run to the door and greet Ty. The remote tumbles from my lap as I shift in the seat to stand. I reach forward, bending off the seat of the sofa to pick it up as an ear-shattering *boom* and *crash* rock the house, sending me sprawling in shock.

Mack screams for me from his room, and I find myself on the floor in front of the sofa where I landed. Glass lies all around me, and the night air rushes through the room, chilling me to the core.

Another deafening *boom*.

I scramble on my belly toward the hallway, Mack's sobs ripping at my maternal instincts to protect him before anything else, before I even check the threat. Crunching glass and the soft click of a gun being broken open send my panic past the point of mania and into raw survival mode. The clink of shells hitting each other as they're discharged amplifies my resolve to reach my baby.

Pushing up on the heels of my hands I launch from my crawling position like a sprinter on the track. The snap of the gun precedes heavy footfalls on the carpet, tracking me to Mack's room. I round the doorway, latching my hand onto the frame and swinging my body around the corner without losing any speed. Mack's arms open to me as I rush forward, my own arms outstretched to receive him. His shaking body is barely within my grasp when another boom precedes the drywall in front of us exploding, coating Mack and I in dust and particles.

Tinnitus screams in my ears, disorientating me as I spin to see where exactly the intruder is. My lungs seize while I take in the enormous hooded figure in Mack's doorway, watching us, motionless. He still has one round in the shotgun, but it hangs loosely at his side. A beat passes where the two of us simply eye each other, and I come to understand something essentially crucial to what I do next—he's not here to kill us.

It's simply a warning.

If he wanted us dead, I'd be plastered across the sofa and Mack would be joining me in the afterlife this very moment. My child's body heaves with uncontrollable sobs. I lift my chin and staunchly walk toward the man. He steps aside, letting me pass into the hallway.

I don't push my luck.

As soon as we're clear, I run with Mack in my arms. Where? I don't have a fucking clue—just away. I have no money, no spare clothes for us, nothing. All we have are our lives, and I'll take that any day over the sentimental items in the house that no longer mean a thing to me.

My feet pound the sidewalk, Mack's sobbing having slowed to sniffles. Out of breath, I slow to a quick walk, the night air biting into our flesh as I push on at a fair pace, keeping to the shadows in case anybody else is looking for us.

The ten-minute drive to the clubhouse takes me forty on foot. Mack shivers in his thin pajamas, his little feet icicles as they bump into my knees with my movement. I hold him as tight as I can, my arms aching, and willing my body heat to be enough to keep him from getting sick. The lights of the gate come into view, and I break.

Tears stream down my face, my breaths sucked into my lungs on ragged moans as we near safety. We're going home.

The cameras pick us up as we approach and the gate slides open without hesitation. But salvation doesn't come in the form of a Saint—it comes in the form of a tailored Butcher.

Ty turns from the path he's walking toward his car to check why the gates are opening already. His eyes settle on Mack and I, and his keys hit the dirt.

"What the fuck happened?" he asks, running toward us.

I can't even answer. The adrenalin high has worn off, and my limbs give out. I collapse to the ground, cradling Mack's trembling body into mine, curling myself around him.

"Are they hurt?" I recognize King's voice as heavy boots pound across the yard.

"I don't think so," Ty says. His hands are all over me, tipping my chin this way and that, but I can't even bring myself to open my eyes.

I'm just so tired.

"Carlos," King grits out. "I bet this is that fucker's work."

"Everything was fine when I left this morning," Ty says, hands trailing over my limbs, looking for injury.

"You were there this morning?" Sawyer hollers. "You probably fuckin' laid out the welcome mat, you moron. Why the fuck you think I hadn't been there yet?"

"Daddy!" Mack stirs at his father's yelling.

"Mack, buddy. Are you okay?" I feel tugging against my hold, and crack my eyes open to see Sawyer pulling Mack from my arms.

"He's too cold," I manage to rasp out.

"What happened, sugar?" Sawyer asks, setting Mack down and wrapping him in his jacket.

King squats before me, waiting on the answer as well. A blanket is passed down from somebody and Ty wraps it around my shoulders.

"He was just a . . . message." I whisper.

So tired.

"Come on," Ty murmurs.

Strong arms push under mine and lift me to my feet. My eyes remain closed the whole time, even as my feet leave the ground, but I don't need sight to know whose chest I'm being held against. I let my body relax into Ty's hold, nestling my head into his shoulder, inhaling the scent of safety.

People talk, lights pass overhead, and music is shut off as we enter the clubhouse. But it's all just background noise, inconsequential. Everything I need is holding on to me, and at ease with the knowledge Sawyer has Mack, I shut down.

Several hours later, I wake in Sonya's bed. She smiles

down at me from where she sits on the edge of the mattress and places the back of her hand to my forehead. "How you feeling?"

"I didn't know you were back." The huskiness of my voice rivals that of a pack-a-day smoker.

"Came back first thing this morning." Her eyes mist up, and she reaches out to tuck my hair behind my ears—even though it's already there. "Sweetheart, what happened?"

"How's Mack? Where is he?"

"Sawyer has him downstairs. He's okay, eating and drinking, but he hasn't spoken a word."

My heart shatters. My every worst nightmare has come true—my child was put at immediate risk, and now he's too shocked to talk.

"Can I see him, please?"

She nods, smiling. "Of course."

Sonya stands and exits the room, leaving me alone with my thoughts. Everything I wanted to shield Mack from was condensed into the horror of tonight. I wanted to take him away from the danger, to shield him from what this life involves, but how could I have ever done that? Our house was invaded, our lives threatened, and the only thing I could do was run back to the very people I was prepared to take him from.

How could I make him abandon his family?

"Hey."

I roll my head over to take in the most beautiful sight in the world—Ty standing in the door with Mack in his arms. My little boy's arms are wrapped around Ty's unbuttoned collar, and he looks so *safe*.

"Mack, baby. Can I have a hug?"

He nods, and Ty gently places him down so he can run to the bed. I pull myself up to sit, encasing my life in my arms, relishing the instant Band-Aid he places on my heartache.

"Everybody's wondering what happened," Ty says quietly, taking position at the foot of the bed.

"I bet they are." I let Mack out of my hold and he settles on my lap, leaning his back into my chest. "Are they all downstairs?"

Ty nods. "King sent everyone packing when you turned up. The only people left are the west coast boys and Hooch's bunch." He looks about the room, as though trying to decide if he should continue. "The business we met up about yesterday?"

"Yeah?" I extend my hand when Mack grasps it in between his, letting him play with my fingers.

"I'm guessing what happened with you might have an impact on that."

"Oh."

"Just when you're ready." He nods toward Mack.

I look down at my brave boy, and lift his chin with my finger. "Sweetheart, could you please find Aunty Sonya and get her to give you a glass of milk before bed? You can sleep in Daddy's room, yeah?" It's still dark behind the closed curtains and whatever time it is, he should be asleep. "I'll come tuck you in soon."

He nods, climbs off the bed and leaves. The silence from him worries me, but I try to dampen the fear of what it means by reminding myself that it may well pass; he could be his bubbly self again tomorrow.

Ty sits in silence while I pull back the covers and step out to find a sweater or something warm. He doesn't move as I rifle through Sonya's drawers, coming up with a grey pullover. I tug it on, and look over at him. He's smiling at me.

"What?" I ask with a slight frown.

His lips quirk higher on one side. "You look good."

I glance down at my mostly naked legs, covered by only my small sleep-shorts. "Whatever rocks your boat."

"Come here."

I move to him before I think on it. He reaches out, tugging me into his lap so I sit astride him. Ty's hands wander up my arms, over my shoulders, and rest on the sides of my neck. The pain and torment in his gaze is damn near tangible.

"When I saw you, I just . . . it just . . ."

I dip my head to bring our eyes level. "It what?"

"My world stopped. I feared the worst—that either you were hurt bad, or Mack was, and that things could never be right."

"What do you mean they could never be right? What's right, Ty?"

His forehead touches mine, and his dark lashes fall to his cheeks as he closes his eyes. "I can give you both a happy life. I can give you a home, pay all your bills, and most of all,"—he snaps his eyes open, locking his gaze to mine—"I'd come home to you every day, and be there every night. We could live together, Ramona."

I wanted to hear this yesterday. I wanted to feel like this before a hooded man stormed my home and came fucking close to killing my child.

"I can't do this right now, Ty." I force out of his hold and slip off his lap. Why is his timing always so wrong?

He eyes me with the saddest expression ever, tugging at my resolve to put Mack and myself first.

Tears build, but I fight them back. "You have to understand that this isn't the right time for us to talk about our future," I explain. "You can't drop this on me when I've just carried my child away from the most frightening thing ever to happen to him in his short life."

He drops his head, hands fisting in his lap. "I understand." The tone is cold, detached, and like nothing I've ever heard from him.

"I need to tuck Mack in and then I need to talk to the others." I take a step back, the energy around Ty heavy with his rejection.

"Yeah, you go do whatever you want to. I see where I stand now."

Whatever is happening to him, it's a side of Ty I've never seen, only glimpsed when he had that argument with Hooch. He's quite frankly scaring the shit out of me. I turn and hotfoot it from the room, putting distance between us, pulling away from the magnetism he has over me, fighting to get distance between us before I'm suckered back in.

Before I'm stuck dealing with a man too complicated to love me the right way, once again.

coil the spring

RAMONA Having tucked Mack in to Sawyer's bed upstairs, I make my way into the common room, still disturbed about the fact my child hasn't said another word since we arrived at the clubhouse. He's not the noisiest of kids by all means, but to not say good night? It's too out of character.

The steel staircase is cool, prickling the balls of my feet as I step down to the next tread. The low murmur of conversation dies as I take the last step onto the concrete floor. Lifting my gaze to the room, I find everybody staring back at me in silence.

"How you feelin'?" King asks carefully.

"I've been better, but I'm here, alive, so I can't complain." I look around the place, spotting Hooch, Callum, Bronx, and Mighty at the bar. Vince and Crackers play a game of pool, Jo-Jo sitting to the side with a cigarette, watching their match. Murphy, Tap and Hando are visible out the back doors, sitting on the porch area with brews in hand.

"Where's Sawyer?"

King nods toward the sofas off to the right of where I stand. I walk over and peer over the back of the one closest to me and see him asleep on the three-seater, one leg crossed over the other's shin, hands haphazardly lying on his chest.

"We had to sedate him," King says over my shoulder. "He flipped straight back to the old Sawyer that we all know and sort of love in a you-have-to-'cause-they're-your-brother kind of way."

Damn. It seems the true heart of the beast is still in there after all.

"He wanted to ride out to sort out Carlos on his own," King explains. "Took four of us to wrestle him off the bike. Fingers is fixing the damage now."

"I guess I missed all the fun," I mumble.

A chill sweeps the room, my senses hyper-aware as footsteps cross the concrete floor behind me.

"Drink, Ty?"

I twist and watch Bronx hold up a bottle in Ty's direction. He shakes his dark locks and keeps on walking through the back doors.

"Moody fucker," Bronx mumbles pouring himself another drink.

"Everything okay there?" King asks, coming to stand beside me.

"I don't think so, but it's not important."

"I don't think he sees it that way." King nudges his large shoulder into mine, having to bend at the waist to reach my level. "You ready to tell us what went down at your place?"

"As ever." I plaster on a smile for his benefit, and head over to the bar.

The men congregate around me, Callum throwing me a blanket to wrap over my bare legs. Mighty passes me a juice. "Get those sugars up, yeah?"

I could cry, but if I did I know it'd never stop. These guys are all brothers to me, giving the term they use on each other so flippantly such heart. They look out for me, protect me, and treat me like blood. How could I leave them? How could I have ever thought they'd abandon me?

"When you're ready," King coaxes.

I take a last look around at each of the rough, bearded, and scarred faces, all waiting patiently on me, a tiny redheaded woman, to speak. "It was a message, a threat or a reminder. He could have killed us if he wanted to, but he didn't."

"You have any idea who it was?" Vince asks.

I shake my head. "It had to be one of Carlos's goons. His face wasn't familiar—what I could see of it."

"Your house is pretty smashed up, Mona."

I frown at Callum's statement. "You went there?"

He nods. "After you passed out. Mighty and I took a quick ride over to talk to the boys in blue."

"We've got a guy on the payroll who can make it all go away," Mighty adds. "You don't need to worry, Mona. Just let us look after everything for you."

"It scared the hell out of me," I recount. "He shot the front window in, blew another one somewhere in the living room, and then shot over my shoulder while I was holding Mack in his bedroom." My knees shudder at the memory, my flesh dimpling. I pull the rug tighter around my legs and clutch the juice for something to ground me.

"The whole place was trashed, Mona," Callum says quietly. "Your furniture, smashed. Your stuff you had boxed, everywhere."

My gaze keeps flicking between his eyes, yet I have no idea what I'm looking for. He isn't lying—the silence of all the men around us confirms it. An overwhelming urge to shower grips me, the need to wash this feeling of violation off of me.

"Did they take anything?"

"Don't think so," he answers, shaking his head. "Just smashed it all up, made a real mess of the place to make a point."

"Why would he do this to me? I mean, why now?" I've been Sawyer's old lady for more than five years. I've never met his father, but he's also never bothered me before. It was as if we had a mutual ignorance of each other's existence. "Is it because we got Elena to move?"

King shakes his head, drawing my focus to him. "No, I don't think so. She's safe, away from here now. We think it was because of what happened when Sawyer went home."

"What did happen?"

Some of the guys duck their heads, avoiding my gaze,

while others look to King for the answer. I join them, eyeing our president, my friend, silently pleading for the truth this time, not just another bullshit answer of 'business'.

"You were used as leverage, Mona. Carlos had been following you before we even went to Elena. If Sawyer didn't do what Carlos wanted him to, he threatened to harm you."

My gut drops, my legs so damn useless I'm thanking the stars that I'm sitting. "And Mack?"

King nods jerkily. "Yeah, and Mack."

He moves to say something more, but I lift my hand, slipping from the stool. The blanket drops from my legs as I stagger on autopilot through to the ladies and fall to my knees before a toilet, hurling everything I haven't eaten into the bowl.

I'd thought that the intruder was my nightmare come true. I'd thought that Mack's silence was the thing that would break me. But little did I entertain the idea that things could be so much worse.

So. Much. Worse.

"Mona, you okay?" Callum calls from the door.

All I can do to answer him is emit some animal moan from deep in my gut. There are just no words. Mack's safety doesn't exist anymore, and it's entirely my fault. It's solely because I picked the wrong man to have a child with—unplanned or not. How could I bring a child into this? How can I risk the kind of merciless torture, the slow death Carlos would afford us, regardless of the fact Mack is only a child?

What kind of selfish monster was I deciding to keep him when I clearly can't escape this life?

I can't believe I'm doing it—thinking that I should have aborted. I heave bile into the bowl again. What kind of mother thinks things like that? What kind of mother is so horrified at what could happen to their child that she actually thinks it could have been better not to have them at all?

I'd never wish to lose what I have; I'd never wish to give up the beautiful boy who makes my days worthwhile, but if it meant he didn't have to die as a child, he didn't have to experience pure fear at the hands of his grandfather, I'd turn back those hands of time and make that choice.

Callum crouches beside me, jamming between the stall wall and where I kneel at the bowl. He moves my hair out of the way, wiping the sweat from my brow with the back of his wrist. "Oh, hell, baby girl. What are we going to do with you?"

"I don't want him to hurt Mack, Callum."

He twitches a weak smile. "We won't let him, Mona. We wont let him."

switch off

TY Even from the far end of the porch, I can hear the commotion going on inside. The boys are arguing over what to do about Ramona, what level they're going to get involved in Sawyer's shit.

I kind of have to side with the ones shouting the loudest on this—why does Sawyer deserve to have their lives on the line when he was so happy to take them for fun?

King's bellowing at them about the code, about loyalty, and Hooch is backing him up. 'A brother never walks away from a fight.' 'A brother never gets left on his own.' Blah, blah, fucking blah.

Reason number one why I'm happy I don't belong to one of these fucking outfits—I don't have to blindly walk to the slaughter because some fucking asshole wearing the same colors has one hell of a messed-up home-life.

Bronx steps outside, nodding at Murphy, the only man

remaining here with me. I turn my head away as Bronx approaches. Whatever he has to say, I don't want to hear it.

"What the fuck did you say to Ramona up there?"

Yep, didn't want to hear it.

"None of your fucking business."

"Whatever it was, dude, you've got her pretty messed up. Well, not as much as she is now, but you gave her a good fuckin' head-start."

I give in and look over at him as he casually takes a swig of his beer. "What's wrong with her now?"

"Callum told her what they did to her place after she left. She's heaving her guts out in the ladies."

"Because her house got trashed?"

He frowns, giving me that *are-you-really-so-stupid* look I hate. "No, because Carlos threatened to hurt her and Mack if Sawyer didn't play the game, dude." He lifts his eyebrows, as though coaxing me to finish.

"And Sawyer's not playing the game."

"Exactly."

It pains me, I won't lie, but she's made it pretty fucking clear she doesn't want a bar of what I have to offer. "I'm sure her *old man* will look after her."

Bronx snorts. "Did you see him? Dude can't even take a piss without help. Boys have him so fuckin' jacked up in there just to keep him placid."

"Maybe so, but he's the jackass she picked, so she can deal with that."

Bronx scowls, leaning forward so his elbows rest on his

knees. "Is that what this shit is all about?"

"Perhaps."

"You're a fuckin' tool, man."

"Yeah? Well fuck you, too."

Silence hangs heavy as he glares at me. I brace for the onslaught of words telling me how useless and heartless I am, telling me to get my shit squared away, but it never comes.

The fucker stands and leaves without another word.

Go on, asshole. Walk away like everyone does.

I catch Murphy's eye, who has watched the whole interaction. "What?" I snap.

"Bro, bitches don't wait for long."

"Fuck, that's deep," I mock.

He lifts his hands in surrender, tipping his head to the side. "Giving fair warning. You may just wanna check what it is you're so fuckin' angry about before you blow the chance at having whatever you've got on somethin' that isn't her fault."

I just stare at the guy. What sort of fucking message is that?

He matches my unimpressed stare. "Fuck, layman's terms: realize it ain't her you're angry at."

The guy gets up from his chair, stubs his cigarette out, and heads indoors. I stare out into the night, rolling the idea around in my head. Of course I'm angry with her—she hasn't chosen me. But the more I think on it, the more the table tips toward what he was saying. Why *didn't* she choose me? Because of a misplaced loyalty to the man who fathered her child.

I can understand that. I still feel a duty toward my dead sister more than two decades later. Sometimes the heart can't let go of the small amount of joy we get from our attachment to another in fear that if it did, the sadness would fill the space and take over. We cling to those attachments, however frail, in fear of the unknown.

I want Ramona to see me as the answer, not a risk. The connection is there between us, but I have to prove to her that history doesn't matter to me. I don't care who the father of her boy is—I just need to know that he's not the man she's thinking about at night.

Sulking when it seems like she *is* thinking of him, assuming Ramona's putting her loyalty to Sawyer before us without any proof, isn't the way forward. If I have any real chance at making her happy with her decision, I need to figure out how to first find balance with my own. Which means I have to do exactly as that smarmy fucker said—realize it's me I'm angry at, and sort that shit out.

I have to go back and settle the dust from my past—find a way through the cloud that stops me from seeing what's ahead.

The ruckus indoors has quelled by the time I drag my sorry butt into the common room. Everybody has disappeared except for Bronx and Jo-Jo, playing pool, and Callum squatting before Ramona, who's curled up in one of the armchairs. On closer inspection, Sawyer's feet protrude over the arm of the sofa opposite them.

I make my way to the bar, snagging a bottle of water.

As much as I'm gagging to get shit-faced and find another hooker to roughhouse me, to distract me from this mess in my head, that isn't the way forward. If I'm going to be the man she needs, it's going to take a hell of a lot of self-control, and what better time to start than now?

Callum's head swings up at the rattling I'm making opening and shutting the fridge door. He stands, pats Ramona on the knee and stalks my way. *More of the same bullshit, I bet.*

"You got your head screwed on yet?"

"Didn't realize it was loose," I snap, uncapping the bottle in my hand.

"I don't know what's going down between you two, but shelve it. I need to head out for a bit and somebody needs to be with her. Sawyer's useless, Bronx is heading out shortly as well, and Jo-Jo,"—he glances over at the guy—"is too fuckin' shady for my liking."

"Why me? Get one of the old ladies to babysit." I have things to do, ghosts to bury.

"I get the feelin' it's you she needs to talk to." His gaze penetrates mine, questioning, testing.

I take a swig of the water, holding eye contact, and then recap the bottle before slamming it down on the bar. "If you think she wants to see me, you've got your wires all crossed up. Right now, she needs her old man to balls up and take care of her. I'll be back later when she's finally realized he's no good for her."

He doesn't move from the bar as I stalk around it. I snag my keys from my pocket and head across the room toward the exit. The heat is on me, and there's no need to look her way to know that Ramona's also watching me leave. But staying won't help anyone. The tension is too thick between us, the wounds too raw. She needs someone to hold her hand? Get an old lady to do it. I'm in no state of mind to be licking her wounds for her.

I've got old wounds of my own that need cleaning.

immersion

RAMONA It's three in the morning—I should be sleeping. Yet here I sit on the edge of Sawyer's bed, watching Mack sleep, with a cup of warm coffee in my hands. My head's in turmoil, the ever-changing thought patterns building toward a dull ache in my right temple.

Ty left. And he hasn't returned like he said he would.

King and Tap rode out with instructions on where to try finding him from Bronx. They're worried about what Carlos might do, or more so, what his goons might do if they happen across him. Right now they need him—so do I.

They just shot up my house and trashed everything I own.

Mack's little hands twitch with his dreams. What I'd do to be able to see inside that head of his and know if it's tonight's terrors he's dreaming about. I lift the blanket a little higher over his shoulder with my free hand and slowly rise from the mattress to head downstairs.

Sawyer is groggily pulling himself into a sitting position when I enter the common room. His face has red pressure marks where he's been laid up against the sofa for too long. I seat myself on the armchair opposite and take a sip of coffee while he rubs his head with both hands.

His green eyes lift and find me waiting. "Mona . . ."

"I'm okay," I assure him, holding my free hand up to stop him from talking. "Mack's asleep in your bed. He's okay, I think."

His pupils constantly grow and shrink, a war raging within. "I wanted to ride out and string that fuckin' asshole up with his own guts."

"I'm sure you did."

"I would have taken a photo to show you what I did for you both."

"That wouldn't have been necessary." I force my coffee down.

"He went against the unspoken code; he broke the rules. Wars aren't waged at home. You never take it to a man's family." Sawyer frowns and scuffs the heels of his boots.

"I think he broke that rule when he sent his men to Elena's, don't you?"

"That wasn't my family." Loaded silence hangs around him.

I'm afraid to move in case it sets him off. "We're okay,

Sawyer. He didn't hurt us."

I lurch back as his entire torso twists to his left, the force of his right fist tearing a hole in the worn seat cover. "Fuck him!"

With shaking hands I manage to get my coffee to a flat surface, placing what's left out of the way to wipe down the remainder over my legs.

Sawyer's gaze flicks across me as I rub the liquid into my skin. "Sorry."

"It's okay," I say, taking a steadying breath. "You're angry—I get it."

"I promised myself I wouldn't scare you anymore. I made a promise that I'd be better." He flops back into the seat, lacing his fingers over his head.

I run my eye over the curves of his muscular arms, instantly remembering what it was that attracted me to him in the first place. He's strong, self-assured, but he doesn't put it out there to show off to the women around him. He's so damn unsure of himself that he hasn't got it in him to flirt. It was always me who chased him, me who told him all the things he should already know.

Sawyer sighs, turning his head to meet my gaze as I settle on the couch beside him. "You should go," he murmurs.

The words sting, lancing straight into my heart. He's never rejected me before. "Why?"

"You need space to see that you deserve more, Mona. You're so blinded by your need to look after me when we're close that you can't see what I'm doing to you."

"You aren't doing anything to me but being damn frustrating right now."

His eyes search my face, flick across my body, and return to hold mine. "What do you want to do with me? Why did you move closer?"

I want to hold you close, rock you in my arms until you feel better. "I wanted to give you company, support. I wanted to just do this." His breath huffs over the top of my head as I nestle in, my head to his strong chest.

"Can't you see that's the problem?" he asks.

I tip my head back so I can look at his face. "What is?"

"You just want to cuddle me. You want to be my mother."

I rear back, frowning. "I do not."

"Mona," he drags my name out an extra syllable. "When was the last time we fucked?"

Doing my best to swallow away the rising heat flushing my neck and face, I think hard on it. When did we?

"Exactly," he says, startling me from my timeline. "The week before I left, you never touched me once. I've been back here a day, and right now we're sitting here on our own with Mack asleep and taken care of. If you wanted me like that we'd be fucking."

I was so busy freaking out about my own situation last night when I saw him I never though about his needs. As much as the thought disturbs me, I ask, "Is that what you want to do?"

He throws his hands down. "Hell, no."

Thank fuck. My chin hits my chest, and I press my

tongue against the roof of my mouth, willing the tears of shame to fuck the hell off. I'm relieved that he doesn't want to take me to bed—I don't want to muddy the waters when I'm trying to find a way to break things off—but still, that rejection sliced in to me. Am I not enough? Does he think another woman can fix him?

Strong fingers encase my chin, tilting my face toward him. "Sugar, don't you go gettin' it in your head that it means anything bad about you. Girl, you're the prettiest woman in this place—any guy would want you on their bike. I've just taken advantage of your goodwill for so damn long that I can't get past that. I can't love you as anythin' more than a companion because I know you fuckin' deserve more than me. Baby, I've tried—it just ain't happenin'."

"So what you're trying to say is that you want me to move on, find another man who'll treat me better than you?"

"Yes and no." His hand drops from my jaw, his shoulders falling. "That's the bit I'm strugglin' with."

"You're confusing the hell out of me, you know that? You want me to leave, you don't want to fuck me, but you don't want me to find someone else." Throwing my hands in the air I growl. "What he hell *do* you want me to do?"

"I can't stand the thought of another man touching you."

"But you don't love me anymore, right?"

He heaves a sigh and scrubs the heels of his hands into his closed eyes. "No! I don't want you like that, but I don't want anyone else to have you either." His wide eyes snap to mine, and the mania within sends a shiver down my spine. "I want to keep you locked away like a fuckin' possession, Mona. I want to *own* you, but not *have* you."

I knew it when he first walked in the club, and I chose to ignore all the warning bells going off in my head. He's crazy, unhinged, and I let him take ownership of me. Why the hell did I ever think there'd be a clean way out?

His hand shoves roughly against my shoulder, sending me sprawling over the arm of the sofa. "Go," he hollers. "Get away from me, Ramona."

Isn't this what I wanted? A break from Sawyer? A possibility of a future with Ty? Yeah, it is, except in all my fantasies, Sawyer was giving me a warm farewell and telling Ty to look after me as he handed over the keys, as if I were a God damn car changing hands. I didn't think about the reality of it—that a manic man like Sawyer could never truly let me go, and that Ty wouldn't wait forever.

Fuck Carlos and his fucking men coming into my house. Everything was on track to work out this morning—Ty was mine for the having, he was coming back to spend the night with me, and I had it all figured out that I'd talk to Sawyer about things in the morning.

Yet here we are, hours from sunrise and the whole situation has taken a dive for the worse, spiraling out of control. The sun may be rising on a new day, but fuck having a new start if it means I'm going to have to be doing it with a broken heart.

My old man doesn't want me and the only man who cared about me on a deeper level is missing in action.

Living the fucking dream.

obliteration

TY The sun sets on another day, casting shadows across the stone chapels of the Mt. Washington cemetery. I was born and raised in Kansas City, son of a wealthy member of the local church and a beautiful socialite—both upstanding members of the NRA. So naturally, when my sister died, our hometown was where they'd buried her.

For the last five hours I've sat, slept, and reclined next to her headstone, telling her all about what her big brother's been doing for the last twenty-two years of his life. Yeah, I'm the asshole who put her here, and this is the first time I've visited the beautiful cream marble headstone my parents chose.

"Well, munchkin, it's time to get going. I better head off and face the music."

I touch two fingers to my lips, and then press them to where her name is carved in the stone.

"Last place we looked, and honestly wouldn't have had a clue if it weren't for Bronx."

Fuck it. I spin around and face King, scowling. "Really just wanted some time to myself, brother."

"I get that. It's why we've waited until you were done." He thumbs over his shoulder and I follow the gesture to see Tap in the distance, reclined on his bike. He waves. Behind him, leaning against the hood of his truck, is Malice.

"What'd you drag him into this for?"

"Didn't take much dragging," King says. "Kid's worried about you. Besides, with all this bullshit Carlos has going on, he wanted to head our way and get the rundown on what's goin' on."

I nod, and start to walk toward the others. "You probably enjoyed the excuse to get out and have a ride anyway, right?"

King chuckles as he walks beside me. "Yeah, I did. Fuckin' place is doing my head in. Needed to feel the hardtop through my bars to clear the air in here." He taps a thick finger to the side of his head.

"So you get why I had to leave?"

"I get it," he affirms, "but it don't go givin' you the right to take off without anyone knowin' where you'd be."

"Things have to change," I explain, "and visiting Casey was the first thing to check off the list."

"Bronx said she's your little sister."

"Yeah," I say, giving Malice a quick jerk of the chin to say hello as we approach. "He tell you how she died?"

"Nah. Said that was your story to share."

"Sounds about right." I nod. "He's good like that."

"So, how did she die? I take it she was young."

"Three years old, beautiful dark blonde curls, and the widest smile you'd ever seen." I stop a few yards short of the others and turn to face King. "I shot her."

He immediately frowns, trying to work it out.

"Accident. My parents had a handgun in the kitchen, one in the parlor, and two in their bedroom—all loaded."

King swallows.

"It was only a matter of time, really. We'd been told not to touch, but when you're a curious kid that's pretty much a red flag to a bull."

"Shit, I'm sorry." King wraps his fingers around his chin and drags the flesh downward, making his mouth pop. "Pretty harsh for you. How old were you?"

"Five." I glance across at the others who are waiting patiently. "It's fucked me up pretty bad. I just know how to hide it well."

"We're all riddled with rot, brother. The only way to keep living is to clean it out sometimes, however you choose to."

"What do you do?" I ask, hoping like hell he's just as screwed up as me on some level.

"Get drunk and shoot shit up."

Nowhere even close. "I wish that was all I had to worry about."

"It can be," he says, clapping a firm hand on my shoulder. "You'll get there."

"I fuckin' hope so." Because there are only so many whores you can use and abuse before one of them squeals to the wrong person, and you find yourself face-down in your own blood.

"Come on," King says, walking to his bike. "I believe you've got people back at the clubhouse wanting to know where you are and when you'll be back."

"Bronx sick of drinking on his own?" I say with a laugh.

King turns, winking as he tugs on his helmet. "I wasn't talking about Bronx."

losing

RAMONA *Tap wanted a donut.* The four words King thought would explain the carnage currently unfolding before my eyes.

I'd finally fallen asleep, exhausted enough to shut down despite my buzzing mind. Sawyer had stormed off long ago, taking Mack into Sonya's room when he woke for games on the Xbox. Didn't take a genius to work out Sawyer was simply looking for an excuse to keep away from me.

I can't be sure if it was the yelling, or the rapid-fire splatter of gravel from the yard spraying the huge roller door on the garage. Either way, I sure as hell didn't expect what I found when I stood from the armchair I'd been curled in to see what the hell was going on.

His arm was limp as they carried him in. Of all the things my mind decided to zero in on, that was it; one grey sleeve, dripping with crimson that ran in streams over his tan flesh. That's the one thing I can't shake even now.

Gloria has been roused from her sleep, driven in on the back of her old man's bike, still in her nightgown. She's crowded at the pool table by Bronx, King, Tap, and Malice. The rest of the boys filtered in afterwards, and they're now scattered around the surrounding furniture, watching what's happening.

Nobody sees me; nobody pays me any mind as I stand off to the side, also watching what's going down. I'm a ghost, unimportant in their mission to save Ty's life. Bronx's deep voice murmurs in a low rumble, his face close to Ty's as he talks to him constantly, trying to keep him conscious. Ty's eyes flutter erratically. He's fighting to stay awake, fighting against the pain of what Gloria is currently doing.

Her hands are coated in his blood—King's also painted red. There are two fragments on the table beside Ty's shoulder, but from what's being yelled between those working on him, there are two more they can see.

She can't stitch him up until they're all out.

A hospital could fix this; the ER is equipped for exactly this kind of wound. But none of us have health insurance, and none of us want the attention from the authorities. Injuries are club property as much as the member who receives them is, and Ty is as close to a member of this club as he can get without actually wearing a patch.

My eyes zero in on a droplet of blood pooling under the rim of the table's timber frame. It grows, swelling, and gaining size before it finally drops to the floor. Another forms, building, hanging, and falling. The deep red pool beneath the table grows.

A flick of the wrist and Gloria has another fragment out onto the table. I shuffle a little to the left, closer to his head. Bronx's gaze flicks up to me, but he doesn't stop talking to Ty. I'm here in body, but a spectator in mind. My thought processes have shut this down to no more than a horrific movie playing before me, detaching me from the idea that I know the people in this room, that what's happening hurts me as much as their faces all show it does them.

A low moaning breaks through King and Gloria's chatter. My panic sets in, my palms slick with sweat. He can't be giving up; he can't be succumbing to the pain, the wound, all of it. *Not yet*. Bronx's eyes snap to me once more and I realize the most disturbing thing of all—the moaning . . . is me.

"Mona," King snaps. "Get your ass upstairs."

My breaths are erratic, my nostrils flaring, and my feet are as heavy as concrete. I'm not moving—I'm not leaving yet. "Can't we call in a doctor, take him to the ER and leave him there? There has to be something else we can do. He's going to die!"

"Mona!" King hollers. "Go! You're not helping!"

Like a disrespectful child, I cross my arms over my chest and stomp one of my feet.

Rage like I've never experienced flashes in King's gaze as he pulls free and charges around Gloria to get to me. Bloody hands shake my shoulders as he lowers his face to my level. "You quitin' makes him think *he* needs to quit," he hisses through clenched teeth. "Now get your fuckin' ass upstairs and we'll come get you when we're finished."

I swallow back my fear, and shake my head.

"Fuck!" he roars, shoving me back hard. "Callum, get her out of here."

"No!" I fight against Callum's strong arms as they wrap around my torso from behind, trapping my arms against my sides. "I want to be here. I need to be here!" If he goes on this table I'm not waiting it out in another room. I want to be there when he dies. I don't want to leave things unsaid like I did with Bruiser.

"Mona," Callum murmurs in my ear, "let it go."

"No," I wail, my body giving up on me and falling limp in his arms. "No, Callum. Don't make me leave."

"Get her the fuck out of here!" King screams, arm and hand directed at the stairs. "We're trying to fuckin' concentrate!"

I steal a last glance at Ty as Callum drags me away, his hand wrapped firmly about my upper arm. Ty's eyes slip closed, Bronx tapping him on the cheek to open up. I yank against Callum's hold, but he's a big guy of nearly six-foot, muscular, and solid as a rock. I'm just a flimsy little girl of no more than five-seven. What chance do I stand?

Bronx straightens, looking at King. Something is uttered between them, but because Callum has me to the base of the stairs I'm too far away to hear a thing. Ty's shoulders slam into the table, his body going rigid as Gloria steps back, lifting her hands clear. Ty's blood flies from her fingers with the movement and lands on the concrete floor behind them in tiny little dots.

Three perfect circles of crimson.

Somebody's screaming, and I know it's me, but the scene it just too surreal. None of it can be real. This morning he was fine, this morning the boys went to get him, and a little more than three hours ago King had called to say they were coming home.

Callum grimaces each time my fists strike him about the head and shoulders, but he battles on, his arms locked around my waist as he struggles to get us up the stairs without tumbling backward.

Gloria has moved away from the table, giving space to Malice and Tap who are now working CPR. Malice's mouth covers Ty's, Tap furiously pumping at his chest. Bronx is pacing, hands in his hair and the look on his face echoes the feeling in my heart.

It's all over.

Callum crests the landing, shoving me hard toward the bedroom. "You need to let them work, girl. I know you're hurtin', but you can't be down there screamin' at them when they're doing their best."

"What the hell is going on?" Sawyer asks behind me.

I turn to face him, tears across my face, snot bubbling from my nose. Nothing comes out of my mouth but a bunch of garbled guttural noise.

"Ty's seizing on the table down there. Gunshot. They were ambushed at a stop on the way back." Callum's voice is strained as he explains.

"Shit." Sawyer scoops me against him, wiping my face with his sleeves, struggling to find a dry patch by the time he's dealing with my nose. "You're scarin' Mack, sugar. You need to pull yourself together."

Mack. If seeing Ty struggle to stay alive rips my lungs from my chest like this, then how the fuck could I survive something like that happening to Mack? I need to get him away from this life; I need him to *want* to stay away.

Sawyer steps back as I charge by, marching into Sonya's room and grabbing Mack from the floor. He looks quizzically at me as I drag him from the Xbox and out to the landing like the mad woman I am.

"What you doin'?" Sawyer asks, stepping in my way.

"Move," I growl in a voice that's doesn't resemble my own.

Shouting and commotion downstairs continues as they struggle to bring Ty back from the brink.

"Mona," Callum warns, hands raised. His eyes tell me exactly what he's not saying: *'You've lost the plot, and you're acting crazy.'* He shifts to block my access to the stairs.

"I need him to see," I explain feebly. "He needs to know why he can never be one of you." The words pain my throat. I'm forcing them out with such hate.

"Like fuck," Sawyer exclaims simultaneously as Mack looks up at me for assurance.

"Mom?"

It's crazy, it's wrong, and I can see all of these things, but I'm so over the pain, so over the heartache, so over the *worry*. I just want to shock the hell out of him, to show Mack what this life entails—that people you love *die*.

"Mom!" Mack shouts, tugging his shirt out of my hold. He backtracks to Sawyer, standing offset behind his legs.

I stare at the hands that trapped my child. I stare at the arms they're attached to, arms that lead to me, the monster who was about to drag her child down to witness a grown man bleeding to death on a fucking pool table.

All to prove a point.

Looking at the shocked and stunned faces around me, I think I've done just that. I've proved that I've finally lost it all together.

melt it down

RAMONA The face staring back at me in the mirror is a girl I haven't seen in a long, long time. Her eyes are red and bloodshot, her cheeks and under her eyes puffy from too many tears. Her complexion is blotchy, and her hair is a damn mess. I'm pretty sure I have boogers sticking my hair to the side of my face—who would know?

Things went quiet downstairs a short while ago, but I missed the change—I was too busy howling my eyes out into Sawyer's shirt like a damn banshee. I expected him to push me away. After all, I'm upset about a man who isn't him, a man who, for me to have such a connection with, I would have had to be sneaking around with while I was still Sawyer's old lady.

But he held me. He even rubbed my back as I fought back the urge to vomit I had cried myself into such a stupor.

And now he's downstairs finding out what's happened to Ty for me. King said they'd send somebody when they'd finished, but nobody came. I can't fight the panic that twists my gut in knots when I assume the worst—they didn't come get me because they don't know how to tell me.

Acid swims in my gut, surging up my throat before dying down again. Do I want to know if it's the worst? Can I take that kind of news?

My gaze snaps to Sonya behind me in the bathroom doorway. She arrived at the clubhouse amidst the chaos, saw Callum drag me up the stairs and came to join us about the time my legs gave out, and I fell to the floor lamenting what I'd almost done to my child.

The boy who stared at me as if I were a stranger.

I've never broken like that in front of Mack. He's never seen what happens when Mommy doesn't cope. Until then, I'd always managed to restrict my tears to when I was alone, sobbing quietly into a balled facecloth in the shower. Not any more. The truth is on the table, and my greatest fear is I've done irreparable damage to my own flesh and blood.

"Mack's had his dinner. He's happy doing some puzzles in the kitchen with Sawyer. They found an old jigsaw one of Callum's nieces left behind. Mack doesn't seem too worried about the fact it's a Disney princess he's putting together." She smiles softly, stepping in to the room. "You okay?"

"Who have I become?" I ask, turning to face her and

dropping on to the side of the bathtub. "I'm a terrible mother," I mutter, shaking my head. "It should be me looking after him."

Sonya perches beside me, bracing her hands on the edge. "Why? Sawyer's his daddy; he's just as important to Mack."

"I know. I guess I'm used to being the one who's always there, ready to make him feel better. But this time, I'm the one who hurt him."

"You didn't hurt him," Sonya says carefully. "You just opened his eyes a little wider to the world around him. He'll be okay. He's a resilient child, and you've done a hell of a job bringing him up right."

My chin trembles and I ball my fists in an effort to distract myself with the pain of my nails digging into the heels of my hands. I won't cry again. I'm not even sure if I have any tears left.

"Hey, Sonya." Callum steps into the doorway, his face solemn and *pitiful*.

"Where's Sawyer?" I ask, worried what having Callum come back instead means.

"Looking after Mack. He asked me to come to get you."

A stake driven through my chest wouldn't hurt this much. "I don't want to know," I sob. His expression gives it all to me as clear as black and white. "Don't tell me."

"You need to hear what I have to say," he urges softly.

Sonya takes hold of my hand, squeezing.

"Just listen, Mona," Callum pleads.

My head trembles side-to-side like a leaf in the

summer breeze. "Can I see him?" It's the only thing that'll convince me, the only thing that'll make me believe.

"Of course you can." Callum holds out a hand.

I take it and let him lead me out of the bathroom and down to the far end of the landing to the stairs. As we descend, Sonya trailing behind, I see why they didn't come to get me straight away. The place is spotless. A prospect throws a wet rag into a bucket as we approach, bundling up most of the cleaning supplies, and heads away from the immaculate floor. Sonya picks up what's left and follows after him.

The pool table is gone.

"He's over here." Callum guides me to the sofas where King, Bronx, Malice, Tap, and Hooch all sit around either on the armchairs, on the back of the seats, or positioned on the floor.

I can barely make out where they've positioned Ty through the damn water filling my eyes. Callum lets go of my hand as I come to stop among the men. Bronx reaches out an arm, and tugs me to his side. My hip crashes into his, and I relish the comfort of his huge arm shielding me from the scrutiny of the room as I wipe away the tears.

Ty's stretched out on the longest of the four sofas, a blanket over his body, arms folded beneath. A sob jams in my throat and I cough, choke and splutter as I step closer and fall to my knees beside him to be sure.

It moved. The blanket moved.

My hand trembles wildly as I reach out and place it on his chest. My elbow flexes with the rise and fall of his ribcage. I turn and look over my shoulder at Bronx. He nods. King smiles, and gestures for me to turn back to Ty.

"It was close," Malice says quietly beside me as he drops into a squatting position.

"It's a miracle," I whisper.

"He's always been a stubborn fucker." He chuckles softly. "Always has done everything on his terms."

Hooch stands and places a hand on my shoulder. "We'll give you a minute, yeah?" He turns away with a gentle squeeze. "Come on, Tap."

"I just wanted a donut," he mumbles.

"I know you sorry ass motherfucker," Hooch teases. "Let's get you drunk."

"I'll be in my office," King offers, rising from the chair he'd been in. "Bronx, you want to join me? We need to run over some shit."

"Sure," Bronx replies, following King across the room.

Malice moves to stand, but I place a hand on his arm and still him. "Can you stay?"

"Sure." He settles onto his butt, crossing his legs at the ankles, and propping his knees inside his elbows.

"What happened?" Confident his breathing isn't going to stop, I trail my hand up to Ty's face and brush his beard with the backs of my fingers.

"Crossed the wrong guy. From what the asshole said while he was waving the gun around, I get the feelin' it was some pissed off pimp."

I cut my gaze to Malice, and he winces apologetically.

"He hasn't spoken to you about his habits yet?"

"Clearly not," I murmur, returning my eyes to Ty's ruggedly handsome profile.

Malice sighs, the subject not an easy one to divulge, evidently. "He had a relatively okay upbringing, and then something happened which changed it all. I met the hopeless fucker on the streets, scrounging for food, beaten pretty badly."

I frown as I continue to caress Ty's beard, moving to run an index finger over his eyebrows. "He told me he'd been homeless."

Malice nods. "He's got it in his head that he needs to suffer for what happened, why he left home. Usually, he pays whores to dish it out for him."

"Dish what out?" I ask. *So many secrets.*

"Pain. They hit him, cut him, and hurt him however he wants." Malice fidgets with a ring on his middle finger. "He gets the hookers to abuse him as a kind of release, figuring they get paid for it so it's not as bad as if he asked some girl at a bar."

"That's pretty warped." I understand the requests; on more than one occasion I was asked to do similar. But to think that only a hooker can give him what he needs? Why? Surely he doesn't believe that there's no chance of him finding a girl who could give him that—pleasure laced with pain?

I know I would if he asked.

"Yeah, it's a little messed up," Malice agrees, "but it's how he's always been, ever since I've known him. He's tried to see shrinks about it, but they tell him he has to find a passive-aggressive output like golf." Malice looks to me, and smiles devilishly with the corner of his mouth. "Golf."

I meet his smile and laugh. "Yeah, I can't see that helping either." I withdraw my hand and turn so my back rests against the sofa. Letting my head fall back onto Ty's thigh, I roll it to the side and look at Malice. "Why doesn't he let it out like most of the guys around here, with a gun or his fists?"

Malice drops his gaze to the floor and smirks. "He's never been great with his fists. I mean, he can fight his way out of a paper bag—he's not that bad, but he's nowhere near as good as the likes of Bronx."

"So guns then," I say. "Why doesn't he go to a shooting range and let off the steam?"

Malice's dark eyes hit mine with force. "You'll never catch him with a gun in his hand."

I ignore the chill racing over my flesh, and focus instead on the warmth of Ty's body under my hand. "Why not?"

"A gun is the very thing that made him run away from home. He shot his sister, fatally, playing with his dad's handgun."

As tragic as that is, and as much as I have an overwhelming urge to sit up and pull his sleeping form into a hug, I can't figure one part out. "Why did he run away? Surely his parents wanted to support him after such a tragic accident?"

Malice smirks, discounting the idea. "They put *all* the

blame on him for it. Sure, he pulled the trigger, so ultimately it was his burden, but they didn't take an ounce of responsibility for the fact a *loaded* gun was accessible to a child."

"That's sick," I murmur.

"Yeah, it's pretty fucked up," Malice agrees. "More than what he does, if you ask me."

I twist my neck and look at Ty's pale face. "What did he do to piss off the pimp?"

Malice winks. "Free pass is over, sweetheart. You can ask him that." He nods toward the sofa.

I shoot up on my knees, leaning over Ty after I realize his eyes were open . . . are open. Clutching his hand nearest me between mine, I just smile. What could I say to make this kind of pain go away? Nothing. So why bother trying to fill the moment with empty, pointless words? Instead, I offer him the only thing I need him to know. "I'm sorry."

His lips don't move, but he blinks. He blinks, draws a loaded breath, and then shuts his eyes again, succumbing to sleep.

Malice and I sit with him for a while, shifting around in an effort to get comfortable while staying close, talking about any manner of things that don't involve the club, guns, or my severely messed up love life. Ty remains sleeping, never stirring while Malice and I chat. His body is in survival mode, shutting down unnecessary stimulation while it heals. Chances are he'll be asleep for hours yet.

"I think I might go see how Sawyer's getting on with Mack," I tell Malice.

"Sure thing. I'll stay here."

"Is Jane okay without you? She doesn't mind being on her own?"

"Yeah." He nods. "She's staying the weekend at some retreat with her mother; they're trying to repair their relationship. It's good for her . . . I think."

"Hope it works out, then."

"So do I," he murmurs, lifting his eyebrows briefly, his lips pressed flat.

"Thanks," I offer, "for hanging out with me." I steal a last look at Ty. "I honestly thought he was gone when Callum dragged me up the stairs."

"We all did."

I walk away with that last comment playing over in my mind. No matter what the guys tell me, I have a feeling I'm never going to be able to fully grasp just how close they were to losing him.

Sawyer lifts his head as I enter the kitchen and gives me a tip of the chin. "You better?"

"Yeah."

"Good." The intense stare he holds me under lets me know he's expecting me to never pull a stunt like that again. Hey, I agree. It wasn't exactly my finest hour.

"Almost done?" I ask Mack.

He nods, studiously putting the final pieces into the puzzle. Princesses in colorful gowns swing around a ballroom, flanked by their respective princes . . . and a beast. The parallels I could draw to that picture.

"How long?" Sawyer asks, his line of sight glued to Mack and his puzzle.

"A little under a month," I answer.

"So the whole time I was gone?"

"Not really," I say, fidgeting with the edge of the counter. "It's been . . . complicated."

"Is he good to you, though?"

"Can we not talk about this now?" I pointedly flick my eyes across to Mack.

"You right for five minutes while I talk to your mom, buddy?"

Mack nods, looking between us.

"Cool," Sawyer answers. "You've done a real good job there."

Mack smiles. My heart melts.

"Step outside," Sawyer demands gruffly in my ear as he passes by, heading for the door.

I follow him into the hall, and gasp as he shoves me roughly into the wall. He pins me in place with a large hand to my shoulder as if he were a lion grounding his prey.

"He treats you well?"

"There've been hiccups," I admit. "But he's good."

"You fucked him yet?"

"What business is that of yours?" I hiss.

"Every bit my business," he seethes. "I told you—just 'cause I don't want it doesn't mean I like the idea of somebody else manhandlin' you. I fuckin' meant it. If he's dipping it in you, he better be ready to put a ring on your finger and treat you like a fuckin' queen."

"I'll go ask him, shall I?" I narrow my gaze on him.

His nostrils twitch and he glares right back at me. "Stop being a cunt, Ramona."

"Stop being so fucking demanding over something you have no say in anymore."

His hand drops and I slump slightly, finding my feet again. "I'm struggling, Mona."

"Clearly," I bite out, doing my damnedest not to raise my voice in case Mack hears us.

He paces to the far side of the hall, leans his wide shoulders into the wall, head forward, and slumps against the wall so we're eye-level. My chest weighs heavy with the memories those sharp green eyes provoke. As tortured as our relationship was, he still provided for us—he still put us first the best way he knew how.

"I'm thinking of heading out to Cali with Tap's crew."

"Why?" I ask. Los Angeles is more than twenty hours from us. How the hell can I get Mack to see him on any sort of regular basis? I can't afford that.

"You need space from me. If you plan on getting something started with that guy," he says, jabbing a thick finger toward the common room, "you need me out of the way. If I'm anywhere near you two while his hands are on you, I'm probably goin' to put him right back where is now."

"What about Mack?" I whisper. "Does he get a say in this?"

"He's almost five, Mona." Sawyer frowns. "I'll visit for birthdays and Christmas."

"It's not enough."

"It's enough that he'll keep better memories of me. The less he knows about what a fucked up psychotic maniac I really am, the less likely he'll end up like me. He needs influence away from this life, and I'm countin' on you to find it for him."

He worries about the same stuff as I do? "Why Cali, though?"

Sawyer rubs a hand over his face, sucking in a sharp breath. "You're moving to Fort Worth, aren't you?"

Right. "I'm not sure anymore." My legs fold and I slide down the wall to sit. "I only wanted to move to get Mack away from all of this violence, this pain. Now I think that the comfort he gets from being around people he's grown up with is more important. These people are his family."

"It follows you, this life. You know that."

"I always hoped if I buried my head long enough things would change, but I'm starting to see how wrong I was."

He chuckles quietly, and slides down to sit as well. "Never gonna change, baby. It's been this way since our parents were suckin' on the tit. Nothing's going to change before we're both six feet under."

"Yeah, well I hope whenever that is it's a long time from now. I want Mack to not know what it's like to grieve people killed too soon."

"Sugar," he says softly, "Mack will grow up and be his own man. You can't protect him from everything. I know you don't want him hurt, you want him safe, but baby, his grandfather is Carlos motherfuckin' Redmond. Mack ain't ever going to be safe." He drops his head and mumbles something else I don't quite catch.

"Pardon?"

Sawyer twitches a guilty smile and shrugs a shoulder. "I said, until I kill my dad, that is."

My head makes a dull thud against the wall. "Are you still planning on doing that?"

"How else am I supposed to give you two protection?" His boots bump my thigh as he stretches his legs. "Besides, I've been lookin' forward to it for the last fifteen years of my life. It's kind of what gets me up in the morning."

I just shake my head. He's right—nothing's going to change around here, and the sooner I stop fighting it and learn to control what I *can*, the better off we'll be.

The door to the kitchen inches open. "Can I come out?"

Sawyer chuckles, and waves Mack over. "Sure, buddy. Can I get a cuddle?"

Mack smiles shyly, and then scoots in record time into his father's lap. He nestles in with his back to Sawyer, smiling at me.

"You joinin' us?" Sawyer asks with a mischievous smirk.

Not wanting to disappoint Mack, I scoot over and wrap myself around them both, squishing Mack between our bodies, my legs outside of Sawyers. His large arms encase us all and we sit there on the floor of the hallway as a family, enjoying the intimate moment in the least homely of settings.

My eyes shut, and just one last time, I enjoy how it feels to share being a parent with the man I still admire.

whiplash

TY My first conscious thought as I test my aching limbs is how much of a fucking bitch it is when your lapse in judgment comes back to slap you upside the head full force. Retribution hurts like a motherfucker. No wonder the boys love dealing this shit out, if this is how our enemies feel afterward.

I had a gut feeling that hooker I left at the park would go south, and I chose to ignore it. Guess I almost paid the ultimate price for my tendency to be a jerk.

"Morning, sunshine," Bronx mocks from beside me.

I reach out to smack him one, and bellow as my nerves all fire to life in one inferno of pain.

"Hold there," he says. "I'll grab the shit Gloria left for you."

My attempt at asking who the fuck Gloria is comes out in raspy barks.

"Dude, you've been asleep for close to a day. You'll be

parched." Thick fingers dig in between my head and the pillow, and as gently as a man like Bronx can muster, he wrenches my head upward.

My eyes fly open with the searing pain in my chest. "Are you trying to kill me?" I scratch out in broken notes.

"Think you proved that's impossible." He laughs to himself as he twists and returns with a drink bottle.

I wrap my lips around the fast-flow top, and guts back several large helpings before he rips it away. I make sure my protest is clearly audible. I could have easily drunk the Atlantic and not felt satisfied.

"Too much and you'll be yundering it all over my lap, dude." He taps the side of my jaw. "Open up."

Bronx places a couple of horse pills on my tongue and then hands the water back. I manage to lift a hand this time to take it from him, the pain reduced to the surface of the sun rather than the blazing infernos of hell. The pills catch in my throat and without a second thought I belt myself on the chest to dislodge them.

Worst. Mistake. Ever.

I swear every dog in a ten-mile radius replies to my howls of pain. Bronx curses as he fiddles with a large bandage under my right pec, muttering his frustration as my eyes water with the hairs being ripped from my flesh on the tape. *Enough with the suffering already.*

"Only a few spots of blood. I'll keep an eye on it, but you have to be careful, man. You might rip open the sutures Gloria gave you."

Who the fuck is Gloria? I just stare at the monkey,

confused.

He smirks. "Right, you were out to it for the most part. Gloria is one of the old ladies. She stitched you up when we dragged you in."

"My car?" I ask.

"Trashed, dude. He made a right fuckin' mess of it before he came inside."

Imagery of the diner we'd stopped at on the way back here flashes in my mind. I try to think of what the pimp looked like, but all I get is dark hair, a flash of silver, and screaming. The rest is a colorful haze of nothing.

"The guy?" I ask. "What'd they do with him?"

Bronx twists his lips, and darts his eyes to the right. "Uh, I guess the diner's cleaner double-guessed their previous assumptions about a bad day at work?"

A chuckle tickles the back of my throat, but I fight it back, not wanting to shake my body in such a way. I lift my head a little from the pillow that's jammed under it and take a look around. My legs are covered in what appears to be the same blanket Callum gave Ramona the other night.

"Where's Ramona?"

Bronx smiles knowingly. If I could reach that far I'd rip the look right off his face. "Out with Sonya getting some groceries."

"She's out?" I yell—well, try to yell, grasping at my sore throat.

"Yeah. But Callum's with her. I think she needed to get out, break her cabin fever."

"Excellent," I huff to myself, flopping back on the pillow. One of the women who tops Carlos's hit-list is out in the open, and the fucking vice president of the chapter accompanies her. It's bloody Christmas for the mad bastard.

Malice walks into the room from the back porch, breaking into a jog when he sees I'm awake. "Hey, man!"

I lift a weak hand in acknowledgement.

"His throat's worse than a whore who's given head all night," Bronx explains, fondling his jugular.

I glare at the idiot.

"Nice analogy, man," Malice says with a scowl. "Real classy."

"Fuck, you know me," Bronx replies, standing. "I'm all class." He sweeps his hands the length of himself. Malice and I exchange a knowing look.

"Yeah, well take that class out of here and have a shower. I'm pretty sure classy folk can afford a fuckin' bath."

Bronx flips Malice his middle finger and leaves.

"You gave us all a bit of a scare." I watch one of my oldest and best friends take a seat on the floor beside me. He tucks his knees inside his elbows and stares off into space. "You going to quit with that shit now?"

I gesture to my chest. "Surviving that was a fluke. Don't know if I'd have as many props with the man upstairs next time."

"You've got to find another way to deal with that shit," Malice bites out. "You can't just go around getting other people to hurt you in an effort to expel all your self-hatred and expect no one to get upset."

"I don't expect that at all. He was her pimp," I say. "It was his job to get upset."

"He shot you in the chest with a .44 Magnum, man. That's not just upset. He was a man with a vendetta."

I frown a little, holding his gaze. *What's he getting at?*

"The whore was his old lady, man. Mother to his kid." My gut sinks. What a right fucking mess for the woman—all because of my fucked up behavior. "Tap looked into it."

Speaking of which. "How is the guy?"

"Still pretty cut up that his rumbling gut put us in the place to begin with."

"The shit would have caught up with me eventually, either way." I gesture for the drink bottle.

He passes it over. "I'm just glad it was a fucker who thought drinkin' before he went out lookin' for you was a smart thing to do. If he'd been sober he would have aimed a little better and we wouldn't be talking, man."

"Yeah, I know."

The final words from the pimp ring through my head. *'You wanna try and punch a hole out my girl's head? I'll blow one out the back of yours!'* A shudder ripples the length of my spine. I royally fucked up, underestimated what I was doing and how much it hurt the people involved. Now there's a woman without a husband, a baby without a dad. I'm not sure it's even possible to feel worse than I do now. I deserve everything I got.

"Does Ramona know what happened?" I ask, fingering

the blanket over my legs.

Malice shrugs. "Sort of."

"What do you mean 'sort of'?"

"She knows it was an angry pimp, and that you fuck around with whores for a pastime."

What the actual? I shunt myself up using my elbows. "Who told her?"

"I did." He holds my angry gaze, firm, challenging. "If you'd been honest with her, it wouldn't have come as a surprise. That's on you."

"Fuck man, what I do to get release isn't really the kind of thing you bring up on a first date. Fuck, we haven't even been on a date yet. When the hell was I supposed to tell her? Were you expecting me to hand her a disclaimer, or something?" What the hell does she think of me now? Will I ever get a look in, or is my habit of taking out my anger on the person I'm truly pissed with—me—going to seal the deal?

"Can you help me get up and in the shower? I feel like I have a weeks' worth of scud caked on me."

Malice nods, and rises to help me stand. Together we manage to get my weak body up the stairs, despite it taking us the better part of twenty minutes to scale them. I hobble as best the pain will allow into the bathroom, thanking Malice and assuring him I'll be fine from here on in. He holds up a finger and comes back a short while later with my duffle.

"Retrieved this from the mangled wreck of your car before we took off."

"You're a lifesaver. Don't suppose you grabbed my laptop?"

He nods. "It's charging in King's office." He turns to leave, and then hesitates. "Don't forget to keep the thing dry." He points to my bandage, drawing circles in the air with a finger.

I give him a thumb up and shut the door after he leaves. The ache in my limbs is intense, and every time I move too quickly my head spins with an extreme case of vertigo. All I can put it down to is the massive amount of blood I lost. A good feed after this shower and I'll be ten times better.

The water is heaven, and I swear in that moment to never take the simple pleasures like water streaming out of a metal pipe for granted again. The run-off turns pink as blood washes out of my hair, and off my body. Most of it will be mine, but the thought sticks with me that a good part of it could be his too—the pimp's.

The stupid fucker barely had time to recover from the recoil of his gun before Tap and King rained down on him with theirs. I vaguely recall Bronx ushering a couple of kids in the diner out of view of the gore, but the rest is still taking its time to come back to me in dribs and drabs.

The burn, the pain, it was so intense. And all I could think about was Casey. Is that how she felt the day I shot her? Is that the same agonizing burn she experienced as everything around her faded? To die by gunshot would have been poetic, and in a way I never fought it.

Which disturbs me greatly.

If I'm going to show I can be enough for Ramona and prove to her that I can take care of Mack as well, then I need to fear death. Not in that all-encompassing way that the majority of the population does, where they inhibit their lives in case they so much as get a scratch. No, in that *if* I get injured like this again, I'll throw the Reaper a big fuck you and fight to survive.

I can't give in because of sins past. I can't keep looking for new ways to hurt myself to try and balance out what I did to Casey.

I suffered enough the day I left—there's nothing else that needs to be done.

back to the start

RAMONA The blanket lies on the floor and the cushions are empty. The very first thing I notice walking in to the common room as Sonya and I carry the groceries through to the kitchen is *he's gone*. I case the place as I continue on my path. The Cali boys are hanging out at the bar, Sawyer sharing a drink with them. King is in his office, on the phone and yelling at the person on the other end. *Nothing new there.* Mack watches Jo-Jo and Malice as they carry in the new pool table. Hooch reclines on one of the armchairs with a joint, watching the guys struggle to work out how to get it through the back doors. Mighty's voice floats in from the porch and he pushes ahead through the doors with Crackers and Murphy in tow.

They're all here except for the most important person of all.

"I can take those," Callum says, nodding to my bags. He

holds his already laden arms out for me to hook them on. "Go find Ty."

He doesn't have to offer twice. I slip the plastic handles over his arms and give him a quick peck on the cheek as I dash up the stairs. Hand on the bannister rail, I look out over everyone once more and catch Sawyer as he gives me a tight nod. He's still pissed with the idea, but the man will just have to get over it. He's said himself that he doesn't want me, so in theory, he has no claim over me. Possession isn't his privilege anymore.

I follow the sounds of the shower shutting off and head down to the bathroom. Steam seeps out the gap under the door, the muffled shuffles of somebody drying off audible as I hesitate in the hall. Do I wait? Is that too eager? What if he's still mad?

I find a comfortable spot on a footlocker in the wide hall, positioned under a framed picture of the club's first president on his Triumph Bonneville. It's a picture I've looked at a thousand times, lost myself in wondering what it was like for them back then when booze was the currency and all they had to worry about getting in trouble with the cops for was running over the speed limit.

A low groan sounds behind the door. I lift my gaze to the dark cedar panels, wondering if he needs help getting dressed. Surely his wound is causing trouble? A hiss follows, yet still I war with myself as to whether knocking would come off as creepy. I know I'd be a little disturbed if somebody had been sitting outside the bathroom, listening to my every move.

Fuck it—how's he to know I haven't just turned up?

I push off and march up to the door, knocking on it with a determined beat. "Hey, it's me. Are you okay?"

Muffled swearing precedes the handle rattling before the door swings open. "Hey." He's dressed in only his jeans, droplets of water dripping from the longer strands of his hair.

I swallow thickly, averting my gaze to the steamed up mirror behind him before I become a complete mumbling idiot. "Do you need a hand? I mean, with your injury and all it must be hard doing things like getting dressed."

He chuckles. "Yeah, it is. But that's not what I was having trouble with." He steps back, crossing to the basin and points to the gauze that's perched on the edge alongside a roll of tape. "I'm having trouble taping this on, since I can't lift my right arm very high."

"Oh. I can definitely help with that." I pick the roll of tape up and rip off a few lengths, hanging them by one end off the edge of the basin.

He lifts his arm slightly as I pick up the square of gauze. Bringing it to his chest, I stop and sigh at the mess that is his wound. Red angry skin pinches around the stitches Gloria gave him. The incision flares open, the raw flesh pink and inflamed from the shower. Just looking at it hurts.

"It's fine," he says, watching me eye him. "Only hurts when I breathe."

My lips curl up at his dry humor. "Best you stop doing

that then." I bring the gauze to cover it, careful not to press on the heart of the injury. "Can you hold this with your other hand?"

He places two fingers just under the top edge and watches me intently as I lift the strips of tape and place them over the edges, securing the bandage in place.

"I think that'll hold. First aid isn't my strength."

He runs a quick finger over the tape, giving it an extra press. "Looks okay to me."

I move back, taking a seat on the closed toilet to watch him finish dressing. He struggles with the right side of his T-shirt, and I step up briefly to straighten it out for him, lifting the fabric out from his skin as I bring it down over his ribs.

He turns to face me as he finishes up by cinching his belt. "Malice said he told you a bit about what happened."

"Yeah," I answer quietly.

Avoiding eye contact, he fusses with the toiletries on the vanity. "How does that make you feel toward me?"

"I hadn't really thought about it."

"You must think I'm some sort of freak, or really fuckin' messed up."

I sigh, crossing my arms over my stomach. "A freak, no, but messed up, a little."

"She was the first one I'd hurt. The first I ignored when her eyes asked me to stop."

My flesh chills and I rub my hands up my arms. "What do you mean? Malice said you get them to hurt you."

Ty faces me, hands propped behind him on the edge of

the basin. "Usually, yeah. But that one time it was different. I wanted *her* to hurt."

"Why are you telling me this?"

"Who else do I tell?" he asks. "I'm giving you all the details so you can make an informed decision."

"About what?"

"If you're stayin' with Sawyer, or leaving him for me."

"It's over," I whisper. "We're already over."

"I don't get the impression he feels that way." He rubs his left hand up and down the thigh of his jeans.

"It's complicated. He's given me his blessing to move on, but he still struggles with the idea of it." After a beat, I ask, "You still going to doing it?"

"The hookers?"

I nod. "Will you hurt any more?"

He shakes his head, shame etched into the lines across his forehead. "No. I don't think so."

"I'd need you to be honest with me, Ty. I've had to deal with a lot of shit from Sawyer, and all I ask for is the truth. I can't hack being lied to again."

"I understand." Ty fidgets with a worn thread on the denim. "You moving still? I thought you'd be gone by now."

"I don't think we're going to move anymore. Mack needs the stability and protection these familiar faces can provide." My gut flips—he must think I'm so damn ungrateful. "Can you cancel that advance you gave me for the rent?"

He nods. "Yeah, it's no issue."

"I'm sorry. You did so much for me and now I've just thrown it back at you."

"You have to do what's right for you two." He sweeps his hand over the smooth surface of the bathroom counter. "What about your place here? Were you renting? Are you allowed to keep your lease after what the gunman did?"

Pressing my lips together, I shake my head. "It's not rented; Sawyer owns it."

Ty's eyebrows shoot up. "Why's he not staying there, then?"

"Moving on. He'd rather we had use of it."

"I was looking forward to it, you know." His amber flecked eyes catch the overhead light as he looks up at me. "It sucks. I've got nothing to go home to now."

I fight the guilt that assails me seeing the disappointment in his gaze. "Where does that leave us?"

Ty's rich eyes snap up to mine. "My offer still stands, you know. You and Mack can come live with me."

"We can't."

"Why not?"

How do I explain it to him? How can I get him to see this from my point of view? "I need the space to find myself again."

"Didn't know you were lost." He smirks.

I pick up a nearby towel and throw it at him. "You're such a smartass." He barely ducks the flying fabric, not recovered enough yet to try and catch it without hurting himself.

"Seriously though, Ramona. Do you think you can handle living back at that house?"

"I don't know. I guess we'll stay here until things die down and the place is fixed. I really don't know."

"How long before you think you'd want to move again?"

I shrug. My train of thought hasn't reached that station yet.

Ty moves from where he stands to balance his behind on the toilet with me. Our shoulders are jammed together, even after I shuffle right to the edge to give him room. He braces his elbows on his knees, and leans forward, head hanging.

"You okay?"

"Started to feel a bit faint." He makes spinning motions with his hands beside his head, grimacing. "Everything's turning, even when I'm standin' still."

"When did you last eat?"

"Uh, a pie at the diner."

"Then get your ass down to the kitchen and I'll hook you up."

He peeks out from the corner of his eyes, a smile playing on his lips. "Can you help me get down there?"

"Sure," I say with a chuckle. "Wouldn't want you breaking your neck on the way to eat. Imagine that headline."

Ty stands, leaning on me with an arm slung around my shoulders. "Fuck this sucks."

"I imagine it does," I say, leading him from the room. "Getting shot hurts, from what I've been told."

He catches my eye and chuckles at my sarcasm. "I meant, it sucks having to rely on you to lead me around. I think I checked my masculinity at the door when they dragged me in."

"Suck it up, princess," I say with a hint of humor. "Just shut up and enjoy being looked after for a bit."

He hesitates at the head of the stairs. "Only as long as it's you who looks after me."

I push up on my toes, pressing a chaste kiss to his lips. "Guess I better go tell Callum to get out of the nurse's uniform then, huh?"

He laughs, clutching his side as he starts down the steps, leaning heavily on the rail. I move past him, walking down below his position in case he faints—not that I'd have a chance in hell of catching him.

Sonya appears at the base of the stairs and moves aside to wait for Ty. "The walking dead," she teases.

He smiles back. "Yeah, may as well be. I think it'd take a head shot to bring me down."

"Glad to see you're up and moving." She gives me a nudge as I help Ty off the bottom step, giving him my shoulders again. "Look after him, sweetheart."

Ty nods in her direction as she jogs up the staircase. "See? She thinks you should be the one looking after me, too. Sure you won't fit that nurse's uniform?"

I shrug. "If not, body-painting one on is always an option."

The shocked look on his face is priceless.

location, location

RAMONA "This is so good, Ramona." My name curling off his tongue still does all manner of warm things to my insides.

I lean across the counter, resting my chin in my hands, and watch him finish off the banana pancakes I'd made. "You must be feeling better?"

"Full, but still pretty much dead," he says with a smile, quickly dropping it at the pain in my expression. "Shit, sorry for saying such a dumb-ass thing." He scrubs the heel of his left hand up his forehead through his still damp hair.

"It's okay. No harm, no foul."

Ty's fingers brush over my forehead, pushing a stray lock of hair away. He watches his hand as he slides his fingers though the lengths of my hair. "I'm sorry about what happened before I left."

"No." I trap his hand under mine, hyper-aware of the

tingles firing off beneath the contact. "I should apologize too. I've been stringing you out."

"Hardly. You've done what you had to do. I started this knowing you had an old man looking out for you. I put you in this position."

"I've told you, he's not my old man any more." How long will it take before Sawyer's name isn't permanently attached like a ball and chain to my own?

Ty's hand retreats as he exhales loudly. "Are you sure you're okay with that? You said you still love him."

"I love him, but not *as* a lover, Ty. How many times do I need to say that before you'll believe it? He's the father of my child, and he means a great deal to me. There's a side of Sawyer that only I know, and I'll always love him . . . just not like that."

Ty frowns, pushing his plate aside. "Have you spoken to him about . . . you know . . . us?"

I nod. "I honestly thought he would have taken the news harder, you know? I mean, he's just not the kind of guy to let his woman be taken from him. . . at least, he didn't used to be."

"Something pretty fuckin' monumental happened while he was gone, you know."

"I just wish I knew what, or *who* it was. They've managed to achieve doing what I failed to for years."

"Perhaps he was never your problem after all?"

"Perhaps," I muse.

Ty runs his hand over the smooth steel of the counter. "The world works in mysterious ways. Whatever happened to him, whatever it did to you, I'm just thankful it brought us to where we are now."

"Which is?"

"Talking about a future where we're free to explore what it is that started this thing between us all those weeks ago."

I lean forward, resting my chin in my hands. "What was it, you think?"

He props his elbows on the counter, moving closer. "There aren't words that can do it justice."

"Cop out," I tease.

"You name it then," he challenges, leaning back.

I run my fingers over the swirls in the counter. "I guess . . ." What? He's right, there aren't words that adequately describe the way a person can bring every cell in your body to life, the way their presence alone can lower your heart-rate, and that a simple word from them is all it takes to breathe easy. "You have a point," I cede. "There aren't really words that explain it the right way."

He smiles, looking deep into my eyes. "I wish you'd reconsider moving."

"I can't. Not yet."

Ty drops his head, shaking it. "I know, and I understand, really. The wait's going to be torture, though."

"We'll work it out."

"Yeah, we will." He pushes from his stool, and rounds the counter to where I stand. "In the mean time . . ."

I smile, lifting an eyebrow to coax him along.

". . . can we go get that nurse's uniform for you? I'm

feeling rather tired, Miss. I think I need to be put to bed."

Laughing, I give is beard a little tug. "One track mind, you men."

His hands find my face, and he leans in to take my lips in a slow, sweet kiss. "Babe, with this face, that heart, and such an amazing smile, can you blame me?"

"I guess not," I say cupping my hands either side of his neck. "I feel a lot the same way."

Ty's forehead touches mine, his eyes closing. "Fuck gettin' shot. All I want to do is take you upstairs and worship every inch of you. It's like the universe is conspiring to keep us apart."

"Perhaps," I say with a laugh. "But you have to admit, it's going to make it all the more special when we are together that way."

"Jesus, woman. Don't torment me like that."

•• • ••

With the added motivation to take it easy on himself, Ty's recovery proceeds well over the next few days. His range of movement improves considerably, and I think he's enjoying the excuse to hang out with Mack most of the day, just chilling.

Sonya's been great, finding excuses to have Mack with her in the kitchen, or helping her with the washing so Ty and I get some time alone. We talk, kiss, and sometimes do nothing more than sit in silence while we watch a movie, just enjoying being around each other.

We're cuddled close on my bed upstairs one afternoon when I decide it's time to question him about the only thing I'm still not clear on. Ty's chest rises and falls under my head as I draw lazy circles around his covered wound.

"Can I ask you something?"

He shifts his head to look down at me, propping his right hand beneath. "You know you can."

"The things you got the hookers to do for you—do you still crave that?"

His throat bobs, the sound of him swallowing loud in the otherwise quiet room. "Do you mean the pain?"

I nod.

"Nowhere near as much as I did before you," he says. "Why?"

"I just wondered, is all."

"You give me the same release, Ramona, just in a different way."

"But if I could do that for you, would you want me to?"

"You'd inflict pain on me, if I asked you to?" His voice is strained.

I roll so my chin rests on the good side of his chest, and look up at him. "If it's what you needed, yes."

"Why?"

I push up and over him, kissing his forehead. "Because you mean that much to me."

"Baby . . ."

There's air between us, and then there's not. Then there's just our air as we come together. My hands are in his hair pulling, coaxing, and testing. I hesitate as he slips his tongue between the seam of my lips, and he pulls back.

"You okay with this?"

I nod, letting my gaze fall to his chest. "I don't want to cause you any pain though."

Ty's hand gently covers the adhesive bandage sitting just underneath his right pectoral muscle. "Baby, this pain is nothing compared to what's it's been watching you these past days and knowing I wasn't allowed to touch you."

"I would have let you."

His eyes darken, and the familiar tingle spreads from my toes to the tip of my nose. "I wouldn't have been able to stop myself, though, and then I would have ended up doing all sorts of damage and makin' it even longer that I had to wait."

The speed with which he moves takes me by surprise. Ty rolls, taking me with him in the process and pinning my body beneath him. His face betrays his pain, but his actions tell an entirely different story. He holds himself above me, staring down into my eyes while he shakes his head.

"He's a fool," he says, tracing my features with his thumbs, "to give this up. A damn fuckin' fool."

I smile as his fingertip grazes my bottom lip. "You make me sound like I'm something special." I'm just a girl who stumbled into a lawless life, searching for a place to call home.

"To the right man, baby, you are. To me you're fuckin' everything."

His hips push in between my legs, and I part them without a second thought. Our lips come together once more, his hands wrapping around the top of my head and holding me with a fierce ownership, yet still gentle.

I wrap my legs around his hips, crossing my ankles behind him. Ty's lips pull, suck, and tug at mine—a feverish, hungry man, looking for his last meal. I'm begging to be devoured. A low groan reverberates within his chest as I move my hands to the top of his butt, pressing my fingers into the firm flesh and urging him closer.

Breaking our kiss, he stares deep into my eyes, muttering once more, "A damn fool."

I answer with a hand on his belt, fumbling to unhitch the buckle.

He groans, and swats my hand aside. "Not yet." Before I can ask why, he's moving down my body, a devilish grin on his lips as he goes.

My hands are in his hair, tugging at the locks I've been longing to tease for so damn long. Blood rushes through my veins, priming and swelling me as he gently works the button and zipper of my jeans. He gives them a little tug at the waist, and I shuffle so he can slip the denim and my panties out from under me. The urgency is in his heaving breaths as he undresses me, but the care is in the slow way he does it, relishing every inch of skin he reveals with a gentle touch of his finger or brush of his lips.

My eyes flutter closed, soaking in the sensations of a man who adores my body, cherishes it, and wants to spend his time appreciating it. Sex with Sawyer was always just that—sex. He never gave me oral; he never kissed me anywhere but on the mouth. Sometimes I struggled to tell if he fucked me out of anger or love.

I guess looking back, knowing what I do know, it was always just a variation of anger or frustration.

But this? Ty's fingers trail a path down my calves, his tongue flicking over the rise of my ankle. Every touch is a show of adoration, thought out and executed with care. Ty's hands slide up my legs, heading for home as he gently lays kisses in their wake.

I'm hanging on the edge.

A gasp falls free without thought as the rough pad of his finger brushes over my sex: once, twice, three times. Each builds the buzz of my nerves to a deafening hum. My fingers knot in his hair, tugging him up, desperate to bring his mouth to mine.

But he resists.

Placing his hand over mine, Ty urges me to loosen off. I ease my grip, and quiver in anticipation as his heated breath caresses me right *there*. The rush of air as he inhales alerts me to just how wet I am for him, the room temperature chilling me in its wake.

"You smell so damn good," he mutters, running a finger through my folds. His finger pops from his mouth. "Tastes even better."

I groan, clenching my fists in his hair again. He chuckles, and then leans in to sweep the flat of his tongue the length of my sex. *Holy hell*. I've forgotten just how intimate the act is, how erotic.

"Good?"

I groan some more. He's lucky he can get that much of a response out of me, my mind such a mess of pleasure.

His tongue lavishes me with another long sweep, but this time pauses at the hood, flicking the hard tip across my sensitive nerves. I squirm at the assault, equal parts trying to get away, equal parts trying to get more.

He settles into a rhythm, teasing me with his tongue. I settle into the sensations, enjoying the building tension deep in my gut when he works his fingers over me, spreading and teasing. Garbled sounds are all I can make, my hands yanking in his hair a little too hard at times, making him growl into my pussy.

It's good.

I tug again.

He catches on.

"You keep yanking on my hair," he murmurs, muffled by my wet heat, "and I swear to God I'll walk out of here."

I release his locks from my grasp, moving my vice-like grip to the bed.

"Good girl."

Ty continues, licking, fondling, and building my desperation to feel something, anything inside of me. I begin to beg, shamelessly, and without regret. "I need you in me, please. I need something inside of me. Please, Ty."

He hums between my legs, quickening his tongue and pushing me to the brink of coming. I fight it. As amazing as it would feel I know it could be better, if only I had something *inside* me. He continues, and I reach out with my right hand, shoving his head away.

He smirks, his lips glistening with my arousal. *Fuck me dead.* I need a picture of that for posterity.

I open my mouth to say something, but snap it shut with a throaty groan as he thrusts two fingers inside of me, curling them to rub that sweet spot deep in front. I push back, meeting his pumping hand hit for hit.

It's still not enough.

Riding his hand, I tug on his head, urging him to move up me. He shuffles over my body on one elbow, his fingers still buried deep. Ty catches my mouth with his, plunging his tongue deep, mirroring his fingers. It's all I can do not to come on the spot.

My fingers work his belt without hesitation, my heightened arousal giving me freakish dexterity. Nothing's going to stop me. He sure as hell doesn't try, either.

Ty's belt flicks aside, slapping me high on my inner thigh as it does. I shudder at the extra sensation, the sharp sting heightening the delicious pleasure he's thrusting into me. As I reach inside the waistband of his boxers, Malice's words hit me like a damn truck.

'He pays whores to do it for him . . .'

I still, as does he. "What's the matter?" he pants.

"Are you clean? Do you get tested?"

His eyelids droop. "Regularly. I'm always protected, so you can take me any way you want me, baby."

God, yes. His cock springs free with the gentlest of tugs. I glance down at the smooth flesh, red and straining at the tip, and literally drool. Ty chuckles, wiping the dab of saliva away with his free hand, and then smearing it over the tip of his glistening length.

Best. Sight. Ever.

He gives me a few more pumps with his fingers, rubbing my clit with his thumb, and then withdraws. Ty's gaze holds mine as he licks the digits clean. Nudging him with my knee, I coax him off me, and move us so that I now straddle him where he lies. I position myself, and watch his jaw fall wide, his eyes sliding shut as I slip onto him with a groan. He stretches and fills me, the position I'm in on his lap with my legs wide allowing him to sink as deep as he can physically go.

"A damn fool," he groans, his head lolling back.

Taking my time, I rise and fall over him, enjoying the way his face changes with each thrust and pull of my heat. Tentatively, I reach up and run my thumb over his lip, his eyebrows, down his nose, all the while continuing to ride him at a leisurely pace. On the second sweep, he turns his head and sucks my thumb into his mouth. I gaze into his dark eyes, watching the mood build behind the rich brown flecks as he runs his tongue around the top of my thumb.

My pace builds, but not as quickly as his need. Ty's hands grasp my backside, lifting me from his lap, and slamming me down hard. I gasp, part in pleasure, part in pain at how deep he's managed to seat himself with the motion. He repeats the movement, his forearms flexing under my hands as he slams me down again, and again.

Skin slapping, breaths gasping, uninhibited desire—I want to stay in the moment forever.

His jaw set rigid, his eyes screwed tight, Ty growls as he continues the assault. I moan, whimper, and groan at the pure shots of ecstasy firing through my body each time he hits deep. His movements lose fluidity, become jerky and desperate. On one descent he misaligns us in the slightest way, but enough to make it hurt. I cry out in shock and pain as he wrenches me up quickly.

I expect to see an apology in his eyes, but instead I find raw hunger; the pain drives him to some higher place.

Silently, he sets me down and lifts my hands, bringing them to his throat. He maneuvers them so I'm throttling him, my thumbs over his jugular. A beat passes, each of us staring deep into the other's eyes, asking and understanding. As he lifts me up, I press on his throat, giving him the extra push he needs. His eyes fall shut, his movements becoming quicker the more pressure I give him.

He's an animal. It's the only way to describe the brutal assault he dishes out. His hips bruise my thighs, his thrusts hard and unforgiving. I grip his neck hard, his breath raspy as it vibrates past the restriction of my hands. A roar builds in his chest, breaking free as I drop my hands. He comes, jamming his thumb over my clit, rubbing hard. The friction, the pulse of his length, and the raw desire painted across his features set me off. I come hard over him as he twitches a final time inside me.

Realizing my eyes are shut, I crack them open to find

him grinning at me, his chest heaving with his ragged breaths. The smile is infectious, and I find myself grinning back, even though I have no idea what he finds so amusing.

His abs crunch between us as he pulls close and dots a kiss to my nose. “If this is what recovery is like, I think I need to get shot more often.”

conflict of interest

TY

She giggles, and apologizes as she climbs from my lap, hand between her legs to catch my cum. It's cute. Fuck, everything about her is cute: that slightly upturned nose, her long dark lashes, the way her red hair frames her face.

Damn, I want her again.

First, painkillers. There's something to be said for losing yourself in the moment. Everything about her bouncing that tight little butt on my cock had me ignoring the fact my chest hurt like a motherfucker. Getting shot in your side will do that to a person.

The cramping pain rips through my chest as I try to stand and I cede defeat, falling to my back on the bed. Ramona finishes cleaning herself up with some tissues and leans down beside me as I laugh hysterically at the predicament.

"You okay?" Her wide eyes search my face.

I choke back my laugh. "Babe, I'm fucked—literally."

She moves her gaze to my bandage, and her hand lifts to brush gentle fingers underneath the tape. "It's bleeding."

"Shit." I push myself to a sitting position, and twist to check it out. "It doesn't hurt too much more than a burn, so hopefully that means it's fine."

"Perhaps we should get you downstairs to have Gloria check your stitches anyway."

He grins. "What are we goin' to say we were doing?"

Ramona laughs, covering her mouth with her right hand. "I have no idea."

I take her hand, and tug to hoist myself up. Ramona struggles not to tip over, digging her heels in. It takes more effort on my part, but it's okay—she tried.

Crashing and yelling filters in from the common room, and Ramona catches my gaze. "What the hell now?" She tugs her jeans and panties on in record time, and we head for the commotion.

We walk into a warzone. Ammunition is flying, and there are casualties strewn all over the common room. King has his head in his hands at his desk while the woman I assume is Elena is hurling glassware at the wall beside his door, insults renting the air like gunfire. A few members are hanging around, witnessing the carnage, staying out of the way, and looking every part as reluctant to join in on this as I am.

"Hey!"

The Latin woman spins to her left and sets her sights

on me. "Who the fuck are you?"

Ramona looks around frantically for Mack, heading over to the boys to ask about him.

"You might want to tone it down a little," I tell the crazed woman. "There are kids around, you know."

"Don't try and reason with her," King calls out from his position of safety. "She doesn't listen."

"Oh, that's fucking rich coming from you!" She spins back to him and proceeds to march toward his office. He jumps up from his seat and strides out to meet her. "How long have I been telling you that I don't need your help," she hollers, "and yet you still have to keep your nose in our business."

"Yeah, because funnily enough we have a shared interest, Elena." King stops nose-to-nose with the woman. "You expect me to walk away from my kid?"

Speaking of the 'kid' . . . I look around the place but come up short. Where is *their* kid? "Where's Dante?"

"Garage!" they shout in unison.

I skirt the pair as they continue to go at it and head over to where Bronx sits at the bar. "How long have they been fighting?"

"Mmm," he says, twisting his mouth, "about ten minutes. The boys are getting worried they won't have anything left to drink out of." Bronx gestures to the snowdrift of glass shards beside the wall.

"I've already had to resort to this," a prospect says, holding up a plastic *Dora the Explorer* cup.

"Fuck me." King walks over, rubbing his head with one

hand. “That woman is incredible.”

“Intolerable, I would have said,” Bronx mutters.

King shakes his head, taking a stool and gesturing to the prospect for a drink. “Nup. I meant incredible.”

Both Bronx and myself stare at the guy. After that showdown he’s love-struck? She looks a bunch of unnecessary suffering to me, but hey, each to their own. I swivel in my seat to see ‘Miss Incredible’ snatch up a leather jacket and keys from a table, and storm toward the door.

“Are you sure she should be going out?” I ask, aware that Carlos probably still has a tail on her.

King looks over his shoulder and sighs. “For fuck’s sake.” He slams back his drink and races off after her.

Bronx is chuckling beside me, watching the spectacle unfold. I eye him warily. Sure, it’s a good thing he’s relaxed in light of what’s coming up, but I want to be sure he’s taking this job seriously, and not going to ruin it for all of us.

“How’s your head?” I ask.

He directs his smile to me, and answers, “A little rough after one too many the other night, but okay.”

It’s not what I meant, but I continue with the issue he’s brought up. “Dude, you don’t drink.” He’s a health nut, and vehemently against putting alcohol in his temple . . . usually.

“Yeah, well I’m practicing for the role.” His eyes are vacant. He doesn’t believe this bullshit either, but I let it slide.

"You got time later to go over your backstory?"

"Sure." He takes a swig of water, and recaps the bottle. "Have to be this afternoon though—I'm going back to the Red Lion later to 'mingle'."

I nod. We agreed at the start of this that before Bronx has his staged introduction to Edward's crew, he'd make sure he was seen in a few of their haunts to become a familiar face to them. There's nothing more suspicious than a guy who turns up out of nowhere, trying to join in.

"Who you going with?" As much as he's the purpose of these visits, I don't like the idea of him walking into uncharted territory without at least one person on his side.

"Nathan here has offered to ditch the colors for a night and expand his horizons," Bronx says with a playful wink in the prospect's direction. "Thinks he might find himself a nice English broad there." Bronx regards the guy for a second and continues. "Man, you need a road name, stat. Nathan is so . . . proper." He wrinkles his nose at the kid.

Nathan nods in solemn agreement. "Totally agree, but I haven't done anything to earn a name yet."

"Who knows?" Bronx says, raising his bottle of water in toast. "Maybe tonight's the night."

"Maybe." Nathan nods to acknowledge the gesture.

"Ty!"

I spin around and face King as he marches towards us, Elena trotting to keep up, her skinny arm in his firm grasp. "Where did Ramona go?"

"To find Mack."

"Keep a watch on this one, boys." King shoves Elena toward us, and heads for the stairs.

She drops on to a stool and reaches over the bar for a bottle of bourbon. Screwing her nose up, she takes a swig and replaces it. "Ugh."

"If you don't like it, then save it for those of us who appreciate the stuff." Nathan swipes the bottle up and moves it out of her reach.

She barks out a laugh. "I'd rather a glass of wine, but I doubt you rough lot have that."

Nathan produces a bottle from the fridge beneath the bar. "I'd offer you one, but . . ." His gaze drifts to the mass of glass across the room.

She sighs, and drops her head into her arms. "I have an issue with anger," she admits in muffled tones. "I lose my temper a lot."

"You don't say," I mutter. "You guys have a dustpan or anything? Should probably clean that up before the kids get near it."

"I'll do it," Elena offers. "It's my mess, so I'll clean it up."

"I'll show you where Sonya keeps the cleaning stuff," Nathan offers, and walks out from behind the bar to show her the way.

They leave the room, and I take stock of who's left. A couple of women are in conversation over on the sofas, and there are three older guys hanging out on the back porch. Satisfied they're all out of earshot, I lean across to Bronx. "Are you sure you're okay? I worry, man."

"Fine," he says flatly, waving me off. "Don't get yourself

wound up over things that aren't happening, Ty. You're good at that."

I frown at the guy as he walks away toward the backyard. Twiddling a bottle opener between my fingers, I watch him step outside, strip off his shirt and start running laps around the grass area. It's the first time I've seen him do something relatively 'normal' for weeks.

I've got to wonder what exactly this role is going to do to the guy. He's getting so involved with playing the part that I kind of have to wonder if he'll even remember who he is by the time that this all blows over.

I can't shake the sickness in my gut that tells me I'm slowly bringing my best friend to ruin.

home comforts

RAMONA "Sorry about that. She's calmed down now."

I look up from the impromptu game of 'I spy' Mack, Dante and I had started to find King leaning in the doorway. We've been holed up in Sonya's room waiting for the fireworks downstairs to end after I found the boys heading toward the warzone from the garage.

"Is she always like this?"

He smirks, and shakes his head as he enters. "Only when she's upset." King moves to sit next to Dante on the bed. "How you doing?"

"Good," he answers simply. "Mom doesn't want us to move."

"Yeah." King nods at his boy. "She doesn't. Do you?"

Dante nods. "I want a new room."

I pull Mack onto my lap and cross my arms over his

chest as I watch King with his son. The love he has for his child is clear, but so is the pained conflict. He wants to protect his family, but how can he be expected to do that when he's running such a dangerous operation?

"Would you two boys like to come help me make us all something yummy for dessert tonight?"

Both boys turn their heads toward me and nod.

"What can we make?" Dante asks.

"I hadn't decided," I answer honestly. The idea was totally spur-of-the-moment. "What's your favorite?"

He looks at King, then at me. "Same as Dad—chocolate steamed pudding with lots of cream."

King twitches a smile and then looks at Dante with nothing less than blatant adoration. "You know that?"

"Mom always makes it for your birthday."

King's brow furrows as he studies his sons face. "I don't see you guys for my birthday."

Dante nods, my heart swelling with the sentiment he's revealed. "I know. Mom makes it anyway."

King turns his head away, hiding his face. I give Mack a little squeeze, and tap Dante on the arm to get his attention. "How about you boys go and find your mother, Dante, and ask her if she'd like to join us?"

"Sure." The two kids clamber off the bed and tear out the door, laughing about who's going to get to the stairs first.

I turn my focus back to King and give his knee a nudge with my foot. "You okay?"

Red-streaked eyes look up at me. "We could have been

such a good family."

"What do you mean 'been'? You are."

"I mean, the proper way, you know? With two parents in the same house."

I frown, drawing parallels to my own situation, and the amount of times I'd wished Sawyer was home more often. For years I harbored the guilt that Mack didn't have a stable, predictable home life; there was one parent on the road more often than not. But after time I let it go, realizing that the fact Sawyer was away a lot didn't mean he loved Mack any less. If anything, it made the nights he did come home more special.

"Just because you two are separated, doesn't mean you love your boy any less."

"I wonder if he's going to look back on it and regret not having more time with me when he's older," King admits. "I don't want him to be angry at the kind of relationship he was born into."

"He'd be selfish to be. His parents love him; that's all that matters."

A pregnant pause fills the air around us before King sighs, rubbing a hand over his head. "I've been trying to work out what we're going to do for you two, Mona. You can't go home, but I know you don't want to have Mack here all the time. Especially with everything that's been going on lately."

"I think we'll adapt," I say, shrugging my shoulders. "I can work out what we'll do. We can always take over one of the rooms up here, force a couple of guys to share so we get a room to ourselves."

He lifts his gaze to mine, smiling. "I almost forgot."

"What?" His smile is infectious.

"I have something to show you." He stands, holding out a hand. "Come."

I take the offer and let him pull me up, nudging me first toward the door. Unsure where we're going, I hesitate in the hall.

"Head down to the garage," he instructs.

"The kids are probably waiting for me."

"It'll only take a minute."

I do as told, and make my way through the clubhouse until I'm standing just inside the door to the garage. Fingers is tinkering away on Sawyer's bike over on the far side, sunlight streaming in through the half-open roller door. He lifts his head, and gives us a tip of the chin to acknowledge our presence.

"Almost done, Boss."

"You manage to get that dent in the tank out?"

Fingers nods. "Hell of a job, but I got it."

My eyes roam the work surfaces, and the bikes in for services or repairs. What did King bring me down for? Turning my head to face the boys after the conversation stopped, I see King coming toward me with two boxes stacked in his arms.

"What's this?"

He places them at my feet, gesturing for me to open them. "I sent Mighty and Dog back to your place the other night."

Squatting, I pull the unsecured flaps open on the boxes and look inside. Mack's books are stacked to one side, a few of my DVDs holding them up, and Mack's Marvel figurines tossed haphazardly in the free space on top. Tears welling, I open the other one, surprised at just how much I missed having something of my own. The second box is filled with more practical items like clothes, my phone, the charger for it, my makeup and hairbrush, and my purse, complete with all my cards and the papers Ty gave me outlining our rental down-payment.

"King . . ."

"I figured you might need some of that stuff."

Standing, I lean over the top of the boxes and pull his huge frame in for a hug. Fingers chuckles behind him as I squeeze the living daylights out of the man. He's such a big softie, always thinking of everyone's best interests. The stuff in the boxes may not be valuable, but their sentimental worth and the small joy they'll bring Mack and I is immeasurable.

"Thank you," I whisper, leaning back.

"Any time. Now go and make me some chocolate pudding. I'll take these upstairs and decide who I'm going to kick out of a room for you." He glances down at the boxes, and most evidently, at the slip of paper sticking out of my purse.

I follow his gaze down. "Did you read that?"

"Yeah," he says lifting his face. "I wanted to be sure it wasn't some threat or the like before I gave it to you."

I stare at the paper, decisions rolling through my mind.

"Are you still going?" King asks.

I shake my head, unable to meet his gaze. "I don't think we could. Mack needs his dysfunctional extended family." I lift my chin, meeting King's welcome eyes. "I need them, too."

"We might not be the best influence, Mona, but we'll always be there for you both."

"He's loved here," I say, fighting more unwanted tears. "And with everything that's been happening this week, that's what matters the most."

"It's not over, yet. You know that, right?"

I drop my gaze, unease swirling low in my gut. "Yeah, I know."

"It's the life we chose," King says, placing a hand on my shoulder. "We've just got to make do with the hand we're dealt."

Frowning, I shake my head and look into his eyes again. "No, King. It's the life we fell into, and what we do with it is what makes us the people we are."

His lips quirk in the corner. "Go make me some sugary sin in a bowl."

Pushing up to my tiptoes, I give the big lug a peck on the cheek and then turn to head indoors. A week ago I was ready to leave this all behind, unsure what the nausea I felt every time I'd thought about leaving really was. I'd thought that it was nerves, and that I'd get past it once we were settled. But now, I can see that the feeling would have never left. What I felt wasn't jitters at the unknown, it was the sick dread you get when you know things are never going to be as good as what you have in that moment. It was the ill uncertainty of leaving behind the best part of my life to do what I thought was right.

How wrong I was, and how lucky I am to have realized the mistake before I pulled us away from the only real family we've known. We may not live in a conventional house anymore, but this is the only place I've ever felt home.

As I walk into the kitchen and see the welcome smiles of three people I'll happily spend my afternoon with, I realize that when it all comes down to it, it's the people around you who make you feel home—nothing more.

back to business

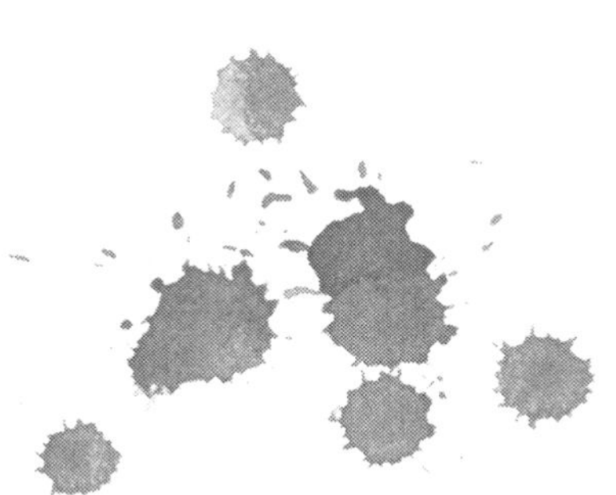

TY King comes in from the garage carrying two boxes in his arms. He props them on the edge of the bar, eyes fixing to me as I sip at the bottle of water before me.

"What?"

"I need a hand with something." He turns his head and eyes Sawyer across the room, chatting with Tap. "Sawyer!"

"Yeah?" he hollers back.

"I need a hand with something."

Sawyer casually saunters over, his jaw firm, his steely gaze locked on me. I smirk back, knowing the implication of why I might be happy is driving him nuts.

"What needs doing?" he asks King as he comes to a stop beside us.

"I need a room here for Ramona and Mack. Who do you think we should double up? Fingers and Frog?"

Sawyer's gaze flashes to me, a slight twitch to his brow

giving away his unease at discussing the subject with me around. "She can have my room," he offers to King. "I won't need it for long."

My ears prick up at this little admission. *Where's he going?* I don't need to wonder much longer.

"Just been talking with Tap about transferring over to the west coast."

King frowns, rolling his lips this way and that as he thinks the offer through. Sawyer and I remain still, waiting on his answer. Is he going to be mad that Sawyer's leaving? Or relieved? I know I'm over the fucking moon at the thought.

"Fine," he barks. "Get your ass upstairs and start sorting out what you're taking and what's staying. Put the shit you want relocated in the garage. I'll get Nathan to box it and ship it when you're ready."

Sawyer nods, turns to Tap and gives him a 'we're cool' tip of the chin, then heads up to his room.

I meet King's burning stare with a shrug. "Took me by surprise."

"Don't pretend you're not happy about it," he drawls, his face impassive. "You probably planned the whole fuckin' thing."

I start to sweat under the scrutiny. Has my hatred for Sawyer finally started to ruffle feathers the wrong way around here? I mean, I know they don't approve of what he does, but I kind of discounted the fact he's still one of their members.

King's lips curl into a mocking grin. "Just shitting you.

I'm cool with it. The change will do both him and Ramona good. Bit far away from Mack, but it is what it is. They'll work around it."

"Can I ask you something?"

He nods, leaning an elbow on the boxes.

"Nobody's fronted me about Ramona. I expected to get grief about it, you know? I took one of your brother's woman." Not stealing another member's lady is one of the golden rules. Having me, an outsider, do it—shit, I expected to be brushing knuckles the day I got here.

"Not many people were fooled," King drops casually. "The ones who were soon got set straight when you showed an obvious interest in her."

I lift my eyebrows, surprised. "What's the deal between them?" I ask. "Ramona said they'd called it all off, but he sure as fuck doesn't act like it."

King curls one side of his mouth toward his nose and tips his head to the side briefly. "I can't speak for the guy. Maybe she can fill you in." He hoists the boxes into his arms again. "Anyway, we better get to it if we're going to have this sorted by dinnertime."

"We?"

"Yeah, we. I'm not finished talkin' to you; you're comin' upstairs with us."

I start to protest. "But—"

"Nothing. Big boy pants on and headin' for those stairs, now."

Asshole. He's forcing Sawyer and I together knowing that we'll either sort things out or establish hierarchy by the time the dust settles. I don't move.

King hesitates beside me, clearing his throat. "Did I fuckin' stutter?"

Begrudgingly and with a huge sigh to let him know how much so, I turn and slide off the stool, nabbing my bottle of water as I step away. "Fine. I'm coming."

Sawyer is piling clothes on top of the bed when we enter, King dropping the boxes to the right of the door. The look I receive is no less than I expected—a dagger of hatred intended to scar me six ways from Sunday. He turns his attention to King, the look of sheer disgust melting from his features. *Asshole.*

"They can have the bed. Too bulky to shift."

My eyes dart to the double-sized frame, the mattress stripped bare underneath his pile of laundry. An intense need to go shopping grips me; no way is she having the bed they probably conceived Mack in, not if I'm staying over. At least it's only for a little while.

I find both men watching me. "What?" I snap.

"You look like somebody stole your last fuckin' cookie, is what," King answers. He glances between Sawyer and I. "You fuckers have to sort this bullshit out, get your differences squared away."

"You're askin' a little much, ain't you Pres?" Sawyer remains with his back to me, casting a sideways glance at King.

He lifts a finger at Sawyer, ready to speak, but just shakes his head instead. Turning away, he body-blocks the two of us, facing me. "Can you go down to the kitchen and ask Sonya or Ramona—whoever you come across first—if they have any empty boxes we can use?" King asks. "Maybe this wasn't such a hot idea after all."

No fucking kidding.

My feet are itching to leave that damn bedroom. Why does she have to stay in there? *Of all places.* My brow is deep set and my fists tight by the time I push through the doors to the kitchen.

"Hey," Sonya greets, thumbing over her shoulder at Ramona and the boys measuring out ingredients into a large bowl. "If you want something different, now's the time to speak up."

"Do you have any boxes we can have?" I ask her.

"What size? What you need it for?"

"Packing up Sawyer's shit."

Ramona pauses in her instructions, the boys both looking up to see what's taken her attention away from the baking at hand.

I meet her inquisitive stare, ignoring the glimmer of sense I have to talk about this rationally.

"I'll go see what we've got," Sonya says, eyes darting between us. "There's some stored flat in the supply cupboard."

"Thanks," I mutter as she leaves us.

"You helping him pack?" The surprise is evident.

"In a manner of speaking," I bite.

"Dante," she says, ducking her head to the kids, "can you measure out two cups of flour from here, and Mack, I need three teaspoons of this over here." She fidgets with a set of metal measuring spoons, passing him one. "This size."

Stepping back from the workbench, she tips her head for me to follow. We walk through to the large pantry, Ramona slightly closing the door behind us. "What's the matter?"

"You're staying in his fuckin' room?" I blurt out.

"Am I?" she snaps back, hands on her hips. "All I knew is that King was going to sort me a room—I didn't know which one."

"Well you've got his," I hiss. "And the bed I'm sure you've fucked him in plenty of times."

She ducks her head, pinching forefinger and thumb to the bridge of her nose. "Ty . . ."

"He's going to be everywhere, isn't he?" I thought that I could do this—take on her past without a care as long as they were over. But maybe I was wrong? The jealousy consuming me is too strong to ignore, the need to be seen as the top dog, the guy who's in control, overwhelming.

"It'll only be a problem if you let it." Her face lifts, her irises dark. "Now get out. Go find somewhere to cool off and think through how irrational you're being. I've got dessert to make."

She twists her body to avoid colliding as she moves by me, heading through the door and rejoining Mack and Dante with the sunniest fucking attitude in the world. Striking out, I knock a bag of rice off the shelf with my fist, cursing under my breath as the contents spill over the floor on impact. Salvaging what I can, I slam it down on the shelf, spilling more. The grains skitter under the shelving with each mad swipe of my boot.

Fuck him. He never cared for her in the right way, but the fucker is going to be ingrained in her life from here on out. She can't even make a clean break from the guy since they share a child. Things would be so much easier if her ex was somebody a little less . . . narcissistic. But no, she had to go and shack up with Sawyer motherfucking Redmond.

Nursing my injuries, physical and mental, I storm through the kitchen, snatching the flattened boxes Sonya holds out to me as I pass. There isn't any way in hell I'm taking these upstairs and facing that asshole, so naturally when I pass a prospect at the base of the stairs, I reach out and catch him by the collar, sending him up with the goods.

Bronx straightens in his seat, attention pulled from his phone in his hand. "What's wrong now?"

"Nothing," I snap, ruing the harshness of my tone. "Can we get out of here?" I'm trapped without my car.

Bronx stands, grabbing his jacket off the back of the chair. "Sure. Anywhere in particular?"

"Wherever I can be distracted for the next few hours is fine."

He nods, accepting, and heads for the door.

I trail behind, wearing my cowardice like a lead vest. If I can't swallow my pride and accept her past, then what hope does our future hold?

baggage

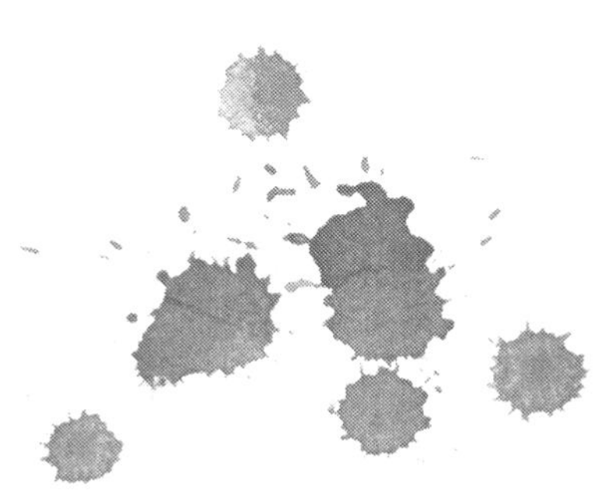

RAMONA His damn outburst has *me* mad at Sawyer—how backwards is that? I train my focus on the boys, making sure they follow all the steps as they prime the dish for the dessert and pour the batter in. Dante opens the door of the wall oven, and Mack hands me the dish to place on the rack. We stand together for a moment, watching it start to sweat under the heat.

I *am* the damn cake.

The heat from Ty and Sawyer is akin to the heat the cake gets from top and bottom. I'm in the middle, wearing the brunt of their anger at each other. And it's not fucking fair. They push too hard and I'll split, probably leaving the same amount of mess in my wake as a damn cake would.

"You think King will like it?" Mack asks, breaking me from my thoughts.

"Yeah," I answer, giving both their shoulders a squeeze. "I think he'll love it."

"Hey, Mack," Dante asks. "You want to see my Ninja Turtles?"

Mack nods furiously, his eyes alight. "Sure."

The boys tear out of the kitchen leaving me with the cake and too many damn representations of my life in its chocolaty center for me to stomach. I set the timer, and escape to the fading hues of orange sun that lavish the porch.

Tap is reclined in one of the plastic lawn chairs, tipping it on the back legs precariously. One eye cracks open as I pass by and take a seat of my own.

"Holding in there?"

I smile genuinely at him, and fidget with a speck of batter on my jeans. "Yeah, I think so."

"Boys still being tools?"

I snort. "Are they ever not?"

"Yeah, I get ya." He lets the chair find stability, extending his legs out in front. "You cool with Sawyer shifting our way?"

"He can do what he wants," I answer, staring out at the lengthening grass across the yard. Seed stems wave lazily in the light breeze.

"That's not what I asked."

I turn my head and take a good look at the man beside me. He's rough around the edges in that wilderness loving way, but beneath the facial hair and plaid shirt is a strikingly handsome man. The Tap I was introduced to as a newcomer to the club was a lot skinnier, a lot younger, and a darn sight quieter. He's changed, as we all do.

“I won’t lie,” I answer, looking to the grass again. “I hate that he’s moving so far away from Mack, but the guy had a point.”

“What’s that?”

“If he sticks around, I’ll never let him go. I’ll keep babysitting him, kissing his boo-boos when he falls. He needs the space as much as I do to find his feet.” Pinning Tap’s gaze with mine, I frown a little. “Do you know what happened when he went home?”

Tap shakes his head slowly. “Hooch won’t say, and I’m not stupid enough to ask Sawyer directly. I kind of figured it was fuckin’ bad though, whatever went down. I mean, it had to be—Hooch’s sister was murdered right after his old man.” He shakes his head again. “It’s harsh, that’s for sure.”

“He was different at first, when he got here.”

“Yeah, he was. I think he’s trying real hard to get back to that, too.”

We each sit in contemplative silence, staring out across the barren back yard. An old jungle gym sits idly in the back corner by the second garage, and I wonder how easy it would be to fix up for Mack given the amount of time we’re spending here now.

Boots on the wood draw my attention to Hooch as he wanders outside to join us. “Any of you guys seen Ty?”

My face flushes with heat. “He not here?”

“Can’t find him anywhere.”

Tap’s eyes dance across my face briefly before fixing to Hooch. “Overheard him talkin’ with Bronx as they headed out to Malice's ride. Said they were headin' to Hooters to watch some game."

My throat catches as I swallow. *He's escaping me.*

"Thanks. I'll hook up with them there." Hooch spins and leaves.

I feel the burn of Tap's stare before I meet it. "What?"

"You two argued?"

"You sure you're not wasted in this life?" I snap. "I mean, you're pretty onto it all. Maybe you should've been a detective. A profiler even?" Why is it everybody in this damn place makes my business theirs?

He glowers, cocking his head off to one side, and ignoring my sharp sarcasm. "Was it about Sawyer?"

"Fuck!" I cry out, throwing my hands up as I stand. "Who else would it be?" If Tap wants to know why I'm upset that badly, then he's about to damn well get the whole nine yards. I march across the porch to ease the rage buzzing inside. "He's mixed up in everything. He ruins everything he fucking touches. No, scrap that, he ruins everything he bloody well looks at. He doesn't even have to touch it, just *breathe* over it."

Tap watches me rant and pace with a humorous smirk. "You done?"

"No," I answer honestly with a smile. "But I'll stop."

"No," he says, waving the backs of his tattooed hands at me. "Carry on."

I frown at him for a moment, struggling to work out if he's serious or being facetious.

He catches on to my uncertainty. "Mona, you've been

here almost as long as I have, right?"

I nod. It's been years since we've crossed paths, but regardless, our knowledge of each other goes a long way back.

"In *all* that time," he says, "I have *never* once heard you complain. Always there to help, but never asking for it. You ask me,"—he lifts an eyebrow—"you've got a hell of a lot of suppressed shit to get off your liver, woman. So by all means, carry on."

I hesitate for another few seconds, and then pick up right where I left off. Tap sits in silence, big arms crossed over his flannel and leather-clad chest, nodding where appropriate and offering grunts in the more intense parts.

I walk, sit and stomp my feet like a child, all the while spieling off all the things that have pissed me off during the last five years. By the time I'm done, my breathing comes easier and my head is ten times lighter. I lean back in the lawn chair, the early notes of dusk now faded into a dim black around us. Somewhere along the line the outdoor light was turned on, and moths flap at the bulb.

"Feel better?" Tap asks, shadowed by the light behind him.

"Yeah, heaps. Thank you."

"Glad to be of service. Do you think we could eat though, because I'm fuckin' starved?"

"Shit!" I cry out, leaping to my feet. "Dessert!"

raw truths

TY

Bronx taps away on his phone as a velvet-haired woman stops at our table to clear the empty bottles. "Sawyer's headin' out to Cali tomorrow."

"Part of the inner circle now, are we?" I swirl what's left of my fourth beer inside the bottle.

His phone hits the tabletop with a smack. "Stop being a douche. Jo-Jo messaged me. He heard it from Hooch."

The notion he might be leaving to get away from Ramona and I twirls through my head like a damn fruit fly, never relenting. Would he leave because of that? *Don't be so fucking stupid.* Of course he's not—it'll be business. Always is.

"Surprised King's letting him go, what with the threats from Carlos and all that," I say. "Mind you, knock the asshole off and it's one less thing for him to worry about. Maybe that's the plan."

"Keep your wet dreams to yourself," Bronx snaps, a

grimace contorting his face. "The west crowd can look after themselves. It's probably more a case of King gettin' sick of so many broody fuckers mopin' around the joint."

"Perhaps." I shrug.

"You goin' to talk to Mona when you get back?"

I cut my gaze to him as he signals the waitress over. "Since when do you call her that?"

"Mona?"

"Yeah. I've only heard the guys she's known for a while use her shortened name."

"Firstly," Bronx says, passing his empty bottle to the waitress for an exchange, "saying her full name just seems like unnecessary work, and secondly, dude—only old people or toffs prefer to use people's full given name."

"I'm letting that slide."

"So you goin' to talk to her?"

"Does a brown bear shit in the woods?"

He takes the new brew, and tips it towards me. "And there, just like that you fuckin' swing into sailor mode."

"More than just sailors are crass, you know."

"Anyway, you never asked how our first trip to the Red Lion went."

"How did you go at the Red Lion?" I drawl.

"Stellar." His throat bobs with two long pulls. "Especially since you keep putting off going through my back story like you said you would." He gives me a smart-ass smirk. "Good thing I'm so fuckin' good at what I do, huh?"

"Settle down." I roll my eyes and take a swig of the drink before me.

"Are you supposed to be drinkin' with your pain meds?"

"Bit late to notice now isn't it?"

"Guess so. But back to the Lion—"

"You were the one who deviated."

"Back to the Red Lion," he stresses, "I met a guy called Taylor."

My ears perk up, my sour mood shelved for the time being. "Eddie's guy?"

"That's what I wanted to ask."

"Well? Do you have a full name for me?" I pull myself up a little straighter, working the stiffness out of my chest.

Bronx glares back at me from the other side of the table. "Dude? Really?"

"What?"

"Do you go 'round askin' everybody you meet what their surname is?"

Point taken. "What did he look like then?"

"Short, as in, came up to my shoulder. Dark hair I think—hard to tell since it was close cut—and a hard-set jaw that looked like I'd bruise a knuckle or two on it. He had the weirdest fuckin' dress sense."

"The guy's a skinner."

"They stuck in the eighties or somethin'?"

"They just have a distinctive sense of dress."

"You can fuckin' say that again," Bronx mutters as I catch a familiar face approaching over his shoulder.

"You assholes forget to invite me?" *Hooch.*

"I was kind of hopin' for a quiet afternoon." I eyeball

him over the bottom of my upturned bottle.

"I need a favor," he states, taking a free stool.

"I'm not finding a stripper."

"Not what I was askin'."

"Why should I help anyway after you tried to smash my face in?" *Have a cry, Ty. Have a cry.* When the fuck did I become so whiny all the time?

"Fists fly all the time in our world, brother. You best be lettin' that go or you'll find yourself the only one with a problem."

Again—reasons why I'm glad I'm not an MC monkey . . .

"What do you need?" I eye him suspiciously, running my fingers over the neck of my bottle.

"A beer first." He signals the waitress and points to what we're having. She delivers it in record time, standing close enough to press her D-cups into the back of his arms as she places the cold bottle on the table. "Thanks, sweetheart." Hooch places a huge hand on the opposite side of her face and tugs her in to give her a sloppy kiss on the cheek. The woman walks away glowing.

Asshole.

Downing at minimum half the damn thing before he stops to swallow, Hooch places the bottle down and leans on an elbow to bring his face close.

"King tells me that you can locate people."

"Haven't had any trouble so far," I reply.

"I've got somebody I need you to find. But I need to know you can keep it to yourself."

I stare at the idiot blankly, circling a hand before my

face. "Does this look like the town gossip?"

He grunts his response, and then turns to Bronx. "You trustworthy?"

Bronx just glares.

"Right," Hooch says, leaning back and taking another long swallow. "Thick as thieves."

"The saying had to come from somewhere," I reply drolly.

His eyes narrow on me. "You pull this off and I swear here and now, hand to my colors, that I'll apologize for doubting you and tryin' to deck you in front of whoever is at the clubhouse when you deliver the proof."

Interesting. "What's the challenge?"

"I need you to find my sister."

"Which one? I thought they were both pretty easy to find, since they're six feet under."

His lips curl on one side, a menacing glint in his dark eyes. "You sure about that?"

Ohh . . .

waiting game

RAMONA He never came back for dinner. The boys still didn't roll in after dessert—which King devoured. Thank God for timers on ovens, otherwise the damn thing would have been charcoal. Luckily the only damage was a slightly dry texture, which I saved with copious amounts of butterscotch sauce.

Still, there was no sign of Ty as I ushered Mack from the bathroom after his shower to our newly set up room. To say I'm distracted would be an understatement.

I sit on the side of the bed, reading Mack his bedtime story, but my head is in another place entirely. The kid's lucky if what I'm saying makes sense. I strain to focus on the words, absorbing my attention into creating different voices for the characters. It works for a little while, all until it's time to place the bookmark in for tomorrow night. As Mack carefully positions the slip of cardboard, I'm staring listlessly at the wall opposite his bed, trying to work out what I need to do for all of this back and forth between Sawyer and Ty to end.

"Night, Mom." I'll never stop feeling relieved at hearing him say that again.

I drop my gaze down to Mack, snuggling himself deeper under his covers. "Baby, I need to tell you something."

He rolls over, holding me in his sharp blue gaze.

"Your daddy's moving to California soon."

He nods. "I know."

My eyebrows shoot up. "Do you?"

"Yeah, he told me."

"Are you okay with that?"

A small smile graces his soft pink lips. "I just want you to be happy."

Chin to my chest, I fight back the tears. "I am, baby."

"No you're not."

Frowning, I stroke the hair off his forehead. "What makes you say that?"

"Because the man with the gun took your smile away."

I don't fight it anymore. Tears crest my cheeks. I swipe them away with the back of my wrists. "I'm so sorry that happened, sweetheart."

"It's okay," he says on a small sigh.

"No, it's not." I run my wrist under my nose, wiping the remnants on my jeans. "It's not okay, baby. It's never okay."

"You were brave, Mommy."

My hearts breaks that we're talking about things like

this, but shatters harder at his cool indifference. "I was scared, too, Mack."

"Daddy says being scared means you're thankful you're alive."

I guess it does. "Did you and Daddy talk about how you felt?"

He nods. "When you were crying about Ty."

His blond hair springs from under my palm as I run a hand over his head. "I love you, Mackie-boo."

"Love you to, Mom." His little face stretches with a yawn. "Night."

"Night, baby."

After tucking the blankets into his sides, I head out of the room, taking a last look back at my success in life as I switch the light off. My breath catches in my throat on a gasp as I turn the corner into a hard chest.

"Hey," Ty murmurs, touching the sore spot I've just slammed against. "I was coming to find you. Can we talk?"

"Sure." I take a step back and nod toward the stairs. "I'll make us a coffee, huh?"

"I'm fine, but you go ahead." His hand twitches at his side, almost as though he's unsure how close I want him.

Heavy boots shadow my bare footsteps as I lead us into the kitchen area. Ty takes a seat on one of the stools next to the workbench, and watches my movements as I pour myself a hot cup. Steam rising, I carry it across and set it down to his right, pulling out a stool for myself.

"Where did you go?"

"Out for a couple of drinks." He leaves out the name of

the establishment, I wonder if on purpose. "Had a good talk to Bronx. He helped me clear the mess in here." Ty taps a finger to his head.

"It's been a hell of a week. I think we're all a little unsure of ourselves right now."

He drops his head between his shoulders, running a hand through the dark locks of hair. "I'm sorry I flipped out with jealousy before."

"He's never going to lose a role in my life."

"I know."

"He's Mack's father, and even though he didn't treat me the best for the time we were together, he's the reason why I'm no longer hopping beds in this place."

He cringes at the concept.

"It's harsh," I say, "but it's the truth."

"It's not the whoring that I have a problem with most," he says, scrubbing a hand over his face. "It's the fact so many other guys touched you." A smirk graces his lips. "Gives me a heck of a list to work through if I ever feel the need to defend your honor."

"You make it sound so bad," I say with a laugh, smacking him on the arm. "There weren't that many."

Ty's face grows deadly serious. "You never need to justify yourself to me, Mona. We do the best with the path we're given—that's all there is to it. If anyone ever gives you shit about it, first you remind them that you're alive and happy, so who gives a fuck what you've done to stay that way, and secondly,"—he smiles—"you come get me."

"I just want you to understand that the Sawyer you

guys all see is Sawyer the biker. Sawyer the dad is an entirely different creature now."

"It's hard to imagine, but I'll take your word for it."

"He's good for Mack," I explain, thinking back to the conversation I had with my son mere minutes before. "In turn that's good for me."

Ty's shoulders heave with a huge breath, his hands knotted before him on the bench top. "Where does this leave us? I'm dedicated to trying, Mona. I'm not giving you up without a fight."

"You don't need to give me up," I say. "You've got me. We've got the rest of lives to practice getting it right."

His dark eyes capture mine. "The rest of our lives?"

I bump my shoulder into his gently. "Yeah."

His hand curls around the back of my neck, pulling me forward so he can press a kiss to the top of my head. "Sounds nice."

"I'm not moving out of the clubhouse," I whisper, bracing for the storm.

His hand stiffens, slowly easing me back again. "What?"

"I'm staying here."

"You feel safer here?"

I nod. "And these guys are my family. I'm not ready to leave them yet."

His Adam's apple bobs, his eyebrows twitching. "I guess that makes us long-distance, then."

My mouth curls down at the corners when I recognize the clear disappointment in his gaze. "I'm sorry."

"That blows, Mona. That really, really sucks."

"If we're meant to be, it'll work out." Living together just isn't an option right now. Hell, I don't even have a place of my own until it's fixed up. Thanks to Carlos, Mack and I are live-in members.

Silence falls between us while I finish my coffee. The pain I get looking at Ty forces me to keep my gaze trained on the stainless steel worktop. In my peripheral, I know he's just staring at the metal also, hands clasped before him, head hung.

Nothing ever comes easy.

Ty moves next to me, drawing my gaze reluctantly his way. He swivels my stool to mirror his: sideways to the workbench, my legs within his. I lose myself in those deep brown pools, digging a little deeper between each blink of his lashes to see the insecure man within. In that moment, I could damn near kill his parents; the heartache it causes to think of what they did to him, how insignificant they made him believe he is. I'm seriously entertaining the idea of taking their lives for it—I'm that. Fucking. Angry.

"What's going on in that pretty head of yours?" he asks, tilting his chin slightly.

"Have you ever had anyone love you? Like, *really* love you?"

His brow furrows, and his eyes harden as he stares a hole straight through my shoulder. "I don't know. I guess the guys do."

My hand lifts to caress his face, running my palm over his lengthening beard. "Have you never had a long-term relationship?"

Ty's gaze snaps to mine. "There was one girl, for six months or so when I was twenty-one."

"She must have loved you."

"She stole my car, sold it for dirt cheap to get herself two bags of heroin and OD'd."

I swallow back the pity for what drove a girl to that kind of life. "Must have been hard."

"It was, knowing I'd been used. Took me ages to come to terms with the fact a fix was more important than me."

"She was probably in a weak moment. People do crazy things under the influence."

"I try not to think about it." He shrugs. "It's my past."

"She was the only one?" I ask quietly.

Ty nods, holding my gaze. "Only one. Not many chicks go for the smart guy when they've got brawn like Bronx and Malice around."

I give him a gentle tap on the leg. "You're a pretty hot smart guy, you know." Besides, I've had the brawn, and look how that turned out. "I bet most of them were just shy."

He snorts, shaking his head. "Those girls weren't shy." The humor slips from his expression, replaced with curiosity. "What about you?"

"Have I been loved?"

He nods.

I let my gaze slide to the worktop. Sawyer wasn't real love. Aside from him, there's been . . . no one. "Not true love."

"What even is true love?" Ty muses. "Is there such a

thing, or is it just some made-up experience we spend so long searching for that we miss the real thing when it comes along?"

"I don't know what the proper definition would be," I say. "But to me it's complete comfort in your partner. Ultimate trust."

"Never being hurt," he counters.

"Missing them before they go."

"Feeling incomplete when they've left."

"Counting the days until they return."

"And immediately forgetting how long they were gone when they're back within reach." I smile. "Will that be us?"

He shrugs. "I hope so, but only time will tell."

Cupping his strong jaw in my hands, I lean forward, touching my forehead to his. "You're it for me, you know?"

"You can't be sure," he whispers.

"I don't want to know any different."

Ty's hands snake around my waist, scooting me forward on my seat. "I'll come pack your things myself, when you're ready."

"I'll be waiting."

entangled

TY Ramona inches forward, tentatively placing her lips on mine and coaxing my kiss deeper with her tongue. Her smell, the feel of her under my hands, it's all bliss—except today the pain in my chest is severe. I rushed things to be with her, I pushed my body harder than I should have going out for the drink tonight, and I'm paying a fine price for it now.

Keeping my eyes shut, I break our kiss. "I need to rest. I'm sorry."

"I understand." The rejection in her tone causes me to open my eyes, and I find her looking to her lap, a small frown pulling her brows inward.

"If it weren't for this fuckin' wound, I'd lay you over this counter right now." She peeks out from under her lashes, a small smirk tugging on her plump lips. "Probably would have done it earlier, actually."

"You sure you don't want to join the club?" she asks, a

hint of humor in her tone.

"Fuck no. Why?"

"You're about as classy as the rest of these guys when it comes to sweet talking a lady."

My gaze narrowed, I smile. "I bet you ain't no lady."

"You'll have to wait to find out." She shifts from between my legs and off the stool. "Come on. I'll get you settled upstairs."

"You offering to tuck me in?" I tease.

"Might even keep you warm if you're lucky."

I chuckle at her light-hearted response, willingly following her curvy behind as it sways before me. She's barely gotten me out into the common room when Sawyer cuts us off at the stairs.

"Mona, can I have Ty for a bit?"

She eyes him warily. "Why?"

"Just want to have a chat with him, Sugar."

Her gaze flicks between us. I shrug—fucked if I know what he wants.

"All right," she cedes. "But no being an asshole, Sawyer. I mean it. If I hear you've been a jackass, I won't be happy."

He glowers at her. My fists tighten.

"Ten minutes, tops," he answers, holding her stern gaze.

"Tops," she echoes.

Flexing my fingers out, I watch her disappear up the staircase, flashing me a last look over her shoulder.

"What is it you need?" I ask, turning to Sawyer.

He nods toward the sofas. "Come sit."

Not wanting to give him the impression I'm willing to follow his orders, I surge ahead and take the lead. He falls into an armchair, elbows wide on the armrests, while I struggle to get myself lowered with minimal pain. The ache is really setting in.

"I want you to know I'm not intentionally tryin' to fuck with things between you and her," Sawyer grumbles.

I lift an eyebrow. "Excuse me?"

"She deserves somebody who's goin' to look after her, Ty. Can you be that man?"

Does he honestly think I wouldn't? "Why should I have to answer to you?"

"Because I see the way you lost your fuckin' temper just thinkin' about her havin' my old room," he growls, leaning forward, "and I don't like that look on you. Don't bring that shit back to her—it's not her fault. She needs a place to stay, and I have the answer. Deal."

"I'm trying to deal," I grind out between gritted teeth, "but you can't tell me you wouldn't have been pissed at the idea of sharin' *that* bed with her if the tables were turned."

"Fuck yeah, I would have," he says flopping back into the chair again. "I would have had that fuckin' bed down and on fire in the backyard by now."

I can't hold it in—I chuckle at the visual.

"See?" Sawyer says softly. "You get me."

"Yeah, I get you," I say on a sigh. "What I don't understand is why you're tellin' me this shit when you look like you could kill me every time I'm near her. She said you two are over, but fuck, man, it looks anything but on your side."

He shrugs. "What can I say? I don't want to let her go."

"You still love her?" I ask around the lump in my throat.

He shakes his head. "Nah, not like that. She's . . ." He drops his head back, searching for the words. "Did you ever have something as a kid that you cherished? You know, like you'd take it anywhere and everywhere with you because it made you feel better?"

"Like a toy or somethin'?"

"Yeah, like that." He sighs, rubbing his hands over his face. "I had this little soldier thing, made of sacking and hand painted. My mom bought it for me from a market when I was real little. I carried that fuckin' thing everywhere, jammed down in my pocket. It went missin' one day, and I freaked the fuck out."

"You find it?" I ask.

"Nah." He chuckles at the memory. "Turned out my old man had torn it to shreds when I pissed him off one day. He didn't throw it out or anythin' though—the fucker kept it until the next time I was testin' his patience, pushin' the boundaries. He walked out of the room mid-argument and came back in with it—just stood there and silently laid it out before me. Asshole never needed to say a thing. I knew what the message was."

"I don't follow. He wanted you to know he didn't care?"

Sawyer drops his head forward, holding my gaze in an

intense hold. "He wanted me to know that he'd do the same thing to me."

"Your old man is fuckin' whacked."

He chuckles. "Why you think I'm the way I fuckin' am?"

A beat passes before we both laugh at truth of it—fun times.

"Anyway," Sawyer continues. "The point I was tryin' to make is that Mona is like the grown-up version of that. She's that thing the kept me grounded on some level. Man, if it weren't for the guilt she gave me every time I came home, I would have been a fuck-load more careless and got my ass served to me on a platter a long fuckin' time ago."

I understand what he's saying completely. She does the same for me: grounds me, calms me. I lose a little more of the distrust I harbor for the jerk, replacing it with some common connection to the woman with a heart too big for her own good. "She needs to concentrate on herself, you know."

"I know. It's why I'm movin' to Cali."

"To give her space?"

He nods. "She needs to stop worryin' about me and work out her own shit. The woman has no plans for herself; she just follows me around, servin' my needs like a damn maid. I want her to have room to breathe again. I want her to think about what *she* wants."

"What happened when you went home?" I ask. "What made you change?"

"Hooch's sister, Dana," he answers with lifeless eyes. "I

wanted to help her. I've never wanted to help anyone before. It made me step back and see what a fuckin' ass I've been to Mona, using her all this time, destroyin' her in the process."

My gaze falls to the floor between us. This man wages a war on himself—the toughest opponent. I have to at least give him respect for that; after all, I know how hard it is to break past your own propaganda.

Sawyer rises from the seat, and walks across to stop before me, his boots in my line of sight. A heavy hand rests on my shoulder. "Just look after your woman, yeah?"

Your woman. I lift my head and nod. "You have my word."

"Good." He drops his hand and moves away, heading for the garages. "Let's see if Fingers has my fuckin' ride ready yet."

I push out of the armchair, and hesitate after a few steps. "Sawyer."

He stops at the door, and looks at the ground to his right. "Yeah?"

"Thanks."

He chuckles, menacing and quiet. "Don't go takin' a soft moment from me for granted. You fuck her over and I'll be back to claim her, tearin' you limb from limb in the process."

It should unnerve me. I should be angry. But I laugh. I laugh and smile, knowing that he's happy; he's himself again.

"Glad the day will never come," I say, heading for the

stairs.

He laughs as well, the echo fading as he disappears into the garage. Two risers up, I stop and look to the top of the stairs. There's a certain amount of calm now that the air has been cleared between Sawyer and I, but the pang of discomfort in my chest isn't from a gunshot wound—it's from knowing that Ramona wants to stay here, at the clubhouse.

I have a house in Fort Worth.

I can't do long-distance. Just the thought of being nine hours from her makes me break out in a sweat. It's too far away, too far to travel if anything else happens. The threat of Carlos is still very real, and with what we're about to embark on with the drug distribution, shit's only going to get worse.

I can't be that far from her, knowing I'm not doing everything I can to keep her safe.

Turning around, I wander over to the dimly lit bar area and pull out a bottle of water. Crackers walks in from the front hall with Jo-Jo in tow. The two of them head in my direction, laughing and shoving each other playfully.

"You guys after a brew while I'm here?" I point down to the fridges.

"Yeah, all right," Jo-Jo answers, slipping on to a stool. I eye the guy, my hackles rising at the way his cold stare tears into me, assessing, calculating. What Callum said about him being too shady for his liking has never been clearer. Fuck, I don't think I like the guy either, and this is the first real time we've talked directly to each other.

"Grab me one while you're in there," Crackers says, shaking out a cigarette.

Jo-Jo holds his hand out for one. I notice for the first time huge scars on his wrists, jagged circles, as if he's had something driven through the flesh.

Placing their drinks down for them, I grab my water and head for the back porch. Jo-Jo's eyes follow me, and as I take my first step outdoors, he pipes up behind me.

"Not good enough for you, tailor boy?"

Without granting him my full attention, I leave my back turned and answer, "Just making a phone call."

Crackers has a go at Jo-Jo as I wander outdoors and find an empty chair to settle in. Racking my brain I can't find anything other than the argument with Hooch that gives the guy rights to be so cool toward me. What the fuck is it with these guys?

One conflict resolved, and another just started. No matter what else I've fallen short at in my life, I'll always be good at one thing it seems—making enemies without even trying.

comfort

RAMONA Lying back on the bed Ty's been using since he drove up here, I stare at the cracking plaster on the ceiling, playing over the past week in retrospect. So much drama packed into seven little days. No wonder I cracked.

But the details that stand out the most are that Mack is safe—for now—and that things with Ty seem to be progressing. I don't know when he's planning on returning down south, and I won't be asking the question for one simple reason—I don't want to waste the time we have together counting out the hours until he's gone.

Should I have moved, been closer to him? Maybe. It would have been nice to know we were close while this thing between us grows, but I know I've made the right decision. Mack's home, and as much as I fought the concept, I am too.

This is where we belong.

"Thought you might be asleep."

I roll my head to the right, smiling as my gaze falls on Ty, walking toward the bed. "You took more than ten minutes, buster."

He shakes his head. "Nah, the talk with Sawyer was more like five."

I push up on my elbows as he strips his T-shirt off—awkwardly. "What were you doing then?"

Ty toes his boots off at the foot of the bed, smiling. "Had to make a few phone calls." He climbs on to the mattress with me, positioning us so I lie in his arms, my back to his front.

"Club stuff?"

"No," he whispers, his breath sending goose bumps racing across my flesh. "You know what you've never asked me?"

I shake my head. "It can't be that important if I haven't, I guess."

His lips press against my shoulder blade, laying a kiss. "I love it that you haven't; it means it doesn't matter to you."

"Are you going to fill me in on the secret?" I ask with a hint of humor.

"You've never asked me what I did to go from being homeless to having enough money that I don't need to worry about what's available when I want to help somebody."

Am I going to piss him off again my making the wrong assumptions? "I sort of thought it must have had something to do with the stuff you Butchers do: payoff's, bribes, that kind of thing."

"Most of that goes straight to the other guys."

"What else do you do, then?"

"Property," he reveals.

I roll in his hold, turning to face him. "You own houses?"

He shakes his head. "I own the company that manages them, builds them and sells them on to investors."

"How do you do that with what else, you know, you do?" Surely it makes things tricky when the two worlds cross over.

"Titling. The whole thing's done through a private trust, so if you wanted to know who was behind it all you'd have to do a lot of digging. Took my parents over ten years to find out."

"You keep so quiet about it," I say, running my fingers though his beard. "I never would have known, or even guessed."

"That's the idea," he says. "I don't like people knowing, because then I'm not just a guy who's good with information—I'm a rich guy who people assume thinks he's above them. I'm not. I'm just the same as anyone else—I just have more to fall back on."

The doors that kind of buffer could open for a person like me . . . There are so many things I want to do for Mack, so many options I want to give him, but money always ruins the dream. How can I enroll him in a sports team when I can't afford the gear? How can he have music lessons when I can't afford the tuition, let alone the instruments? I can't even take him on a holiday anywhere special; every time the savings I put aside for the trip grew, something else like car repairs came up, which drained the fund.

Placing a hand on his chest, I tap my fingertips against his collarbone. "Can you show me how to do something like that? How to invest, build something for myself from next to nothing?"

His lips quirk up on one side. "I could . . ."

"But what?" I frown. Does he think I couldn't do it? I'm not smart enough?

"I don't need to."

"Why?" I ask. "I want to know how to give Mack and I more security. I want to stand on my own two feet, Ty."

"I know." He wraps a hand around the back of my neck, and pulls me close to kiss the top of my head. "Which is why I made that phone call."

I pull my head back and stare at him, perplexed. "I don't follow."

"Baby, Sawyer and I talked about you. He wants you to be happy, cared for, and looked after."

"Yeah?"

"I can't do that if I live nine hours away."

My heart hammers in my chest, slamming against the restriction of his body pressed into mine.

Light dances in his rich brown eyes. "I asked for the title of my house to be transferred to your name."

"I don't want to live with you though," I say, missing

the point. I thought I'd explained why I wanted Mack and I to stay at the club. Maybe not well enough . . .

"I'm not asking you to," he says, barely containing his smile. "It's your rental house now—your income."

"What?" I push against the good side of his chest, sitting up. "Seriously, what?"

He shrugs, as if it's no big deal. *It's a fucking house!* "I'm going to move my stuff here, and run my business remotely," he drops casually. "You don't like the idea?"

I smack my hands against my knees, bouncing beside him and giggling. "Are you fucking kidding? I love it." I hold his gaze as I fall serious. "I'm paying you back, though. As soon as I can, I'm repaying you."

"No, you're not," he growls.

"Ty," I admonish. "I told you I don't like taking things I can't repay, and I damn well meant it. It might take me twenty years, or even forty, but I'll pay you back. I'm taking the gift, this one time, but only as a leg-up. You aren't giving me something that monumental for nothing."

He smiles, shaking his head. "It's not for nothing, baby. Trust me."

"I'm repaying it."

He chuckles, pulling me down to lie with him again. "Whatever, now stop wriggling around. I just want to lie here with you while my pain meds get to work."

"I'm sorry. I'm just so freaking excited. You've given me a house," I say, the words sounding surreal from my lips.

"I have," he murmurs into my hair. "Now, be quiet and let me rest up for later."

I frown, restricted from looking up at him by his tight hold. "What's later?"

"Me feelin' good enough to celebrate with you."

"Ty, it's late at night and Mack's in bed. We can't go out. Besides—"

"I never said we'd leave this bed," he mutters, "did I?"

No, he certainly did not. I lie in his arms, doing what I can to relax, but the anticipation is too much. I creep a hand down his body until I reach his belt. He grumbles as I flick the belt open.

"What are you doin'?"

"Nothing."

I slip my hand inside the open denim, and tuck my fingers beneath his boxer briefs.

"Baby," he murmurs, wriggling to help me get my hand around his semi-erect length.

"Shut up and let me say thank you, would you?"

epilogue

RAMONA Two months have passed since Ty gave me his house. I could have been ungrateful, taking it as an insult that he felt I needed to be given a home—that I couldn't possibly earn it myself. But I understand him, and he understands me.

My pride would have gotten in the way—hell, it pretty much did. I don't ask for help—I struggle along on my own, fighting fire with a hose that has a kink in it. But my personality is the type to persist until all options are gone. I would have kept going battling away against the odds until our lives, Mack and mine, burnt down around us.

His personality is the kind that sees where help is needed and gives it without a second thought. He knew that if he'd given me what I wanted and taught me to do it all myself, Mack and I would have been toeing the bread-line, stuck at the clubhouse with no extra cash to go on holiday or have day-trips to amusement parks or the like before I made my first profit. The two of us would have gone mad with cabin fever, and Ty saw that. He's been there, done it, and experienced it.

So why then should I look a gift horse in the mouth? Why not use his experience to my advantage and graciously accept the amazing head-start I was given. After all, if roles were reversed and it were me with the capability, I know I would have done the same thing without thinking twice.

So I accepted. And I don't regret it or feel guilty about it one little bit.

Malice and Bronx have both told me how much it's changed Ty, being with me. He's lighter, relaxed, and hasn't touched a whore since before he was shot, which pleases me no end. I wouldn't be with him now if he had. That part of him is healing—he no longer feels the need to punish himself so severely for what was nothing more than a childhood accident. Yeah, okay, every now and again he asks me to hit him, or choke him in the heat of the moment, but hey, when his face shows such pure ecstasy when I do, who am I to deny him?

Sure, I feel like being physically ill every time I think about that side of his past, all the women he paid for sex, or abuse—I'm never really sure what to class it as. But who am I to judge? Once upon a time *I* was a woman who gave men a brief respite from life, who gave them a moment of happiness to help them get through the shitty week that followed.

Breaking from my thoughts I glance across the

backyard at the clubhouse to where Mack helps Malice, King and Ty put the finishing touches on a fort. Vince squats off to the side, helping Dante stir a pot of paint. King decided the kids needed their own escape when things got too tense inside, and so, here they are building a monstrosity that rivals the square footage of the house Mack and I used to live in.

It has two levels, a slide hacked from the old play-set, and ropes and a chain to hang off and climb on. There's a 'secret' hatch, a balcony on the upper level, and a turret that the kids can poke their heads out of and fire the wooden guns from. It's a child's dream. Hell, I wish *I* were a kid again looking at it.

Sonya steps out onto the porch with me, placing her hands on her hips as she watches the men work, a dishtowel slung over her shoulder. "You got a minute to help Elena and I plate up some lunch for these brutes?"

I nod, rising from my chair. "Sure."

Elena's been steadily coming in to the clubhouse more often now. King figured if Carlos's threat wasn't centered on her, then there was no reason why she should have to stay in hiding and miss out on the support being around the rest of us would give her and Dante.

Plus, I think he was missing the chance to hang out with his son as much as he does these days.

"You heard anything from Sawyer lately?" Sonya asks as we walk through to the kitchen to join Elena.

Ty told me everything about what the club is doing shortly after he moved up to Lincoln, saying he wanted me aware of the risks we were bringing down on ourselves should things go south. I panicked at first, knowing what Carlos is like, and the hurdles the boys are up against trying to take him down. But as Sawyer once pointed out, and as I firmly agree, if any of us are going to live our lives outside of fear, tyrants like Carlos have to be removed.

Knowing what the club has planned, I realized the true reason Sawyer went west—to keep Carlos away from his family. It hasn't quite worked.

"He rang a few nights ago and spoke to Mack," I answer, "but nothing other than that. I think he's coming over soon; said something about organizing a day to hang out with Mack." I pick up a knife and use it to slip the pizza slices onto a large plate.

"He probably just wants to check up on the job Ty's doing of looking after you." Sonya gives me a sly wink as we organize the food onto trays to carry out to the porch.

"Probably," I say, a touch more serious. "Wouldn't put it past him."

Five weeks ago, Bronx went deep cover.

Three weeks ago, Carlos firebombed the clubhouse.

Another warning. Another flex of his muscles. The fire burnt out half the garage and damaged two of the bedrooms upstairs. But King, being a stickler for safety, had a fire plan in place and the sprinklers put the flames out quickly before there was too much destruction to the main living area.

Fingers cried when he saw the state of the garage. The

whole thing was incredibly heartbreaking, given that fixing the boys' rides is that man's pride and joy. King promised him he'd rebuild him a better workshop, twice as big. Fingers stopped crying and smiled, hugging King around the waist. The boys still give him shit for it.

I catch myself looking around the place sometimes, wondering what life *would* have been like if I'd moved. Would I be back by now? Or would Ty and I have started living together? Who really cares? I'm happy now, and that's all I could ever ask for.

"Grub's up, boys!" Sonya yells across the yard as the three of us emerge with the spread.

Six heads lift and turn our way, the men soon drifting toward where we set the homemade pizza and enchiladas down on the outdoor tables. King dives straight in, burning his chin with the hot cheese dripping from the pizza. Malice cops a backhand to the chest for laughing at his misfortune.

Ty takes an enchilada on a throwaway plate and settles into one of the chairs. Patting his leg, he tips his chin for me to join him.

"It's coming together well, eh?" I say, looking at the fort as I lower myself onto his leg.

He balances the plate on his other thigh, taking a glance at the construction. "Yeah. I think the kids will love it."

I catch some meat that falls from his lunch as he precariously lifts it to his mouth one-handed. "I can move so you can eat properly."

He finishes his mouthful, shaking his head. "Nuh-uh. Took me long enough to earn the right to have you sitting on my knee—I ain't givin' that privilege up in a hurry."

He grumbles when I stand to reach across the table and snag myself a slice of pizza, and then wraps me in his arm when I return. We eat in silence, simply enjoying the afternoon for what it is. Ty shifts every so often under my weight, but every time I try to move, he firmly pulls me back in with a tug of his hand on my hip.

"Look," I finally say. "If you're uncomfortable, just let me sit over there on the spare chair."

I glance across to the empty seat, contemplating making a dash for it, when the silence of the rest of the group strikes me. Slowly lifting my gaze, I find them all watching me with interest.

"Have I got sauce on my face?" I ask, dabbing my fingers to the corners of my mouth.

King grins mischievously while Sonya blushes beside Vince. Elena hands Dante another slice of pizza and ushers him to a seat. Malice grabs Mack by the sleeve as he tries to leave, quietly ordering him to sit as well.

"What?" I cry out, frustrated that they're all looking at me as though I'm some sideshow attraction. "What's so amusing?"

Ty's hand squeezes my hip. "Babe?"

"What's going on?"

He places his plate down on the porch beside his chair, and then leans forward into me, reaching into his back pocket. My lungs grow heavy, my chest compressing.

What is he doing?

"I found something I thought you'd like." He reaches forward, placing his closed fist facing down for me to receive whatever he has in his hand.

Shaking like a leaf, I bring my upturned palm under his fist, and wait.

And wait.

And fucking wait.

All the while everybody's smiles grow. My nerves get the better of me and I start to cry frustrated tears.

Ty's fists opens, and something small falls into my palm. I close my fingers over it on reflex to catch it.

"I think you'd have more use for it than me," he says, eyes dancing. Ty tips his head down, motioning for me to look.

I unfurl my fingers, my breath becoming erratic as I take in the white-gold band with square-cut diamond in my hand.

"What do you say?" he asks, tugging me to his side a little tighter. "Will you let me show the world that I plan on keeping you forever? Will you marry me?"

I dance. I wriggle my damn ass about on his lap like a mad woman, while 'oh my God' and 'yes' get mixed up in my squealing. Ty laughs, and Sonya starts a round of applause.

Throwing my arms around his neck, I lay one on him, kissing him as if my life depends on it. "Yes," I cry out, breaking free. "Of course. You don't even have to ask. Of course I will!"

Mack crashes into my side, smiling his little butt off as I pull him up to sit on Ty's free leg. Ty wraps his arms around both of us, pressing his forehead into my temple. "I love you."

"I love you," I whisper back, stroking Mack's hair while I do. "Both."

Everything in that moment is perfect, untouchable, and unbreakable. As I trace a line across Ty's finger where his ring will go, I realize that my search for home is over. That whatever happens now, good or bad, this is where I'll always be drawn to return.

My family.

My loves.

My haven.

Home.

Continue with

Devil SMOKE

Will Bronx break?

BUTCHER BOYS SERIES

Devil You Know
Devil on Your Back
Devil May Care
Devil in the Detail
Devil Smoke

BANJAXED SERIES

Pistol
Loaded
Recoil

OTHERWORLD DESIRES (Paranormal)

Battle to Become
Methods for Mayhem

Acknowledgements

You know what? I've written and published nine books now . . . NINE books. And I still don't feel like a bonafide author. Will I ever? Don't know. I still feel like that not-so-cool kid who's hanging out with the popular crowd, waiting for the day when they get kicked out because somebody better comes along. But I'll keep on writing, knowing that my next book will be better and that what I do is what I love. For that reason alone, I don't think I'll ever stop.

And as I sit here and struggle with all the feelings of inadequacy that EVERY author gets, I know one thing for sure—I'm grateful. I've met so many amazing people on my journey along this long, and mostly lonely, road. And each of them, I can say without a shadow of a doubt, has left me richer for knowing.

My Brisbane girls - Nina, River, Melissa, and Natalie. Talking with you keeps me sane. It's so comforting to know that I'm not the only one who struggles, who has doubts, and who works their ass off wondering if it's enough. I love catching up with you guys—let's keep on doing that.

Lili - I've thanked you before, but I'll thank you again.

You're a fountain of knowledge, and again, it's so good to talk with somebody who thinks in the same dark, twisted ways, but with the kick-ass tenacity of a savvy business-woman. Don't go changing ;)

TGNAFN – what a think-tank. You gals rock, and I love the ideas and encouragement we share.

There are so many more of you awesome creatures out there, lost to your writing cave, slaving away over the marketing fires that I could list if I had endless pages. If anything, I've learnt that being self-published is awesome, because you know what? We can tell the stories how we want to, exactly as they are in our head. Keep doing what you do, giving us epic reads, and most of all, pushing the boundaries.

So to the readers – thank you for giving us a chance and letting us keep sharing the mess in our head that would probably consume us alive if we had no way of bleeding the well.

And to my babies – you're getting older, growing into such awesome little guys. I'm so damn proud of you two: of your enthusiasm and your genuine love for life. You give me the sun on the darker days and I'll never stop loving you with all my heart.

But most of all (and yes, he's not first this time) is my husband. I love you long, babe. You're my biggest inspiration, my grounding, and proof that a crazy messed up mind really can find a happily ever after. It'll never be perfect, but it will always be ours. <3

About the Author

Originally born and bred in Canterbury, New Zealand, Max now resides with her family in beautiful and sunny Queensland, Australia.

Life with two young children can be hectic at times, and although she may not write as often as she would like, Max wouldn't change a thing.

BE SURE TO FOLLOW HER AT:

Facebook – Profile
www.facebook.com/max.henry.9003
Facebook – Page
www.facebook.com/MaxHenryAuthor?ref=hl
Goodreads
www.goodreads.com/author/show/
7555353.Max_Henry
Twitter & Instagram
@maxhenryauthor

JOIN THE MADHOUSE!

www.facebook.com/groups/
346994535466425/?fref=ts

13842995R10197

Printed in Great Britain
by Amazon.co.uk, Ltd.,
Marston Gate.